ABOUT THE AUTHOR

Fight the Best Fight is Marjory Davidson's second novel. Her first, *In Love and Judgement*, was published in 1994.

She has been a correspondent in New York, Washington, Moscow and the Far East and a staff writer on the *Sunday Express*, *Daily Mail* and the *Sun*.

Today she is the Royal Correspondent of the *Evening Times* and *Saturday Times* and is working on both her third novel, *Intermezzo*, and her fourth, *Song of Songs* — a fictional 'Wild Swans' of the West.

Also by Marjory Davidson

IN LOVE AND JUDGEMENT

For Ruth,

who came back into my life

FIGHT THE BEST FIGHT

MARJORY DAVIDSON

POCKET
BOOKS

LONDON · SYDNEY · NEW YORK · TOKYO · SINGAPORE · TORONTO

First published in Great Britain by Pocket Books, 1995
An imprint of Simon & Schuster Ltd
A Paramount Communications Company

Simon & Schuster Ltd
West Garden Place
Kendal Street
London W2 2AQ

Simon & Schuster of Australia Pty Ltd
Sydney

A CIP catalogue record for this book is available from the
British Library

ISBN 0-671-85270-1

Typeset in Goudy Modern 11/14pt by
Palimpsest Book Production Limited, Polmont, Stirlingshire
Printed and bound in Great Britain by
Caledonian International Book Manufacturing Ltd, Glasgow

We are never more totally alive than when the loved one is lying in someone else's arms.

James Kennaway

ACKNOWLEDGEMENTS

I wish to thank Richard Manu for the enthusiasm and creative flair he brought to the design of the promotional material both for FIGHT THE BEST FIGHT and my first novel, IN LOVE AND JUDGEMENT, which was published in 1994.

CONTENTS

BOOK ONE

A WOMAN
IN LOVE

PART ONE

CHAPTER ONE

Glasgow 1953

Edwina Buchanan was acutely aware that within the hour over two hundred men would want to take her clothes off and do the terrible things her mother said no girl should permit before she was married. They were gathering in the ballroom now – rich, respected men whose families had created the city's wealth. Charity fashion galas like this evening brought them out in force to sit on gilded chairs beside their wives.

She blotted her full, scarlet lips and her face assumed the mask of hauteur Barbara Goalen had created and all the models wore. She felt safe behind it because it hid the lack of confidence that lurked beneath the black eyes set in pale Celtic features and the surprising voluptuousness of the slender body about which men sang hallelujahs.

'I am slightly changing the running order of the swimwear.' Margaret Flaxman's powerful timbre commanded Edwina's attention. Mrs Flaxman, whose trim, wiry figure and ebony-smooth complexion took fifteen years off her fifty, owned the Albion Model Agency for which Edwina had worked for nearly three years. 'I need a bit more space between numbers thirty-one and thirty-two. So I'd like you to go on second last instead of last. The order will now be thirty-two, thirty-one and then thirty-three. You'll have no problem with that?'

'That will be fine,' said Edwina, knowing she was being given an order, not asked a question. Though Mrs Flaxman was always helpful when a girl had any kind of problem, no girl ever crossed her even in small things. Those who had done so no longer worked for the agency, and as there weren't many reputable agencies where a girl could get modelling work in Glasgow, disputes were few. There wasn't much money in it either by the time a girl had paid for her make-up, twice-weekly shampoo and set and all the shoes, handbags, scarves and gloves she was expected to have for photographic sessions.

A single white hair shooting straight up from the hair-line on her forehead caught her attention in the dressing table mirror, sharply reminding her that modelling was a short career.

'The scissors, quick!' She swivelled round on her stool in the sprawling changing room and grabbed a tailor's pair from the tray in which Molly, her dresser, kept tools for last-minute alterations. 'I'm getting old,' she mourned, eliminating the offending strand.

She needed to get married before her looks went, and younger, fresher girls came along to claim the best men.

The *crème de la crème* of the Old Aristocracy, titled from the Middle Ages, had been bagged already. Last year a nineteen-year-old American heiress called Virginia Ryan had walked off with the Earl of Airlie's heir, Lord Ogilvy. And another model, Jane McNeill, had snatched the Duke of Buccleuch's heir, the Earl of Dalkeith, from under Princess Margaret's nose and married him at a huge splashy wedding attended by the Queen at St Giles Cathedral in Edinburgh. Edwina had been as green as a Granny Smith.

Marriage into the New Aristocracy, whose fortunes were Victorian and titles early twentieth century, was just as hard to achieve.

At only twenty-two, Viscount Younger's heir, George, a dashing army officer, who had served with the British Army of the Rhine and in the Korean War with the Argyll and Sutherland Highlanders, was already a lot cause. Yesterday her mother had told her he was deeply in love and intended to marry Diana Tuck, a naval officer's daughter from Chichester.

Beyond the New Aristocracy the world fell to the landed gentry, who were often impoverished, struggling to keep up appearances and pay their drink bills, and the nouveau riche, who had made their money in trade and by their entrepreneurial skills and usually lived in horrid red sandstone mansions in Glasgow and the West of Scotland. Edwina pulled a face at the thought of their vulgarity.

'Just wait till August when everyone comes up from London for the grouse shooting,' her mother had said soothingly last week when the ball given by the Queen's Bodyguard in

Scotland, the Royal Company of Archers, to honour her post Coronation State Visit to Scotland, had turned out to be such a bore.

'And bring all the competition with them,' retorted Edwina gloomily.

'And then there's the Scottish season with all the balls in September.' Her mother continued to be irritatingly cheerful.

The brief Scottish season amounted to no more than a series of balls stretching from Royal Deeside to the Isle of Skye and back again and almost invariably involved dreary treks over moor and mountain in the rain because September was virtually the monsoon season in Scotland.

Edwina believed she could have been married by now if she had been presented at court when she was seventeen and had the chance to whirl through the London Season of debutante dances, Royal Ascot and Wimbledon, Henley and Cowes. But there hadn't been the money to pay for it out of her father's salary as a judge in the lower Sheriff Courts and it was only the income from her mother's trust fund that enabled the family to live in style in Edinburgh's New Town.

'I've checked all the clothes are in the right order,' said Molly through teeth clutching half a dozen pins.

Edwina swung round on her stool and eyed the line of garments on a portable rail and the accessories piled neatly beneath them. Nipped-in waists, standaway collars, dolman sleeves and swinging, swirling skirts worn with gloves, stiletto heels, picture hats and parures of pearls bore witness

Rutherford, heir to the Globe Newspaper Publishing empire. He was forty-eight and his raffish looks — the eyes were set in sculpted suntanned features beneath swept-back black hair — could still concentrate a woman's mind across a crowded room.

He was making an introductory handshake at the post-show party last for ever, and Edwina was acutely conscious that only her thin black nylon glove separated her flesh from his.

'I can promise you will have more fun with me than with anyone else,' he said, his eyes daring hers.

'He says that to all the girls,' said Margaret drily.

'Only because it's true,' he assured Edwina, continuing to hold her hand.

'Yes, I'd like to be there,' she said in a voice she knew sounded weak because all of a sudden she wanted Maxwell Rutherford to do all those terrible things her mother said no girl should permit before she was married . . .

CHAPTER TWO

Maxwell Rutherford was certain he would be hanged for the murder of his father.

'Why make me managing director when you cut the ground from under me at every turn?' he yelled down the telephone at the parent who had founded the newspaper publishing empire.

A familiar sense of inadequacy began to diffuse through him. Once again he had done it wrong, not understood what his father and the company needed or seen the direction in which they were going. Once again it had taken an outsider to know his father's will better than he did and the price would be further erosion of his boardroom power. The walnut-panelled office with concealed cocktail cabinet, wardrobe and private bathroom on the seventh-floor executive suite, the view over the River Clyde and the Merchant City, and the glamorous blonde secretary were all symbols of the power his father allowed him to play with, yet refused to hand over. But he wasn't losing this one without a fight.

'I told that sonofabitch you made editorial director, Alex

Robertson, that it was out of the question to send his protégé and yours, Drew Hamilton, to Panmunjon for the signing of the Korean armistice,' he shouted. 'So he goes to you and you overrule me and support him – '

'Because he was right. And he gave me the right reasons for wanting Drew to be there.' James Rutherford's voice was full of the calm authority that enhanced his son's sense of inadequacy. 'If the *Daily Globe* is going to be a truly national newspaper we need to start behaving like one and sending our correspondents abroad like the other nationals do.'

'National newspapers are published in Fleet Street, in London, Father, where your friends, Lords Beaverbrook and Rothermere, have the deep pockets needed to send reporters haring round the globe. We're a provincial morning, Father. And as you've always had such a keen eye for profit I shouldn't have to remind you we don't have that sort of money.'

'Perhaps not in the past. But if we're going to compete in the future we'll have to find it,' James reminded his son.

'And vision, Max. We need vision. A business grows on the vision of its leaders. Alex Robertson has a clear editorial vision of where the papers need to go. That's why I appointed him to the job and why I've supported him over Drew going to Panmunjon.'

Max's fingers started to go cold around the telephone. He heard the controlling parent, who inhibited his whole life, edging into his father's voice.

'You've gone very quiet, Max.'

'Perhaps because I have nothing to say,' he replied laconically.

'Don't be downhearted or discouraged, Max.' The older man's tone was conciliatory and Max felt the controlling parent gaining the upper hand. He wanted to hit his father before he was totally reduced to the psychological level of a small child.

'I am training you to run the company, to show your staff it is your company. One day it will be your company and you must never hesitate to see that your will above all is done and your vision of the company is fulfilled.

'Give people power by all means. You'll have to in order to run the business. But never let them forget that you, like the Lord, who giveth, also taketh away.'

Whenever his father, the son of a late Presbyterian minister, wanted to get his way he turned to the Lord like an Old Testament prophet. Max felt his anger surge again, but it was imploding now, against himself. He closed his eyes and his grasp on the telephone was almost epileptic. Before he had a chance to murder his father he would die of apoplexy, of internal combustion caused by the sustained effort of controlling his rage. He breathed deeply in an attempt to calm himself.

'Max, Max, are you there?'

'I'm listening,' he replied in a reasonable tone.

'Everything I do, Max, is for your own good. One day you will inherit and a heavy responsibility will be yours. And hard though it may seem to you at times, it is my duty as your father . . .'

But Max wasn't listening to the sermon. He had known it off by heart, better than the Lord's Prayer, for thirty-seven years . . . and it never failed to haul him back through time . . .

'You're being sent away to school for your own good,' James was telling eight-year-old Max. 'You can't go on being a mummy's boy. You've got to learn to become a man. You need to meet other boys, who'll become the brothers you've never had and grow up to become the men you need to know in business. I'd have given half my fortune for the chance I'm giving you to be educated. Believe me, son, one day you'll thank me for sending you to a proper school.'

Max sank his teeth into his lower lip till he could feel the blood oozing on to his tongue. It tasted slightly salty but it was warm and the flow was comforting. He looked vainly at his mother, who stood mutely with his nanny a few paces distant. From the moment his father had announced the plans for his education, she had not said a word to save him – though he knew she was suffering just as much as he was at the prospect of the rupture.

'Your father knows what is best for boys' was all she'd said, but the message in her eyes was that she drew no more comfort from her words than he did.

In moments the grand new Silver Ghost designed by Mr Charles Rolls and Mr Henry Royce would carry him away from his home and his parents and his white Scottie dog, Dan Rascal. Dan, who had been whimpering at breakfast and seemed to know his young master was leaving him, had been locked in a shed at the bottom of the garden until the parting was over.

'You'll make lots of new friends at school,' his mother suddenly said in a brittle voice whose cheerfulness was bitterly at odds with the brave sad eyes he would remember on the day she was buried.

'Can't you come with me just to the gates?' he begged her.

'It – '

'That's enough,' James interrupted his wife. 'This kind of women's nonsense is exactly what he needs to grow out of.'

Max knew his father's heightened colour meant he was getting angry, and he was frightened of his father's anger.

'Go with McKerron.' James nodded towards the uniformed chauffeur and offered his son his hand, which Max shook as firmly as he could.

Then he walked slowly from the house.

'It's for your own good,' James reminded the tiny figure in the back of the Rolls before he was borne away from everyone and everything he loved . . .

There was a bitter grimace on Max's face when he replaced the receiver. At forty-eight – at which age James Rutherford had been a newspaper mogul – Max was still an apprentice. Proof that his father was, always had been and always would be his superior by a very long way and in almost every way. And – the worst thing – that was exactly how his father wanted him to feel right now.

'Mr Mackinnon's waiting to see you.'

His elegant blonde secretary framed in the doorway reminded Max that tomorrow he must accede to his father's wishes in his private life as well and start to court that pretty model girl.

But first, tonight, he had to say goodbye to a very dear friend . . .

CHAPTER THREE

The motor launch *Caberfeidh* was leaving a trail of white surf as it skimmed over the sunlit waters of the Firth of Clyde.

'Enjoying yourself?' Max shot Edwina a sideways glance.

'Yes,' she replied, raising her eyes from the immaculately manicured hands spreadeagled on the steering wheel.

Since the evening of the fashion show she had thought about no one and nothing but Maxwell Rutherford. Every day she had spent hours undressing before the mirror, improving the grace of her movements, imagining he was watching her and finding promise and delight in every tiny piece of lace she shed. And she had dreamed of those hands holding her, caressing her, possessing her, making all of her his own. His raffish profile was the last image which drifted across her mind at night when she laid her head on the pillow, where she pictured him, well slept and rampant for her, when she woke in the morning. The rugby scrums in which for years she had defended her 'honour' in the back seats of rickety second-hand cars were history now. Since the night they met she knew she was going 'all the way' with Max Rutherford.

And afterwards he would take care of her because he was older and would know how.

She watched the glaze the afternoon sun lent to his sculpted features and wondered what his fleshy lips would feel like pressed down on hers.

Then her gaze fell once more on his hands. Her body felt turbulent and heavy like stormclouds needing to shed rain. And she yearned for those spreadeagled hands to close around her breasts and encompass all of her.

But she had already waited for him today and she could wait a little longer.

Though his eyes had boldly spoken of his wish to be alone with her from the instant she had stepped on board the yacht, *Marietta*, with Mrs Flaxman and the girls from the agency, he had not even suggested leaving Globe Newspaper Publishing's annual party for wholesalers and retailers until after lunch and the speeches were over.

She was walking disconsolately alone on the deck, thinking he was never going to seek her out, when he had caught up with her and said, 'The best post-prandial digestive I know is a spin on the open sea.'

In minutes they had cast off in the *Caberfeidh*.

Now the gleaming white hull of the *Marietta* must be at least a mile away. The Clyde coast, packed with children with their buckets and spades, was further still. And there was nothing and no one in the world for her except this man and his boat and the wide open sea.

'We're going ashore,' he announced.

'Ashore?'

'Yes.'

'On Arran?'

'That's the idea.'

Alone on the island.

She raised her eyebrows to the towering mountain peaks glittering in the sunshine as he thrust the *Caberfeidh* powerfully towards the island. She didn't care if she never came back!

In minutes they were approaching the coral-pink sands of Whiting Bay, ringed by houses whitewashed and dazzling in the sun. The village seemed deserted apart from the lone figure with a shock of white hair and weathered complexion who greeted Max as the *Caberfeidh* eased up by a wooden jetty.

'Fine weather you're bringing with you, Mr Rutherford,' he said as Max took Edwina's hand and she stepped ashore. 'Everything's been seen to and the car's over there.' He pointed to a white Austin-Healey sports car at the end of the jetty.

'Where are we going?' asked Edwina when she had settled in the passenger seat.

'Paradise,' replied Max, roaring off down the road which circled the island.

Soon they were spinning through open country by the sea, past sunwashed fields and solitary cottages. The Austin-Healey 3000 could zoom at 100 miles per hour, and Max drove like a very young man, cutting corners and racing round them on the wrong side.

Then he began to slow as they descended into a tranquil

wooded valley. The sun had gone — excluded by the tall trees which enclosed the world they were entering.

'Welcome to Lagg,' said Max, his voice sombre now, as if trying to match the change of mood in their surroundings.

Off the main road the Austin-Healey crawled over a bridge by a stream overhung with willow and silver birch. Then it was nosing carefully down a winding avenue of willow locked in overhanging embrace until they came to a clearing where the trees stood back to frame a white house set before a broad gravel sweep.

As Max got out of the car, Edwina stared at the window frames which were painted pale blue like the windows of the crofting cottages. The door was already open and welcoming. It took her back to a different house on another shore . . .

. . . Every summer when she was a small child her parents had rented a whitewashed house on the shore at Elie, in the East Neuk of Fife.

A lot of Edinburgh lawyers had summer homes there and on fine mornings teed off on the golf course from eight o'clock. Edwina remembered waking up to dawn choruses of gulls on days that seemed to last for ever and gazing from her window at the mammary pink tower of the Bass Rock rising up out of the waters of the Firth of Forth. She remembered how her mother was always more keyed up and bothered about making a good impression at Elie than she was in Edinburgh. During a day when guests were expected in the evening her mother was so fractious and flustered that Edwina would go off to spend it with friends and their families. But there were other more relaxed days when her father would take her on the boat from Anstruther to the Isle of May in the Forth Estuary and spend hours telling her about the birds which nested there. These were the only times she had ever got her father's attention . . .

'Come and have a glass of champagne,' said Max, bowing elaborately as he opened the passenger door.

As memories of childhood stirred in the far recesses of her mind, she was unaware of the ease with which her hand slipped into his as he led her to the house . . .

A ceiling fan was sending a current of delicious cool air round a hall furnished with cane settees cushioned in bold floral prints. Through an open door Edwina saw a room dressed entirely in white, and beyond it an open french window led on to a terrace where two tall tulip glasses and a bottle of champagne in a silver ice bucket stood on a white wrought-iron table.

'I hope you approve,' said Max, letting her hand go when they reached the terrace. 'Jockie, who met us at the jetty, and his wife look after me very well here. I asked them to prepare for us . . . suitably . . .'

'Yes.'

Like the house, the terrace was gleaming white. A stream ran below it, with a little white-painted wooden bridge. Marguerites and buttercups and daisies were strewn along the banks of the stream and across the woodland floor and she could see the sea through the trees.

As she sat down she noticed another open french door further along the terrace.

Then her glance was drawn back to Max's hands, now skilfully uncorking the champagne.

For the first time she felt nervous.

But there was no going back now.

Max Rutherford was not a young man she could fend off. He was a mature man with the needs and demands of a mature man. And there was nowhere and no one to run to if she changed her mind. She was totally in his power. He had brought her to the island. And though she vaguely knew there was a ferry to the mainland he was the only practical means of her getting back.

Their eyes met when he handed her a glass. Though she saw more merriment than desire in them, she knew she would never be able to talk him out of . . . anything . . .

'Welcome to paradise,' said Max, dropping languidly into the chair beside her.

'Is that what you call it?' She heard the brittleness and girlishness in her voice and hated it.

'Can you think of a better name?'

Edwina shook her head and pressed the glass to her lips, wondering how long he would talk to her . . . before . . .

'Of all the homes in which my father and I lay our heads, this is my favourite,' said Max easily. 'My mother gave it to me nearly twenty years ago when I came back from Australia. She felt I needed a place of my own after having been away from the family for some years, somewhere I could get away from the business and think my thoughts and dream my dreams. She died less than a year after I came back. I felt guilty that I hadn't spent as much time with her as she would have liked in that last year. The yacht, *Marietta*, is called after her. My father commissioned it shortly after her death.'

'You must have led a very interesting life,' she said, picking up on his reference to Australia. She wanted to know everything about Max Rutherford.

A bitter grin lit his face.

'What is there to say about a life largely wasted?' He shrugged aimlessly.

'I don't believe that.'

'By my age my father had built a newspaper empire. I have done nothing — except be his vassal,' he sighed. 'But I'm starting to get melancholy and I refuse to spoil your afternoon with my acedia.'

'But you must have done some interesting things,' said Edwina, sitting forward, eager to encourage him to tell her anything about himself.

'Your enthusiasm is infectious,' he said, his grin indulgent now. 'You almost convince me.' He took a long draught of his champagne, topped up his glass and relaxed back in his chair. 'I suppose I'd be less than honest if I didn't admit that at least some of it's been interesting. Quite profoundly at times, but it could have been more so if I'd used my opportunities properly and stood up better to my father at critical moments.

'I didn't have to go into the newspaper business but after I graduated from Oxford with a very respectable first-class second in PPE . . .' he saw the question in Edwina's eyes '. . . Politics, Philosophy and English, I knew it was expected of me. And there wasn't anything else I passionately wanted to do.

'So I joined the circulation department at Globe Newspapers as a junior executive and got out and about among the newsagents actually selling the papers — finding out what people liked about them and why they read them, what the competition was up to, and how and where I could increase sales.

'I was really enjoying myself and starting to feel I was building a real rapport with the newsagents after six months when my father decided to rip me out of circulation and pack me off to Australia as a guinea pig for an exchange scheme he'd dreamed up with the Fairfax Group. I tried to make him see sense, that it would at least be better for the company and the contacts I was developing to leave me where I was for a year and I could go to Australia later on. But he'd have none of it.

'"Your passage to New York is booked on the *Aquitania*. You'll sail from Southampton in three weeks" was his answer.

'When I pointed out that New York wasn't in Australia, a great triumphant grin spread across his face, which was wizen even then.

'"I thought you'd like to see a bit of the world on the way to Australia," he said. "So I'm giving you a month in America before you sail from San Francisco for Sydney, calling at Honolulu on the way."'

'Father always knew how to sugar bitter pills. I wasn't

going to turn down that chance even if he was sabotaging my career as a circulation rep.

'I arrived in New York on Black Thursday in 1929. Thirteen million shares had changed hands on the crashing Stock Exchange that day and riot police had been called to disperse the hysterical crowds gathering in Wall Street as dealers obeyed investors' orders to sell at any price.

'I spent a lot of time in our New York bureau — it was the first time I'd come face to face with a big story as it was happening. Now I knew what I wanted to do. I wanted to be a foreign correspondent!'

Edwina watched the light of romantically remembered youth fill his eyes as the years seemed to fall away. She could almost feel the charged, electric air of Manhattan and with all her heart wished she could have been there and shared it with him.

Max took a long draught of his champagne.

'I told my father as soon as I landed in Australia.' He sighed. 'I thought he'd be delighted. He's always said that as news is the core of our business it must come first.

'"You've as much chance of finding a big story in Australia as I have of discovering a kangaroo on Glasgow Green" was what he said. "You need to be in Paris or Berlin, not the outback, if you want to make a name as a foreign correspondent."

'Well, he soon had to admit not all the big stories came out of Paris or Berlin. Three weeks later Amy Johnson landed in Darwin and became the first woman to fly solo from Britain to Australia and the *Daily Globe* cleared the front page for my by-lined story.

'Now Father was encouraging. "Keep up the good work, Max. And you can open the *Globe*'s Berlin bureau when your year is up in Australia. There's going to be trouble in Germany and the world will be hearing a lot more of Adolf Hitler."

'But between one thing and another he kept me hanging around in Australia for five years. And by the time I travelled home across Europe Germany's massive rearmament programme and conscription were sending the shivers through the chanceries. Hitler was quite literally on the warpath already.

'Being back at the centre of things fairly sent the adrenalin coursing through my veins. I was thirty years old and had dutifully served my apprenticeship with my father. Now I was ready to take off on my own chosen career. I met the distinguished American correspondent William Shirer several times in Berlin and every time I told him I was coming back to join him.'

'Did you meet Hitler?' Edwina burst in. Her childhood had been filled with her parents talking about the menace of Hitler in Germany and she had been only nine when war had broken out.

'Not Hitler, but I ran into Ribbentrop and Goering at a party at the British Embassy,' said Max, 'and found them equally unpleasant.'

Edwina was thrilled that he had mingled with the villains who had cast such long shadows over so many of her childhood and growing-up years. It somehow established a bond between them.

'I could hardly believe it when I got back to Glasgow and found out Father had gone cold on the idea of a bureau in Berlin and wanted me to work in the advertising department,' said Max.

'"But we need a bureau in Berlin," I protested. "News first has always been your creed!"

'"That's true," said my father, very conciliatory the way he is when he's determined to get his way. "You've been away a long time. I need you back here for a bit. Berlin's not going to vanish. In fact, you can take it from an old newsman that in a year's time it will be an even bigger story than it is now. A year's not a long time."

'So I gave in and joined the advertising department, but my mother died just as the year was ending.

'"I'm going to need you here a bit longer," my father said as we were leaving the funeral. "I couldn't cope on my own just now."

'"A couple of months, Father. No more," I said, sounding as grim as I felt.

'The Spanish Civil War broke out two months later.

'"I want to report this war from the front line," I told my father. "Everyone's going there and this could be my big chance."

'"But what if you get killed!" cried my father. "There'll be nobody to run the business when I'm gone. If you'd settled down it would be different. You might have a family by now and there'd be a son to follow in your footsteps. But there's no one to be at the side of your poor old father, who's just not as fit and well as he used to be."

'"I'm not going to be killed," I protested. "Professional correspondents don't get killed. Staying alive is one of their skills. Only amateurs lose their lives in war because they don't take enough care, and wander into places no professional would think of going. I'm thirty-one years old and I've got to get my career started before I'm any older."

'But as he always did, my father succeeded in making me feel so guilty about not doing what he wanted that I gave in. I stayed in Glasgow, and when the war came I joined British Intelligence, not the corps of war correspondents.

'I was forty by the time it ended in 1945 and only too glad to get back home to Glasgow.'

The mood between them was sombre now. For the first time she was aware of the lines which cut deep furrows into his brow, swerved around his mouth and fanned out in semicircles from the corners of his eyes.

For an uncomfortable moment a curtain seem to ring up before her and reveal the security she associated with older men like Max and her father as an illusion. She closed her eyes for an instant. That could not possibly be true.

'I'm enjoying listening to you. You really are a very interesting man,' she promised, looking at him like a solemn child as he replenished their champagne.

'And you're a brilliant listener,' he said. 'See how easy it is for you to flatter a boring old man into talking about himself?'

'You're not boring or old.'

'But I'm no longer young.' He enunciated each word clearly and carefully, and left them there — suspended in the air between them as if he was trying to tell her something.

For a moment they sat in silence. Only the rasping of the corncrake and the ocean rolling home beyond the trees filled the air.

'Do you understand what I'm saying, Edwina?'

'Yes . . .' But she sensed she was missing something and felt stupid and naive.

He leaned forward and took one of her hands between his own. But it felt like a gesture of comfort, not advance, and it caused some indefinable sadness to diffuse through her.

'Beautiful, desirable Edwina, you have something more precious than either your beauty or your desirability,' he sombrely assured her. 'You have the whole dazzling prospect of your life. It's the most precious gift you've ever been given, the most precious possession you'll ever have. And it's all yours, so long as you don't let anyone take possession of it.

'Only ever do what you believe in, what your heart knows is right. Don't give up or sacrifice your life doing what others want you to do or expect of you or say it's your duty to do. And never, never feel guilty for not doing what was expected of you.

'I've spent my life being my father's vassal. Whenever there's been any conflict between his interests and mine, I've sacrificed my own. If I can hand you down anything from the years that separate us, it's this, Edwina: never let anyone rob you of your life and what you want to do with it. Not even your parents — most particularly of all, not your parents. They may feel that because they gave you your life they own it, and you owe them for it. They do not and you do not.

'Only listen to what your heart tells you. Obey only its voice. It's your true compass, not the voices of others echoing in your head. You have only one life. For all any of us know we may have only today and there may be no tomorrow. Live the life you're given as you want to. If you think that sounds easy, believe me it's much easier not to.'

Her heart was bursting as he went on holding her hand. Now she knew what she had not understood before, realising that despite his boldness he had been too shy to tell her that he needed her love.

'I was married just before the war to a charming woman who came highly recommended by my father.' His grin was bitter. 'But we hardly saw each other. And by the time it was over we were two completely different personalities to what we had been.

'We were divorced three years ago, and to my very great sadness my wife died six months later.'

'And there is no . . . one?'

'There is no woman of importance in my life now.'

His words rang out in the soft summer air, echoing what her heart already knew — that Max Rutherford was a lonely man who needed her love. And she wanted to love him with all her heart and banish the sadness filling those black eyes from which all trace of arrogance and brazenness was gone.

'So now you know,' he said in a quiet reflective voice. 'Not at all how you expected to spend the afternoon — listening to an old man's story.'

'But you're not old to me.' The voice of her heart and her head agreed with her tongue.

'How very kind you are, Edwina. How thoughtful. How considerate and charming.'

But that was not what he should be saying to her now and not what she expected or wanted him to say. His diffidence emboldened her . . .

'You're a very special man, Maxwell Rutherford . . . to me . . .'

'I'm twenty-five years older than you. That's a huge age gap, a generation. I'm old enough to be your father.'

'My father is ten years older than you are. Age doesn't matter if people . . . understand each other . . .'

'We hardly know each other.'

'I feel I've known you a long time . . . all my life . . .'

How much more did she need to say? How much longer was he going to hold out and torture her? In all her imaginings she had never expected it would be like this. They were right for each other. Couldn't he see that age and the length of time you had known someone were not important? What mattered was what you felt for them and how close you felt.

'Do you know what it is your heart wants, Edwina?'

'Yes.' Her throat was dry, her voice hoarse, her heart bursting and her body close to meltdown. 'I want . . .' This was awful — having to say, almost to ask, to beg for what she'd expected to have thrust upon her. 'I want . . . you . . . to . . . love . . . me . . .'

She had never felt so embarrassed.

'I just wanted you to be sure of what you wanted,' he murmured as he took both her hands in his and they rose.

Then she felt the strength of his arms around her.

And then they wandered towards the second open french window and somehow along the way her headscarf, her shoes and stockings got scattered on the terrace like petals in the summer rain.

Afterwards she no longer felt ugly deep inside. It was then she realised that her mother's crushing mantra — 'You're all top show, Edwina. If anyone ever finds out what you're really like they won't want you' — had been silenced. Max Rutherford had found her out and loved her.

As his eyes held hers, she could see the future now on his arm, her youth and beauty and pallor complementing his mature suntanned looks. They would make a striking couple and the age difference, which didn't matter, would seem like the way nature intended things to be between a man and woman. And she would make small talk with the women about her young children and enjoy the envy in their eyes at the fun she and her husband clearly had creating their family.

It was very much later before she recalled that the crisp white cotton sheets which felt so cool against her skin were already turned down when they entered the room and two tulip glasses and another bottle of champagne in an ice bucket had been waiting for them on a table by the bed . . .

CHAPTER FOUR

They were married four weeks and two days later in Dowanhill Register Office in Glasgow on an August day when islands of creamy cloud floated high across a blue sky and a rare harvest wind freshened the city streets.

The ceremony was attended by Edwina's parents, James Rutherford, Margaret Flaxman and Liza Drummond, another model with the Albion Agency and friend of Edwina's, who took the only photographs and joined the couple and their parents afterwards for lunch at the Spottiswoode Hotel.

'But why the haste?' Edwina's mother had only just managed to edit out the word 'indecent' when the couple presented themselves at her home in Edinburgh's Heriot Row the day after the afternoon in Lagg was followed by a night in Max's Glasgow home.

'Because I am very much in love with your daughter and have no wish to wait a long time to make her my wife,' Max assured Mrs Buchanan.

'Because I might be pregnant,' Edwina triumphantly informed her mother later when they were alone. 'And you wouldn't want your first grandchild to be born too soon after the wedding, now would you, Mother? People might talk . . . It just wouldn't be respectable.' She enjoyed throwing 'respectable' in her mother's face and seeing the old despot reel. Respectable was her mother's favourite, most trusted word, the measure by which she judged everything and everyone. The importance of respectability had been hammered into Edwina's head ever since she could remember. But her afternoon and night of love with Maxwell Rutherford had freed her from her mother's creeds and mantras.

> '"This above all: to thine own self be true,
> And it must follow, as the night the day,
> Thou canst not then be false to any man."'

Max had quoted Shakespeare in the middle of the night.

What Shakespeare and Max said was true. Now she pitied and despised the ageing tyrant, who was finally losing the battle she had waged to demean her daughter from Edwina's earliest childhood.

'Are you sure you know what you're doing?' Her father's approach later in the day was gentler despite a briefing from her mother. 'Max Rutherford may be a few years younger than me but he's still old enough to be your father.'

'But he's not. He's not anyone's father. And now he wants to settle down and have children. We've discussed it already.'

'For a man who's been married before he's left it a bit late.' A plea to have second thoughts or at least wait a bit was written in her father's eyes.

'Max is very conscious of that. It's why he doesn't want to wait any longer.'

'Your mother and I — '

'We love each other, Father,' cried Edwina. 'Can't you at least understand that?'

'Yes, I can,' said her father, giving up the uneven struggle.

'Love's more important than anything, Father. More than respectability,' said Edwina, giving her mother a knowing look as she thought of the armed truce in which her parents lived.

'But I always thought you wanted a big white wedding like Jane McNeill in St Giles Cathedral,' Mrs Buchanan fought back.

'I know sabotage when I hear it,' said Edwina. Her confidence now knew no bounds. 'Leave it, Mother.'

But Edwina would still like to have been married in church.

'It's just I always thought that if I got married it would be in church,' she admitted to Liza Drummond when they retreated to Copland's restaurant in Glasgow after a shopping expedition for her trousseau.

'What matters is that you and Max love each other, not the ceremony,' Liza consoled. 'But I'm sure Max and his father have enough influence with enough ministers that you can get your marriage blessed in church.'

But Edwina was being borne along so suddenly and swiftly and there was so much to do that she never got round to discussing a church blessing with Max.

Somehow it all seemed unreal until the private jet, which took them from Heathrow after the overnight train journey from Glasgow, touched down at Nice airport and Max was behind the wheel of a Renault and the warm winds of Provence were kissing her face like the sunlit breeze over the Firth of Clyde had done only weeks before.

But now she was his wife and as he took the dusty Provencal roads at a far more leisurely pace than the circle road round Arran, the change in her life at last began to seem real.

'Tell me about your life in France,' she said. Her voice was deeper than it had been before her marriage and rang with her newfound confidence.

'You'll find out about it soon enough,' said Max easily. 'Everyone my father and I know is here just now. And I hope you don't find the socialising we may be compelled to do too much of an interference in our honeymoon.'

'I want to meet your friends. I've got the rest of our lives to get you to myself.' She was amazed at how confident she sounded. She was a different person since she became Mrs Maxwell Rutherford.

'Oh, they'll want to meet you,' Max assured her, carefully taking a bend in the road. 'They'll be curious to see who Max Rutherford has married. I'll sit back and enjoy being envied for my wife.' His hand closed over hers in a reassuring gesture.

'Who are these people?'

'The wealthy unscrupulous rogues and pirates and high-way robbers the newspapers euphemistically call the jet set, and their hangers-on. You've read all about these supposedly glamorous people and their coteries. Now you'll meet them in all their infinite ugliness. And you'll soon discover that the principal difference between them and ordinary mortals is that they're much nastier and a lot better at exploiting people than the average individual.'

'But who *are* they?'

'Lord Beaverbrook and Somerset Maugham have villas not far from ours and regularly dine with us when my father's in residence.'

'Oh, I'd like to meet Somerset Maugham,' said Edwina enthusiastically. 'I love his short stories and the way he really understands people.'

'You'd hate him,' Max assured her. 'He's best met only in his books — where he ought to be left. In real life he's a vile, loathsome creature — exactly the opposite of the self-portrait he paints in his books of a sympathetic listener who's so understanding of human foibles. He hates the human race and doesn't hesitate to let them know it.

'As for Lord Beaverbrook, all he and my father want to talk about is politics. But don't worry, you won't have to suffer any such heavy and appalling company. Young people aren't their style. And there are plenty of entertaining villains to amuse you. If the yacht *Shemara* is anchored in the bay, you'll probably meet Lady Docker.' Max grinned. 'She gets a terrible press, but she's enormous fun. She's one of the few jet setters who's a lot nicer than the newspapers make out. Vulgar maybe. But honest — one of the few. I like her. I think you may do, too.'

He gave her an impish grin as he gracefully rounded a corner.

'Well at least they sound interesting,' said Edwina, trying not to feel too let down by Somerset Maugham.

'Oh, they're all a lot more interesting than the stuffed kilts I imagine you've been in the habit of meeting,' he said, giving her a large wink.

They were now bowling through the Provencal landscape of rolling hills and sunbaked farmhouses shaded by black cypresses which shared the world with crooked olive trees and fields of lavender and wheat.

'Over there,' said Max, pointing across the lazy landscape. 'That's where we're going.'

The Rutherford villa had been an olive-oil mill until the sixteenth century when a local grandee had converted it into a weekend retreat. Its ancient honey-coloured walls beneath a roof of mottled slates sheltered behind a high stone wall and tall iron gates at the end of a majestic avenue of plane trees. Though many additions had been made to the house down the centuries its distinct horizontal line on two storeys had been meticulously preserved along with its trellised doorway.

Vaulted ceilings, arches and niches lent an air of mystery to rooms of rough-hewn stone in which elegant French furniture from various periods was set. There were armoires in cherrywood and walnut, and soft furnishings in the colours of the sun filling every open space and corner with their warmth.

'I love it,' sighed Edwina as Madame Metalier, the housekeeper Max and his father employed to look after the villa, brought them 'English tea' in a cool alcove in the living room.

'You mean Scottish tea. *Le thé Ecosse*,' he joshed her when she laid a tray with fine china on a glass table before them. 'Melrose's finest.'

The woman, who was in her late forties and slightly overweight, wore an expression as animated as a statue.

Edwina glanced up at her, smiling, and was greeted by a look of such contempt that her hands started to shake.

'Madame Metalier's all right really.' Max, who had seen Edwina's shocked face, explained after the woman had gone. 'She's been with us for years and is getting a bit set in her ways. It takes her time to get used to people.'

'She hates me,' said Edwina, still shaking. 'I saw it in her eyes.'

'Nonsense,' said Max, pouring the tea. 'You're imagining it. And I really can't stand melodrama. I hope you're not one of those women.'

She had no wish to begin her married life in her husband's home with tears or a scene, and the warming, familiar taste of the tea was having a soothing effect on her.

'I've never been abroad before,' she excused. 'Everything's so strange. Maybe that's what it is.'

Madama Metalier's husband had taken their suitcases up to the master bedroom where they stood neatly side by side at the end of the biggest bed Edwina had ever seen.

'It's enormous! Big enough for a family of ten to sleep in,' she cried, bouncing on top of its cover of rust-red Indian cotton. 'It makes the kingsize in Arran look like a baby's cot.'

'I'm glad you think it's big enough,' said Max, bouncing beside her and taking her in his arms.

She saw the desire massing in his eyes but she didn't want to be taken unceremoniously the first time in this lovely room.

'In a minute, Max,' she cried, springing up and off the bed. 'Let's get unpacked first.'

She took several fluid, long-limbed strides across the floor and prised open two louvred wardrobe doors.

'What on earth is this?' she cried, plucking a white silk robe from the wardrobe and tossing it on to the floor like a filthy rag. 'And there's more!'

The louvred doors concealed a wealth of beautiful silk negligées, peignoirs, patio pyjamas, gorgeous afternoon prints and satins for the evening . . . all belonging to another woman.

Edwina grabbed them from their padded hangers and hurled them with gale-force strength at her husband.

'Whose are these?' she demanded.

Instinctively she knew there was more. She ran across the room and hauled open a drawer in a chest with such ferocity it crashed on to the floor, only just missing her feet.

Sunlight streaming through the venetian blinds fell on a dazzling, intimidating display of slips, French knickers and camisoles that looked exactly as if they had been left there for the express purpose of destroying her self-confidence and peace of mind.

'I'm sorry,' said Max, his eyes filling with pain. 'These shouldn't be here. I told madame Metalier to clear out everything. It's most unlike her to be so remiss. I'll get her to see to them at once.'

'Not so fast,' cried Edwina, trembling as he started to leave the room. 'Who do they belong to?'

He stopped and their eyes locked for an eternal moment when it seemed the world was going to end before he said with quite appalling dignity, 'They belong to a lady called Diana Watson, who was my mistress for a number of years.'

In that instant, between the flash of lightning and the roar of thunder, she knew Diana Watson had been very important to him and probably still was.

As the storm broke she heard her voice demanding, 'Until when?'

'Until she returned to Canada.'

'When?'

'Quite recently.'

'When?'

'Just over four weeks ago.'

'Just over four weeks ago!' The words dropped from her lips. 'But that was . . .'

'Yes. I said goodbye to Diana the day before I took you to Lagg.' The incredible dignity, the respect in which he held this woman, was worse than anything.

'When?'

'The day before.'

'Where?'

'In Glasgow.'

'Where in Glasgow?'

'At her flat.'

'When?'

'In the evening.'

She could not bring herself to ask the next question, but she knew the answer — that he had spent the night with the other woman before he made love to her in Lagg.

'Diana had been important,' he said. 'But it was over between us.'

'But you made . . .' She could not say the words which acknowledged his intimacy with the other woman.

'Perhaps one day when you're a lot older you'll know it's the nicest way for a man and woman who have been close to say goodbye,' he said.

Now it seemed she knew nothing about relations between men and women. She felt stupid and naive and all her old feelings of inadequacy, which his love had seemed to banish, were rearing up. All she could do was grope for information.

'But why, if it was over, were you still seeing each other?' she asked.

'Sometimes when people have nowhere else to go — no one else to go to — they hang on to each other out of fear of being alone. Can you understand that?'

But she understood nothing right now — except that she was in pain and he was far from her and she never wanted to live hanging on to someone without love.

'It was you I wanted to marry,' he said. 'And if you feel I've been less than completely honest with you before our marriage, I apologise. But I didn't think it was that important. It was the past.'

She stared at him uncomprehendingly — until his now haggard expression made her realise he had been as shocked as she was by the discovery of Diana Watson's clothes. She felt a glimmer of understanding at that and seemed to make a connection with him.

'She did it. Deliberately. That housekeeper of yours,' she said slowly. 'She left them there so I'd find them. She hates me. I saw it in her eyes.'

'Oh, I doubt it,' he said. 'Madame Metalier is very loyal.'

'To you probably,' she said. 'But she hates me. She wanted me to find those clothes because she doesn't want me in this house. She doesn't approve of your having married me.' That at least she understood.

'Rubbish,' he said. 'And it's none of her business. I'll go and speak to her and get this cleared up at once.'

Left alone she let out a howl of such anguish that Madame Metalier's husband and the gardener, who were draining the swimming pool, heard her and guessed correctly what had happened.

She wanted to pick up her suitcase and run away. Back to Edinburgh. Glasgow. Anywhere. Away from this horrible house.

She began to pace the room.

She wanted to take a machine gun to that monster of a bed till its feathers flew with the four winds. She wanted to take an axe to the Louis Seize writing desk and armchairs and jardinieres. She wanted to rip the rural prints with a carving knife and hurl rocks at the mirror which ran from the ceiling to the floor till the noise of the shattering was louder than thunder. And she wanted to consign everything that remained to hell fires that would light the skies for days and nights and defy extinguishing until the living, screaming body of Diana Watson was hurled on to the pyre.

Then she stumbled towards the window and stared out at the alien vista of rolling hills, olive trees and black cypresses sheltering sunny farmhouses.

And the tears began to fall.

She had been married to Max Rutherford for scarcely twenty-four hours and she had never been more miserable in her life.

The reasons why she should not have married in such haste came surging forth like some vast artesian well exploding in her heart and brain.

'What on earth do you know about this man?' her mother had remonstrated.

'Enough to know I love him.' The words tripped lightly, glibly off her tongue as she sensed sabotage.

'"Love is patient" . . .' Her father had gently tried to quote St Paul. But, suspecting he had once again been primed by her mother, she had cut him short.

'You're our only child and we only have your best interests at heart,' he had bravely tried again the following evening.

'I'm sure you mean well, Father, but it's my life and I'll live it my way,' she said wearily, trying not to be unkind to him.

They gave up in the end. They had no choice.

'But if you ever need me I'm still here for you,' her father had whispered in her ear before they parted after the wedding lunch.

That had been only yesterday.

Now her eyes were swollen and sore, rueing her marriage. She took off her shoes and stockings and the dress in which she had travelled and tottered towards a door which looked as if it might lead to a bathroom.

But she halted suddenly on the cool tiles at the threshold and drew her breath.

A bath standing in solitary splendour in the centre of the room was reflected in walls lined with mirrors in handsome yellow copper frames. This wasn't a bathroom — it was a pagan temple of bathing. And love.

Tears sprang up to scald her swollen eyes anew. And now the profound sense of inadequacy that had haunted her all her life came welling, too, to compound her woes and banish the brand-new confidence which had come with marriage.

She reeled towards the bath and was violently sick.

Max had changed from his travel clothes into a cool white linen suit and was standing at the bathroom door.

'Western Union made a tramp's dinner of the telegrams,' he said. 'Madame Metalier didn't think we were arriving until tomorrow. But that's no excuse. And I apologise profoundly for the unnecessary pain which has been inflicted on you.'

Edwina lifted her face from the comforting deep pile of a white towel and glared at him.

'We need to talk,' he said.

'About what?'

'Us. Our marriage.'

'It's over. I hate you and I want a divorce.'

'It hasn't even started,' he said, entering the room and reaching out a hand towards her.

'Don't touch me!' she screamed, pulling the towel protectively around her. 'Don't come anywhere near me!'

He stopped and lowered his eyelids for a moment. When he opened them again she was shocked by the depth of suffering she saw in his eyes.

'If you believe nothing else,' he said, 'there is one thing you cannot deny: Diana Watson belongs in my past. She was my mistress, not my wife. You are my wife. And our life together as man and wife is all that matters now.

'Edwina, we are married. We've taken a very solemn step together and we can't walk away from marriage just because there are things we don't like about each other.'

'You married me under false pretences. So our marriage is invalid,' she sulked.

'If I'd thought the past was important I would have told you. But it's just that. It's over, done, and there's nothing you or I or anyone can do about it.'

Dappled sunshine was playing on the terrace and the evensong of the cicadas was filling the cool air as Max sent a champagne cork spinning towards the swimming pool. Edwina watched the expertise with which he filled a tall glass, not losing a single drop or bubble of the expensive vintage. He was very practised.

'Quite sure you don't want any?' He raised the bottle in one hand.

She shook her head. Her fingers were clutched tightly around a glass of iced orange juice. Though a warm bath and changing into a pair of exquisite pink silk patio pyjamas had taken some of the sting out of her turbulent emotions, she was tired and didn't want alcohol blurring her attention as Max told her about his relationship with Diana Watson, which he insisted he must do.

When he had settled on the cushioned lounger beside her upright chair he wasted no time.

'I first met Diana Wetherspoon, as she then was, during Clyde Yachting Fortnight in 1935. I hadn't long returned from Australia, and it was the same occasion that you came along to, my father's annual party for the newspaper trade. Diana's father was a newspaper wholesaler and he brought her. She was the prettiest woman I'd ever seen. And from the moment I saw her I wanted to get her all to myself and spend the whole day running my fingers through her blonde curls and kissing her eyes, which were bluer than the summer sky we were sailing under. But a diamond solitaire the size of a large pebble told the world she was already spoken for. Yet she liked me every bit as much as I liked her, and I'm sure she'd have said a decent goodbye to the miserable soul who had given her the ring – his name was David Trotman and he had some nefarious business with the Stock Exchange in Glasgow – if her family hadn't disapproved of me quite so violently. Neither her father nor mother nor either of her brothers could stand me.'

'Why?'

'Let me tell my story, Edwina. I'll answer your questions later.

'My father was on tenterhooks. He'd have liked me to have married Diana. But once he knew how her family felt he took their side. My designs on Diana were bad for business so far as he was concerned and, as you'll discover, business comes first with my father.

'So Diana married her stockbroker and he took her to London where he'd decided he could make a better living. And in the fullness of time my father found me another bride, a shipping heiress called Elizabeth Johnston, whose father was a second baronet.'

Watching the sunlight play hide and seek on his face as he talked about people who had been in his life long ago, Edwina was becoming acutely aware she had married a stranger. For the first time she was poignantly aware too of the gulf in their ages. And she knew now that it *did* matter.

'Elizabeth was not beautiful but she was an extremely nice woman, and I was confident that we'd get along,' said Max, but Edwina heard the uncertainty in his voice. He was talking too quickly, as if he wanted to get the past over and done with and buried and no more questions asked about it. 'Except we married just as the war was breaking out and hardly ever saw each other for the next six years. I was in British Intelligence and the War Office didn't encourage wives to hang around. And as Elizabeth had no children she was recruited to do war work for the Ministry of Information in Glasgow.

'We were in offices in Victoria in London at one time and

on one fine sunny summer day in 1944 my chief, Colonel
Warrender, suggested we might find some pleasant diversion
from our arduous duties at a lunchtime concert ENSA were
giving at the Whitehall Theatre.

'It was an excellent show, better than any other ENSA
show I'd seen. Then an arrestingly pretty girl came on
stage and started singing "We'll Meet Again". There was
something familiar about her face, but it wasn't until she
smiled at the end of her song that I recognised her. Though
paper was short because of wartime restrictions, Robert, who
could always lay his hands on whatever he wanted, had got
some kind of programme. I asked to see it. And there was
her name — Diana Maria, the one she had used when she
appeared with the Scottish National Players in the 1930s.
They were the leading amateur company in Scotland then,
with high hopes of emulating the Abbey Theatre in Dublin.
Some, like Tyrone Guthrie, who directed them for a time,
became highly successful professional actors and actresses. If
Diana hadn't married that miserable Trotman she could have
made quite a name for herself on the stage as a professional
actress. A lot of people thought she was even better than
June, Lady Inverclyde, who made a name in Hollywood.

'Anyway I managed to persuade Colonel Warrender that I
had some extremely intelligent business to attend to backstage
after lunch.

'Diana was a widow now. Trotman had died at Dunkirk.

'It was wartime. Everyone lived for today because we all
knew there might be no tomorrow. Tonight might be your
very last chance to be happy.

'Diana and I virtually lived together in my flat in Artillery Mansions for the last year of the war. When it ended I wanted to marry her.

'But though Diana's family were now reconciled to the idea of us marrying, my wife refused to divorce me.'

'Why?'

'At the time I thought it was spite, sheer bloody mindedness. If she couldn't have me, no one else would.' He was speaking ever faster. 'So I was forced to keep up the facade of publicly appearing to remain married to my wife while privately Diana and I lived together.'

'That must have been terrible for her.'

He didn't seem to hear. 'Finally in 1950 she agreed to a divorce . . .'

'But she died six months later, so you would have been free anyway then,' cried Edwina. 'What was wrong with her?'

There was a long pregnant silence as Max looked at his expensive leather shoes.

When he raised his eyes to meet Edwina's he said, '. . . of a broken heart.' Now he spoke slowly, in a measured tone. 'She'd always hoped I'd return to her and she couldn't live without me.'

'How do you know that?'

'She said so in her suicide note — '

'Suicide! She committed suicide?'

'Very sadly.' He looked down again at his expensive shoes.

The air was cooler now and a million stars were teeming in the evening sky. For a moment Edwina wanted to think she was playing a part in a film of a Scott Fitzgerald book where the characters played out their unhappiness on nights like this. But as her eyes continued to rest on her husband's bowed head, the notion of a movie faded and she wondered what she had done.

Eventually she said in a low voice, 'But that was three years ago. Why didn't you marry Diana after what people call a decent interval?'

He raised his head slowly and his eyes were unfathomable when they met hers.

'Because it was really over between us even then,' he said.

'But why did her family so object to you marrying her in the beginning?' Edwina repeated her original question.

His gaze remained steady, holding hers when he said, 'Because I had been married in Australia before I met Diana — to a half-Aboriginal dancer.'

'To a coloured woman!'

'Her colour was hardly noticeable.'

'But she was coloured and she was your wife?'

'For six months. My father managed to keep both the marriage and divorce pretty quiet. But the newspaper business being what it is and the way people know each other, word did reach a few people in Scotland, among them Duncan Wetherspoon, Diana's father. Her family considered I had gone native like one of your Somerset Maugham characters, and was not a suitable husband for their daughter.'

'I'd never have married you either if I'd known!' she cried.

This was even worse than his relationship with Diana, who was at least white.

She looked at his hand around the champagne bottle as he replenished his glass, and felt sick.

To think what those hands had once done . . . to a coloured woman . . .

She could never bear for him to touch her again . . .

'My first marriage is probably harder for you to accept and understand than my relationship with Diana Watson,' said Max as Edwina went on staring at him in disbelief. 'It took place over twenty years ago — in 1932. You were two years old then, still in your pram, completely different from the person you are today. Though I was officially adult then, I'm as much a different person today as you are to the little person you were twenty-one years ago. If you can think of my first marriage in those terms, you may find it easier to accept.'

'I think I'd like some champagne,' Edwina said in a low voice.

Their eyes met and held for a very long moment before he said, 'If you wish to sleep alone tonight I'll understand. If you wish to sleep alone for weeks and months I'll also understand. I'll understand for however long it takes for you to come back to me. But it's what I want. With all my heart. I don't want to lose you.'

'I don't want to lose you.'

She thought Max was in the room when she awoke alone in the middle of the night in a guest suite.

Moonlight playing on the shadows of the plane trees

swaying in a breeze was creating weird, fantastic patterns on the walls and the white muslin bedcover.

She sat up slowly and watched them for ages as her husband's words turned over and over again in her mind. They had haunted her turbulent sleep.

She had wanted to be married. More than anything. And like some proverbial knight kitted out in an AI, five star, blue chip suit of armour and riding a Persil-white charger, Max Rutherford had stepped out of the audience at a charity fashion gala and made her virginal dreams come true.

And now she was his wife! The third wife of a man whose first marriage had been to a coloured woman!

She would never have consented to become the third wife of a man of loose morals who had lived with coloured trash if she had known before her marriage what she knew now. At least you knew who people were in the genteel circles of Edinburgh and the Borders, as her mother had always said. And her mother had been right! The legacy of the tobacco-baron culture (if that wasn't too fine a word for it) made Glasgow a wild-west town where the people were carpetbaggers of dubious antecedents.

'He's an old roué,' her mother had said when she was getting desperate, when more subtle means of attack had failed.

'Oh, Mummy, I want to come home,' she cried, pulling the muslin cover over her head and curling up in a womb-like cocoon.

Max was giving instructions to the young assistant gardener

on the far side of the swimming pool when Edwina came down to breakfast on the terrace late the next morning. She had dressed with care in a yellow gingham dress and though she felt wrung out emotionally and had hardly slept she was amazed at how pretty she looked and how almost normal her eyes appeared beneath her light make-up.

'Thank you, Pascal, it's a considerate thought and I appreciate the trouble you've put in to trying to give me what you think I might like, but I don't really want an English border as you call it in my garden in France. Or a Scottish one either.' Her husband's accentless international diction drifted across the pool towards Edwina.

There was a natural authority in that voice, a confident expectation that his will would be done as if it was as much part of the way of things as the rising of the sun. His voice drew her attention to his lean athletic figure, so well proportioned it could have been designed as a perfect prototype for the human male. And she was only just beginning to notice how well Max wore clothes. A fine lawn shirt might look merely expensive on a hanger but on his back it became a stylish, racy thing. The pale lemon shirt he wore open at the neck and tucked into a pair of white trousers conveyed relaxed authority as natural as his voice. If he had been a stranger she knew she would have noticed him, no matter how many people were around. When he saw her and began to walk towards her she could not take her eyes off him.

'Sleep well?' he asked amiably, taking a seat at the table and helping himself to coffee from a blue china pot.

She did not answer, just went on looking at his handsome face with its carved features and brilliant black eyes filled with sadness.

'I don't want to lose you,' he'd said yesterday at the height of her grief. But it had taken a turbulent night half slept, half haunted by visions of hell for her to understand what he meant.

But now in the brightening, warming morning sunlight she understood that for the first time in her life she was needed and wanted by another human being, however flawed. She was not nothing any more, as her mother had always told her. She was something and someone. She was loved . . .

For the first time she became aware of the great breadth of life and its infinite possibilities for happiness – that it was not the narrow thing to be regarded with suspicion and dread that she had been brought up to believe.

They looked at each other across the breakfast table for a long time, across the vast chasm of youth versus experience. And in the fierce light of their gaze the demon of alienation began to flee.

'I had no idea, just no idea what it was like to be loved,' she said eventually, swallowing tears.

'I don't think I had either until I found you were still here, you hadn't fled in the night,' he said, reaching for her hand. And now she did not flinch from his touch.

Without another word they knew they would find their way back to each other and begin again . . .

CHAPTER FIVE

James Rutherford's wedding present to Max and Edwina was a large Victorian townhouse in the heart of Glasgow's West End which he had previously shared intermittently with his son. Its four storeys stood on the rise of Kirklee Terrace by the Royal Botanic Gardens and overlooking the boulevard of Great Western Road, and when the sun shone through its handsome astragalled windows all the most important rooms were filled with dazzling light.

'This will make a fine family home,' said James with a knowing look when he took Edwina's elbow in the pillared hall and led her up the marble stairs on a conducted tour shortly after she returned from her honeymoon. She quickly noticed that the parquet floors, period fireplaces and panelled walls beneath crystal chandeliers and elaborate cornices were all in an immaculate condition that her mother, with her threadbare pretensions to running a salon, would envy. Like the villa in Provence, the house was furnished largely with French furniture from a variety of periods and the *fêtes champêtres* of some of the lesser eighteenth-century French artists hung on many walls alongside the work of the Glasgow Boys.

'It is really so kind of you to give us this lovely house,' she said as they flitted out and in of bedrooms to which the facility of wash basins had been added.

'All I ask is that I can get a bed for the night when I visit my grandchildren if I'm too old and tired to find my way home,' said James, adopting his frailest demeanour as he handed her the keys of the house.

'Oh, I hope you're going to stay with us often long before we have a family,' said Edwina, smiling into brilliant, unfathomable eyes that were as black as his son's.

Though at six feet, James Rutherford was as tall as his offspring and there was no mistaking their kinship, his build was wirier and his expression and manner more alert. At seventy-four he looked more like sixty. And he still missed nothing.

'I hope you're not going to make an old man, who may not have long to live, wait too long for the grandchildren he longs to see,' he said pointedly.

'Not too long,' said Edwina, smiling and suddenly feeling vaguely uneasy without quite knowing why.

Though she wanted to bear Max the children neither of his previous wives had been able to give him, she wanted to have him all to herself for a while. They had been together for so short a time and she was already discovering the demands of his work made tremendous inroads into their private life.

But she also soon discovered she was pregnant.

Marietta Beatrice Rutherford, named after both her grandmothers, was born on 21 June 1954 – the longest day of the year when it was bright in Glasgow till eleven in the evening. Her parents had not been married a year.

But the house was large and the baby had a nanny and a biddable nature, so her arrival hardly disturbed their lives.

The biggest change in Edwina's life was that she saw a lot more of her father-in-law, who doted on his granddaughter.

'I never had a daughter,' he drooled over the cot where the baby lay sleeping on one of his regular afternoon visits to Kirklee Terrace. 'My wife would have been so proud if she had lived to see her. But I know she's up there' – he raised his eyes in the direction of the ceiling – 'looking down and blessing her granddaughter.'

James also talked incessantly about the news, in which he was far more passionately interested than his son. He had started work as a copy boy on the *Daily Post*, running errands for the reporters before he became one himself. His ability to find scoops and unearth scandals had been legendary until he was drawn into management as news editor of the *Post*. Within two years he was editor and it was only another two before his latent entrepreneurial skills flared and with the backing of the British Linen Bank he bought a weekly newspaper in Renfrewshire. From this base he began buying up weekly newspapers whenever he saw a chance or could manage to create one. Five years after leaving the editorship of the *Post* he launched his own daily newspaper, the *Daily Globe*. Though from then on he was increasingly concerned with the business side, his news sense remained as keen as ever, as some editors had learned to their cost. The 5 p.m. telephone call he made to the editor of the *Daily Globe* from wherever he was in the world had intimidated most of them, largely because James Rutherford was one of the few newspaper proprietors who had been a reporter and his news sense remained as alert as ever. He lived, breathed, ate, drank, slept and dreamed news night and day.

Edwina found that listening to him ranging over world affairs with the special background knowledge of the newspaperman with top-level contacts was like having a private line to the hottest gossip in town! She began to read all the newspapers so that she could ask him lots of intelligent questions.

She took a lively interest in the emergence of Nikita Khrushchev as leader of the Soviet Union, the signing of the Warsaw Pact by the nations of Eastern Europe, the Mau Mau terrorist campaign in Kenya and the exile of President Juan Perón of Argentina. She listened for hours to James talking about the resignation of Sir Winston Churchill as Prime Minister and the achievement of his successor, Sir Anthony Eden, in winning the next general election. She was fascinated by the trial and hanging of the blonde model Ruth Ellis for the murder of her faithless lover and the official clearance of Kim Philby as the Third Man in the Burgess and Maclean spy scandal.

But the news which fascinated her most of all in 1955 was Princess Margaret's decision to abandon her plans to marry a former royal equerry, Group Captain Peter Townsend, because he was divorced, and marriage to a divorcee was against the Church of England's teaching.

'His fellow courtiers had as much to do with it as the

Archbishop of Canterbury,' James told her when they dined on the November evening after the announcement from Buckingham Palace. 'They don't like one of their number getting above themselves. They had the boot and the sword into him from the moment they got the first hint of love in the air. The politics at Westminster are a bunfight at a teddy bears' picnic compared to the politics behind closed door at Buckingham Palace. It's medieval what goes on there, but nobody ever hears anything about it.'

Earlier in the year James's attitude to a strike by engineers and electricians which had kept papers published in London off the streets for twenty-six days had taught Edwina a lot about the volatility and cut-throat camaraderie of newspaper publishing. Sales of Globe papers soared during the strike and special editions were produced to meet demand in the news-hungry English market.

'But it's bad for business,' James complained over Edwina's dinner table. 'Some newspapers might not survive the strike. And when a newspaper closes it damages the whole business.'

'But you're making a lot of money out of the strike,' said Edwina.

'That's not the point, and for how long? And if the unions decide to hit me tonight I could lose it all tomorrow,' said James. 'When you read a newspaper it all looks so settled and defined. There's a deceptive serenity about the printed word. It's a mighty volatile business. The biggest problem facing newspapers is that, unlike most other businesses, the owners don't control them. On any night the unions can stop work, fail to press a vital switch, so there's no paper the next day. And the profits are gone. It happens quietly night after night. The bosses are held to ransom by last-minute overtime demands. You pay up or lose hundreds of thousands of pounds. You have no choice.

'One day a newspaper proprietor will come along who'll break the power of the unions, probably a Canadian like Max Beaverbrook. He certainly won't be British because we native-born newspaper proprietors are far too browbeaten and intimidated by the unions ever to stand up to them.'

Edwina listened to every word that fell from James's lips with a rapt expression. She also learned a lot about the newspaper business at the company's frequent social occasions where she met its leading executives — including Drew Hamilton, the fastest-rising editorial star who was editor of the *Evening Globe* and about whom James and Max held violently opposed opinions.

'I've had to give Drew the world to play with and I pay him an enormous salary to stop him going to Fleet Street,' said James. 'But he's an editorial genius, I need him here, and he's worth even more than I pay him. He's also that rare person — the journalist who's genuinely interesting in himself. What journalists do is interesting, but mostly they themselves are not.'

Max could have been speaking about a different man: 'Drew Hamilton is vastly overrated and ludicrously spoiled by my father,' he said. 'The truth about him was revealed in all its vacuity in 1953 after he swanned back from the onerous duty of attending the armistice at Panmunjon at the end of the

Korean War. My father decided he needed some light relief, so he briefly made him diary editor and gave him society to play with. And he came out in his true colours. Like all diary hacks, Drew desperately aspired to be one of the people he wrote about. He may pretend to despise the rich, but he longs to be one of them. That's what drives him. The journalist is by the nature of the job an outsider, but some are seduced by the Cabinet Minister cocktail-party-circuit crap. They want to belong among those they write about. They get too friendly and sacrifice editorial freedom for high-placed friendship.'

In the flesh Drew Hamilton had eyes blue as the Mediterranean in summer, a golden head of hair with the quality of a mane even though it was cut conventionally short, and a way of looking at Edwina that made her feel she was the most important person in the world to him.

But father and son both approved of the *Globe*'s advertisement director, Alex Regan, who resembled a werewolf when he smiled and his canines appeared like stalactites suspended from the roof of his mouth over his flabby lower lip. He wore large horn-rimmed glasses, was almost completely bald, and his broad forehead and skeletal chin stuck out at acute right angles over a scraggy neck. But as he had only recently been widowed he was considered one of the most eligible men in Glasgow and there was no shortage of beautiful women, much younger than himself, willing to drape themselves on his arm on public occasions.

But Edwina withdrew largely from the social scene not long after the Suez crisis broke in the autumn of 1956. She was six months pregnant with her second child and neither

her husband nor father-in-law approved of women in the later stages of pregnancy going out on the town.

Keith James Maxwell Rutherford weighed in at eight pounds, three and a half ounces on I February 1957. He had a thatch of black hair and, according to the nurses, bawled louder than any other baby born that day.

To mark his birth his paternal grandfather presented the Lord Provost of Glasgow with a cheque for £5,000 for various charities. He also wrote a cheque for £5,000 to the Newspaper Press Fund, which Charles Dickens had founded to help journalists who had fallen on hard times. As 1957 was also Globe Newspaper Publishing's golden jubilee, the baby's name was linked to the celebrations which went on all year, culminating in a ball to which the world was invited in James's mansion near Kilmacolm on the anniversary day in November.

James Rutherford's red sandstone mansion, which stood in thirty acres of parkland, had been built in Victorian times and was approached through an avenue of limes ending in a broad gravel sweep. Stairways at either side of the house led to a terrace from which on a clear day, when the sun glinted on the Duchal Moor, it was possible to see for miles over the glorious Renfrewshire hinterland. But when the rain clouds gathered the prospect was as morose and gloomy as the wildest Highland landscape. Fires had been lit and chandeliers blazed, making the house a beacon for miles across the countryside on the dark November night of the ball.

Keith Rutherford and his sister had been brought to sleep

in the house that night. And before he was laid in his cot Keith was carried in his grandfather's arms around the ballroom, hall, dining room, conservatory and all the rooms where guests would congregate.

'In another fifty years when Globe Publishing celebrates its centenary you'll be entertaining guests in this house and will be able to tell them how your old grandfather, who founded the company, made sure you saw something of the golden jubilee celebrations,' James told the baby, who gazed up at him with huge blue eyes that flattered the old man into believing he understood every word.

'Why is Grandad taking Keith and not me round the house telling him about the party?' asked Marietta, pressing her face between the first-floor balusters above the hall.

'Because he's a boy and one day he's going to give a party like this,' replied Edwina, holding her daughter's hand.

'But Keith's a baby and he won't know what Grandad's talking about.' Marietta looked up at her mother.

'I know,' said Edwina. 'It does seem rather silly.'

'Yes. Silly Grandad,' cried the child, raising her voice.

'Shush,' said Edwina, pressing a finger against her lips. 'It's very nice of him to invite us all to stay with him on the night he's busy with his party. And we don't want to upset him.'

But the all-maleness of the Rutherford show was starting to stick in Edwina's gullet. It was father, son and now grandson, all boys together, and women just didn't come into it. She had felt acutely aware of the male chauvinism of her husband and father-in-law ever since the birth of her son. James, who had been so companionable and spent so much time in her company after Marietta's birth, now hardly called at Kirklee Terrace at all. His excuse when she said she missed him was the golden jubilee celebrations.

'They hardly leave me a spare moment,' he explained without apology.

And Max was even busier than ever, constantly working late at the office.

'It's almost as if I've outlived my usefulness to them,' Edwina complained to Liza Drummond on one of their regular lunch dates at Daly's restaurant. 'Now that I've provided the son, grandson and heir they both wanted they don't seem to have the same interest in me any more.'

'You know how demanding Father is even at the best of times, but I think we owe him all our support in his golden jubilee year.' Max had not been sympathetic when she complained she hardly saw him except across a crowded reception room. 'It is after all entirely due to his dedicated efforts to build the business that we live so well.'

She never got the time alone with her husband she had dreamed of as a bride.

'I actually see more of my father-in-law on his own than I do of my husband,' she often said to Liza Drummond in the years between having her babies.

But she wasn't having any more babies, at least not for a while, she had decided after Keith was born. And now that she had produced a grandson and heir, she felt she'd done her duty by the Rutherfords until she and Max should decide another child was what they both wanted to create as an act of their love for each other.

'My next baby will be a true love child,' she told Liza, 'not a duty offspring I'm expected to produce.'

But as she had hardly seen Max since Keith was born there had been little risk of even bringing a duty offspring into the world. When he hadn't been late at the office in some connection with the golden jubilee, he'd been abroad on business. And when a dispute loomed with Globe's Scandinavian newsprint suppliers, James had despatched him to Canada for weeks and months on end to negotiate with a North American company.

But the golden jubilee year was nearly over and with her duty offspring thriving, Edwina intended things would be different from now on. She would be more demanding, assume more of a matriarchal role in her need for her wishes to be considered important and obeyed, become a much more active lover in her husband's life. They'd get the time together they needed because he wouldn't be able to bear to stay away from her!

When she had seen the children to bed she surveyed her reflection in a gilded mirror by the top of James's grand white marble staircase. She'd recovered her shape very well after her children and her strapless black velvet gown, moulded to her figure till it flared below the knees, emphasised her ever-growing voluptuousness. There were diamonds and pearls at throat and ears, and her hair was dressed in an elegant chignon.

She glanced downstairs where her husband and father-in-law were deep in conversation in the hall. The élan with which Max wore expensive suits mocked all idea that clothes were a decent covering for the human body. On him they were an invitation to sublime, unspeakable pleasures, and the formality of evening dress made them seem most sublime and unspeakable of all. He was now fifty-two and for a moment Edwina almost felt jealous that he was still in such commanding possession of his athlete's physique. He was far too attractive for a man of his age, and there had been times recently when she wondered exactly what he did on all those late nights at the office. But after tonight she was going to get him back all to herself and Globe Publishing would have to start taking second place.

She cast one last glance in the mirror. Her old training as a model seemed to diffuse through her limbs. She was about to go on stage again as she had on the catwalk before she was married. She smiled at her reflection and then slowly, as her husband and father-in-law raised their eyes towards her, began to descend the magnificent marble stairs . . .

The guests were circulating beneath chandeliers that shone like stars in rooms banked with scented flowers flown specially for the Channel Islands.

Edwina had been on her feet for every dance and was about to go looking for Max, whom she hadn't seen for ages, when Drew Hamilton asked her to quickstep with him.

'I'd have made an excuse if it had been anyone else,' she

said as he whisked her on to the floor. 'I'm trying to find my husband. Have you seen him?'

'Not since he and the boss said good evening when I arrived,' said Drew. 'He's probably in some quiet corner doing a bit of business when everyone else is enjoying themselves. That's the family style I've observed over the years.'

'He's been working too hard. He needs a holiday and when all the jubilee celebrations are over I'm going to see he gets it,' she said determinedly. But she was enjoying spinning round the floor in the powerful arms of James's favourite journalist and basking in the admiration she saw in his brilliant blue eyes.

She was still humming 'Cherry Pink and Apple Blossom White' after their quickstep when, failing to find Max in any of the rooms being used for the ball, she decided he was probably in the conservatory and wandered through the gallery corridor leading to James's *pièce de résistance*. One of his few interests outside newspapers was horticulture and with the assistance of the Royal Botanic Gardens in Edinburgh and Kew he had created a magnificent semi-tropical garden where Edwina loved to bask beneath the palm trees and sunflowers and delicate exotic blooms on winter weekends and watch the snow gust over the Duchal Moor.

She heard Max's laughter as her strappy sandals lightly touched the tiled floor of the conservatory. He sounded happier and more relaxed than he had in a long time, which added to her mood of quiet elation.

She saw him as she approached the palm court at the heart of the conservatory − leaning forward, an elbow on one knee, his face more animated than she could remember it, 'raconteuring' as he would put it. He's doing a deal or leading the talk up to it, she thought — and having a thoroughly good time in the process. In case she interrupted at a crucial moment, she decided to turn away.

But just as she was turning he saw her.

'Ah, Edwina, come and join us.' He raised a beckoning arm.

She walked towards the palm court where he was sitting on one of the cushioned cane chairs arranged around a pool of water lilies.

Alex Regan was facing Max across a low glass-topped table. The chair between them was occupied by a suntanned blonde woman.

Max lifted a hand in the woman's direction as his wife reached the table.

'Edwina, I'd like you to meet Diana Watson,' he said.

CHAPTER SIX

She would remember the eyes of olive green and the disconcerting warmth that lit them. She would recall the proud head crowned by a fleece of antique gold that fell on shoulders the colour of the sun. She would never forget the acres of bosom slung across a suspension bridge of black chiffon that only just defied gravity and the amazing youth of the woman. But what would kill her was the way he looked at Diana Watson when he introduced 'my wife'. It was a look graced by humility, imbued with pleading, radiant with love. It was a look he had never cast on her and she knew what it meant at once.

'Max has told me so much about you. I'm delighted to meet you.' Diana's highpan Kelvinside accent was modified by a husky transatlantic twang. It was a sexy voice.

'Delighted,' murmured Edwina, taking the empty seat opposite the other woman as she felt herself eddying downwards in an emotional whirlpool. But marriage to Max had taught her to hide her feelings.

'Diana's just come back from Canada and Alex thought he'd bring her along,' said Max, plucking a glass from the drinks bar beside the pool and filling it for Edwina.

'You take out so many ladies you must break more hearts than Casanova,' said Edwina, giving him a watery smile.

'Quite the contrary. I'm a healer,' said Alex, beaming his most werewolfish smile. 'Going out with me does a lot to mend a woman's heart because she discovers there are still some nice decent men in the world when she thought there weren't any left.'

Max gave a bitter laugh.

The silence was so appallingly awkward it seemed like an amateur theatrical company rehearsing a silence in a play. The only sound was the palm trees rustling in the manufactured warm air

Edwina watched the bubbles ebb on the glass of champagne Max had poured for her. They seemed like tears or maybe rain water collecting in the glass. She wondered if it would be good to wash her face in it. Rain was supposed to be good for the complexion, but tears only gave you sore, swollen eyes. But some people said it was good to cry because it got rid of the pain. People said a lot of funny things. What did they really know?

'I came looking for you because I wanted to ask you to dance,' she managed to say in an even tone to her husband as the lifetime of a moment passed. She felt the relief, saw it in their faces, but she was numb as she tried desperately to steady herself emotionally.

As their eyes met, there was a humility in Max's expression she had never seen before. She thought, I'm looking at a stranger, a man I don't know. And then she had the powerful feeling he wanted to ask her for a most enormous favour.

'That's an excellent idea. I can't think of anything I'd rather do than dance with my wife,' he exclaimed, jumping up, unable to conceal his relief. 'And I'll leave the great healer of hearts to carry on his good work for the evening.'

Edwina heard the brittle ring in Diana's laughter, saw the tension easing from the other woman's face.

And as they made their way to the ballroom, she could feel need in Max's hand as she had never felt it before . . .

A Viennese waltz was in progress when Edwina and Max joined the couples on the crowded floor. James was struggling to keep his arms around the extremely fat wife of a leading newspaper wholesaler and a woman columnist on the *Daily Globe* was wrapping herself round Drew Hamilton as if he was a lamppost. The world seemed so normal beneath the light and warmth of the chandeliers that Edwina wondered if she had imagined the nightmare scene in the conservatory. What was so terrible about Alex Regan, who invited out the world of unaccompanied women, bringing along an old girlfriend of Max's? It had been over years ago. Max had said so himself right at the start of their marriage. As she tried to steady her emotions, she told herself she had been imagining things, getting them out of proportion, attaching more importance to them than they deserved. She had done that all her life. Everyone said so — her mother, her husband, her father-in-law. Except she had not imagined the look that had passed between her husband and the other woman. And she was not imagining the way he went on looking at her now with pleading eyes. It was a way he had never looked at her before. He wanted to ask for some vast favour, but her brain was too shocked and muddled to think what it might be . . .

CHAPTER SEVEN

'Share you with Diana Watson!' Edwina stared at Max incredulously.

'It's what I want.' His voice was calm and decisive as they faced each other across the four poster in their suite.

The last guests had not long left the house, and downstairs servants and catering staff hired for the occasion had started clearing up.

'Night about!' she sneered.

'However we can arrange our lives,' he said with the appalling dignity he invariably assumed when that woman's name was mentioned.

'You mean you want me to commit suicide like your last wife did! You want me dead as well so you can carry on with that . . . that . . . trollop!'

'Diana is not a trollop.' His tone was so reverential she wanted to hit him. 'And I mean no such thing. The circumstances are quite different to those of my last marriage. My previous wife and I were no longer lovers.'

'You're drunk! Your brain is fuddled with too much champagne!'

'On the contrary, because this evening was so important I've hardly touched a drop all night. And my mind and heart have never been clearer about what I want,' he said, looking at her with terrifying determination and an earnestness she had never seen in him before.

'But it's not what you're going to get! You're depraved, Max Rutherford. Depraved! And I'm not listening to another word of your horrible, depraved talk!'

She started to stride from the room, but he caught her wrist and forced her back towards the fireplace.

'No, you're not walking out on me, Edwina,' he said. 'You're going to sit down and listen to what I have to say. And you're not going anywhere until you do.'

He was hurting her and his eyes were blazing with a strange, queer light. He didn't seem like himself and she was frightened of the man who pushed her roughly down into a chair.

He strode across the room and poured himself a large brandy from a tantalus on a table by the window.

She watched his tall, lean figure, always at its most graceful in evening dress, and remembered the way he had looked at that half-naked, overripe floozie in the conservatory. A vision from hell blazed across her mind — she saw him doing what he ached to do with that creature. And jealousy, physical and nauseating, shot through her like forked lightning.

Though his step was slower when he recrossed the room, she knew there was no doubting his purpose. He sat down to face her by the embers of a wood fire.

Outside the night was black and still, and the only sound the distant calling of eerie nocturnal creatures she had never heard before over the moor.

Her arms lay tensed along the arms of the chair as she watched him take a large gulp of his brandy. Max had been her life for four years now — her husband, her lover, the father of her children. He had been everything and everyone to her. And she had wanted no one else, no other life. But the man sitting across the fire was different, a stranger who knew what he wanted in a way the man she married never had done. It was as if a facade had cracked open and some other man who had lurked behind her husband's easy manners was stepping out to usurp his place.

Her mind reached frantically for explanations. He had been overworking lately, all year in fact. James had never let him have a moment to himself because of the golden jubilee. He was tired. He needed a holiday. They both did.

They had just never had the time together they should have done.

But she knew that if he had wanted to be with her he would have made the time because people always did find time for what they wanted to do. And he had taken a holiday away from her in Canada in the midst of his negotiations with a new newsprint supplier.

Of course she knew now that he would not have been alone. That baggage lived in Canada. It would have been with him.

Her arms tensed along the arms of the chair as she waited. She was petrified.

'I had hoped this day would never come.' When he spoke at last his eyes solemnly took hold of hers. 'If I'd had my way it wouldn't have happened because we'd never have married.'

But that meant her life was a lie, a game of let's pretend and make-believe. And that couldn't be how it was.

'You don't mean that,' she said in a broken half whisper. 'That can't be true.'

'Edwina, dear Edwina, I had so hoped that you'd understand what I was trying to say to you in the beginning — that I was merely my father's vassal — and refuse to marry me.' She heard the despair in his voice and knew the terrible game of let's pretend had been real. 'I hoped you'd think I was too old for you and so escape being drawn into the nets in which he entraps everyone.'

'But how? How did it happen?' she cried.

'It was his idea that I married you,' said Max. 'He was desperate for me to have an heir. He'd seen you at a fashion show and decided you were the wife for me.'

'What did he say?'

'You may not like it.'

'I want to know.'

'"That one's a good breeder. It's in her eyes."'

'No.' The word escaped involuntarily as the thin veneer of self-confidence which marriage had given Edwina shattered like glass.

'I'm sorry,' he said. 'It was thoughtless of me to repeat that remark. But I'd been married twice and had no heir and my father was determined that I should have.'

And now she knew the game of let's pretend was real

and it explained everything — Max's indifference to spending much time with her, the way James had cultivated her till she produced her son and why both men had virtually ignored her ever since. Once she had given them what they wanted, they had no further use for her, and the pain was crushing and humiliating.

'If it had been possible for me to divorce just after the war, Diana and I could have had a family, but by the time I was free she was no longer able to have children,' said Max. 'So I struck a bargain with my father — if he could find me a bride I would marry and have a family so long as I could keep Diana as my mistress.

'But when he found you, Diana couldn't go through all the horror she'd suffered with my last wife. She left almost at once for Canada and married quickly on the rebound — a man who's still her husband though the marriage is over.

'She and I are both very anxious that we can all be friends . . .'

'No! Oh, you're depraved even to think such a thing,' she cried at this stranger whose eyes were pleading for her understanding as he nursed his brandy. How long did you have to live with someone to know them? How could you sleep with a man every night and nurture his seed within your body and bear his children and still know nothing of what his heart held?

'I know it must come as a terrible shock,' he said. 'And we live in a world where many people lead restricted, conventional, often unhappy lives. What I believe is right may seem depraved to you at first sight. But, believe me, I have thought about it. And I believe that once you've taken time to think about it, you may come to agree with me that it's a civilised and humane way for us all to live.

'Edwina, you're still so young, with most of your life still ahead of you. But that's not the way it is for me. I'm fifty-two years old. Many men have died by my age, though I'm fit and well and not yet the captive of the twelfth chapter of Ecclesiastes, the candle of my time is already burning low. My life has been sacrificed to my father's will. Before it's too late I want to reclaim my life and — '

'Are you telling me I married a ventriloquist's dummy? Or a male model?' Suddenly, like some piece of comic relief sent to stop her brain and heart from bursting, it struck her that the reason he wore clothes with such panache was because he slipped into the roles they represented as she had done on the catwalk. But the pain was getting worse.

'Edwina, that was unkind and uncalled for. I'm trying to make the best of a difficult situation.' He rose and when he had replenished his glass began to prowl the room restlessly.

'Look, Edwina, if you want to take a lover, I'll understand. All I ask is that you're discreet.'

'You mean find someone to fill your bed space on the nights you're with your trollop?'

He winced. 'Please, please don't use that word. Diana's not . . . the name which you called her.'

But her heart was breaking behind her puny insults.

She pursed her lips and looked hard at him.

'Did you . . . did you never love me?' She heard her voice breaking.

It brought him to one knee before her and he took her hands in his.

'Of course I did. And I still do. But try to understand what I'm saying, Edwina. A young girl is not the answer to the problems of a middle-aged man, though many men think it is. They delude themselves. What they're really seeking is the recovery of their own youth and the opportunites that lay ahead. But the years put them too far apart. And I didn't realise it and what I'd lost until I met Diana again.'

'No!' She was crying now as he held her hands.

'Yes. We can make it work for us. I believe if we try we can all be happy.'

But she didn't hear what he said. What she heard was another, much older voice calling to her from down memory lane: 'Edwina, if anyone ever finds out what you're really like they will not want to be with you.' Her mother's words reared up and soared across the years. The real reason Max was going back to his mistress was because he had found out his wife was inadequate and unlovable . . .

PART TWO

CHAPTER EIGHT

Glasgow, 1960

'Ladies and gentlemen, as you know 1960 has been difficult for the newspaper industry,' Maxwell Rutherford told the guests assembled in the first-floor drawing room of the house in Kirklee Terrace. 'Whatever one's political opinions, the closure of the *News Chronicle* in London and its merger with the *Daily Mail*, together with its sister paper *The Star* being swallowed by the *Evening News*, is a serious blow to the freedom of the press. Here in Glasgow we've had our troubles, too, and there cannot be a man or woman in this room who does not bitterly regret the economic forces which brought about the closure of *The Bulletin*.

'But it is not just economic forces which are the enemy of press freedom. Now we have the government wanting to shackle us with a Press Council to hamper our investigations into wrongs that would go unnoticed without our constant vigilance.'

Edwina was acutely aware of the scores of eyes comparing

the mask of hauteur behind which she hid to the statuesque radiance of Diana Watson, who was gazing at Max with a rapt expression a few feet away across the thronged and smoky room. People said it was incredible that a woman of fifty-three could look so attractive and voluptuous and more like thirty, Edwina's age. Edwina knew it was because Diana was lovable and therefore was loved, while she herself sought refuge behind her disdainful mask because she was not. She despised herself for having been far too inhibited to share him with Diana even at the beginning, but she had found the idea nauseous. So she had accepted the truth – that her inadequacy was the reason her marriage had failed – and she had let him go. She had been too ashamed to tell anyone, even Liza, about her failure as a wife and the real state of her marriage. For three years now she had kept up the public facade of being part of a couple while she carried the burden of her pain secretly and cried alone.

But ever since James Rutherford's elevation to the peerage as Baron Kilmacolm in the last Birthday Honours, Diana had no longer been content to conduct her relationship with his son discreetly. Now she swept into public functions on Alex Regan's arm and flirted openly with Max, constantly slipping her arm into his and embracing him with her gaze when he made a speech. And she had divorced her husband in Canada. People were starting to talk.

Looking at Diana's proud cleavage, which she never failed to sport, Edwina felt like a worm, ugly on the outside as well as within. So long as her failure as a wife had been a secret she could handle it and hold her head up in society. But she could not bear people knowing and talking. She wanted to crawl into a hole and die.

'So, ladies and gentlemen, we look to the future with renewed confidence and we thank you for giving your time to be here this evening,' Max concluded his address.

'The elegance of your coiffure reminds me of Jean Simmons's Ophelia.'

The towering figure of Drew Hamilton was at Edwina's side as the applause for Max's speech died down.

'But she was a tragic figure . . .'

'But very beautiful, though not as beautiful as you are,' he said, and those Mediterranean-blue eyes holding hers seemed brimming with empathy and compassion.

She had liked Drew from their first meeting. She liked his easy confidence, the way he made her feel she was the most important person in his world when she talked to him, and his indifference to the power of the Rutherfords. Where other senior company men pussyfooted and watched their words and played a sycophantic game of chess, Drew said what he thought. The company needed him more than he needed them, and both he and the Rutherfords knew it. Since she had been alone she had often felt that if she could talk to anyone it would be Drew because he had known Max and James for far longer than she had and would understand. Recently, whenever they had met on the usual circuit of crowded rooms she had found herself thinking how comforting it would be to rest her head against his broad, handsome shoulders which always looked even broader and more handsome in evening dress.

Now suddenly her need was urgent — she felt tearful, and the longing for the shelter of his powerful arms around her was overwhelming.

'Oh, it's so hot in here,' she said, looking up at him and smiling. 'I need some fresh air. Will you walk with me?'

'To the end of the world if such good fortune were mine,' he said.

And all at once her heart felt lighter. And when he proferred his arm and she took it she felt like sixteen.

They descended the stairs slowly to the morning room where a log fire was blazing.

'Thank goodness it's a bit cooler here,' she said, strolling towards one of the windows. 'Max invites far too many people for our drawing room and it gets so hot upstairs.'

Drew joined her by the window and they stood looking out at the traffic rolling homewards along Great Western Road.

'Busy, busy people leading busy, busy lives,' said Drew. 'Such is life in our great metropolis.'

'Have you had a busy day?' she asked, looking up at him. She felt less tearful away from the drawing room and there was comfort in just having him to herself.

'It's been a slow news day,' he said. 'A fairly routine murder trial, a razor slashing, at the High Court. Britain's Mr Town-Planner-at-Large has weighed into the debate over whether or not the old Merchant City area should be demolished to make way for an Inner Ring Road. He thinks not. He thinks it should be redeveloped so people can live there again. What we need is an Old Firm story, Celtic and Rangers, because nothing sells newspapers in Glasgow like football.'

'But you report the national and international news as well as the local news,' she said.

'Not as extensively as the morning paper, but indeed we do,' he said. 'And it hasn't been a bad year for news either nationally or globally.

'Princess Margaret finally got spliced to her photographer in Westminster Abbey just before her thirtieth birthday and the Queen started a second family with the birth of Prince Andrew ten years after Princess Anne. And we've just had the sensational court decision that *Lady Chatterley's Lover* is not obscene.'

As he ranged over some of the year's foreign stories — Harold Macmillan's speech about the winds of change seeing the end of colonial rule in Africa and the election of John Kennedy as the youngest President in United States history — Edwina felt a wave of nostalgia and longing for the old companionable days when James used to talk to her about the news.

'My father-in-law used to say that what journalists did was interesting, but very few of them were,' she suddenly found herself saying.

'That is a point of view,' said Drew, assuming a thoughtful expression. 'Wherever they go journalists get front seats at the carnival. They know what's going on ahead of other people and they find out a lot more by asking questions other people aren't in a position to ask. So they're very well informed, which makes them interesting to other people. Strip that away and they become less interesting. But strip the law away from lawyers and politics from politicians and the same applies. Take anyone's job away and you diminish them.

'Your father-in-law has a fairly jaundiced view of journalists — chiefly, I suppose, because he has to pay them well to run his newspapers when he'd rather not pay them at all. Journalists are a lot more interesting than a lot of other people and I can't think of any other group of people I'd rather spend my time with.'

'Well spoken. A spirited defence,' said Edwina.

'It wasn't intended as such. It's just the way we are.' He smiled.

'You start work really early on the evening paper?' she said conversationally, slightly changing the subject.

'I'm usually in the office around seven a.m.'

She smiled up at him. The different shades of gold from fine antique to suntanned that mixed and mingled in his hair and face reminded her of childhood summers when the days never seemed to end and she would never grow up.

She didn't know if it was the warmth of his colouring and his smile or because she seemed to have known him for a long time now or the way he was looking at her but all at once she experienced a sense of home and belonging with this man. She seemed to have a place with him . . . something she had not had with anyone for a long time.

She was conscious of the smile that came from her heart to light her eyes spreading slowly over the whole of her face. And he seemed to seize all of it with his eyes.

'Hold me,' she whispered.

The icy dankness of the November night possessed the world outside, but all she was aware of was the pain and chill which had caged her heart for so long dissolving in his powerful embrace. She seemed to be stepping from icy, loveless wastes into an oasis of warmth and joy. This was how life was meant to be — men and women were supposed to hold each other and be close, not alienated and apart. And it was only as he went on holding her that she became fully conscious of the shocking deprivation she had endured these past few years. She had told herself it didn't matter and she could manage better without a man to love. Now she knew she had become too dangerously good at denying her own needs. And a wave of compassion for herself in her appalling loss and deprivation swept over her.

'I needed that,' she said when he at last let her go. 'I'd almost forgotten . . .'

She glimpsed amazing tenderness in his eyes, as if he had needed, too.

'Would you like a drink?' she asked, stepping back and hating the brittleness in her voice because it was so far from her mood.

'I would,' he said and she saw the familiar social smile back in place, masking the need of a moment ago.

'I seem to remember you're a malt connoisseur,' she said, suddenly recalling a heated argument he had had with Max over the various ages and strengths of Glenlivet. 'I think we can oblige,' she said, crossing the room to the drinks cabinet. 'Yes, we've got Glenmorangie and Laphroaig,' she announced triumphantly, producing two almost full bottles from the cabinet.

'I think this evening calls for the peatier flavours of the waters of Islay,' he said, joining her by the drinks cabinet.

She poured good measures into two sturdy glasses and handed one to him.

'Laphroaig,' she announced, raising hers to him.

He took the glass from her hand and placed it alongside his own on top of the drinks cabinet.

Then he wrapped her in his arms in a giant bear hug that was just nice and warm and cuddly and reassuring – as if he did it all the time. And she could not help wishing that he did.

'Is that better?' he asked when he let her go.

'Yes. Much better,' she said, seeing the laughter in his eyes.

'Me, too,' he said. 'We could get good at this.'

And then they were both laughing as he laid his arm along her bare shoulders and they walked towards the fire.

After she had thrown a couple of fresh logs on it, she wanted to cuddle up on the settee with him more than anything. But her husband or father-in-law or anyone could walk through the door. So she dropped gracefully into a big easy chair.

'Slainte,' he said, raising his glass as he sat down facing her across the fire.

'Slainte,' she murmured, her eyes holding his over the rim of her glass.

And now she was dreaming and imagining what it would be like to share a fireside with this man for all of life . . . and grow old with him by the fire when the golden mane was paler and the years had drawn nigh. But she found it difficult to picture him ever being less powerful and strong and in command than he was on this evening when their souls had touched.

She knew he was married and had a family but his wife never appeared at his side on social occasions.

'She prefers to stay away from newspapers. She regards them as the enemy because I spend more time with them than with her,' he had once said to Edwina.

Now she wondered if his marriage, too, was over in the real sense.

Then she realised she was wasting time. If Max walked in, her chance would be gone.

She placed her glass on a table beside her, sat forward in her chair and, pinioning Drew's eyes with her own, asked, 'Will you be my friend?'

It came out so easily and naturally she felt quite pleased with herself.

He immediately put down his own glass and sat forward. And his eyes were shining brilliantly when he said, 'Oh, Edwina, I'm very deeply flattered that you should seek my friendship.'

'I have no one to talk to,' she explained honestly. 'No one. Can we meet sometimes and just . . . talk . . .?'

'Of course we can.'

'Oh, Drew, I'm so glad.' And she wanted to rush over and

sit on his lap. But she looked at the door and stayed where she was. 'So glad.'

'How soon do you want to meet?'

'Em . . . I don't know . . .' She hadn't thought that bit out.

'How about tea at the Spottiswoode Hotel tomorrow afternoon?'

'Oh, yes, yes, that would be very nice,' she said, amazed that it had all been so simple and straightforward.

But her nerves were in knots when tomorrow came. It was over seven years since she'd dated a man and it felt so strange and almost something she ought not to be doing. She was a married woman, a mother now; dating was what teenagers did. Except meeting Drew Hamilton for tea was not dating. She was meeting a friend, like she met Liza. The only difference was, this friend was a man. And she had known him for ages. It wasn't like meeting someone new. So why was she feeling so uncertain, so tentative, so churned up? Maybe she was compromising herself and her husband by seeking the friendship of one of his employees. She was still married to Max; she was the mother of his children and, after her husband, one of them was the heir to the empire for which Drew worked. And what would her father-in-law think if he found out?

'You've got butterflies in your tummy, Mummy. Your hand's shaking,' Marietta noticed when Edwina poured the cornflakes at breakfast.

'I'm going to the dentist today,' she glibly lied.

'Then you should be brave like you tell us to be,' Keith observed solemnly.

Though she had become adept at white lies since she had children, she knew there was no fooling them – and the way they remembered what was said could be torture.

She felt calmer after she'd had her hair done, but then she didn't know what to wear. So she was all churned up and in crisis again.

Studying her reflection in the mirror as she tried on various outfits, she realised her loss of self-confidence had been total, that the real reason she had neither taken a lover nor confided the secret of her shattered marriage to anyone was that it had destroyed the very last fragments of her self-esteem. She had stayed in her frozen place for so long because she believed she was worth nothing and no one would want her. Now in reaching out to Drew she was thinking enough of herself to believe that another human being might want to be friends with her and know her. I've been dead, she thought, gazing at the mirror. I killed myself because I didn't believe I was worthy of being alive. Now I've got to find the courage to live again.

But Drew was a top newspaperman, quick on the uptake and draw, never missing a chance. She knew there was no love lost between him and her husband. Perhaps he wanted to be her friend because he had seen an opportunity to be one up on Max.

Then she remembered how he had looked at her last night when he held her in his arms . . .

* * *

It was just before half past three when she left the house in
a sober grey business suit and white blouse and hailed a taxi
in Great Western Road.

'Central Station,' she told the driver. The station was a
ten-minute walk from the Spottiswoode Hotel. She needed to
walk off her nervous energy and calm herself down.

It was ten past four when she stumbled through the
revolving door at the Spottiswoode and one of her steel
stilettos skidded on the black and white marble floor and
sent her skating across it.

Drew Hamilton caught her just before her face hit
the floor.

'Are your entrances always so spectacular?' he inquired,
laughing. 'I like your style.'

And then she was laughing till the tears tumbled down
her cheeks, releasing her pent-up tension. And she was quite
unaware she was the cynosure of all eyes in the grand marble
reception hall as she went on standing in Drew's arms as if
she'd been doing it all her life and it was her natural place.

'Is Madam all right?' a porter in a blue uniform inquired.

'I think so,' said Edwina, seeing that she had not even
laddered her stockings. 'I'd like a cup of tea.'

'Or perhaps something stronger?' inquired Drew. 'That is,
if you've not already had enough to drink today,' he added,
his eyes sparkling with laughter as he took her elbow and
steered her towards a table in a corner of the lounge.

'You make me laugh,' she said when they sat down. But
now she felt clumsy and awkward and stupid and gauche and
totally devoid of the mystery and excitement a clever woman

like Diana Watson held for men. But he didn't seem to mind. He seemed to like her. And when tea was laid before them she was quite at ease.

'Has it been a slow or a fast news day?' she asked, noticing the extraordinary grace of his movements as he took charge and poured the tea. His fluid gestures reflected his ease with command, which poignantly reminded her of her husband and all she had lost.

'There was an armed robbery at Charing Cross at lunchtime, which we got for the last edition,' he said, handing her a cup. 'Abroad Richard Baer, the last commandant of Auschwitz, has been arrested by the West Germans. And there has been fighting between United Nations and Congolese troops outside the home of the Ghanaian ambassador whom they accuse of trying to bring back the deposed President Lumumba. An average day.'

He treated the world as his parish in the same way she had found so exciting in James Rutherford. But he was even more interesting and exciting because every day he was deciding news values – how much prominence in the paper a story was worth, whether it should be on the front page beneath banner headlines or a few paragraphs on an inside page. Listening to him talk about his job at a length never possible in their small talk encounters at receptions and parties over the years was also safe ground which saved her from making any desperate premature confession that might compromise herself or her husband. But the time went far too fast as he opened a window on the world for her, and it was half past five and she needed to get home to have tea with her children.

'I've done almost all the talking,' he said with an easy smile.

'And I've so enjoyed listening,' she said, meaning every word.

A part of her felt relieved she had got through the afternoon without talking about her marriage and that he had been discreet and tactful enough not to probe, though he must know probably a lot more than she did about what people were saying.

Looking up at his deep blue eyes and broad handsome shoulders when they reached the street, she felt she could trust him.

Before he hailed a taxi for her, they arranged to meet again at the same time the next week, when she began to tell him the story that had started at a gala fashion show over seven years ago.

She wanted to reach out for his hand often as she told her story, but then she would remember they were in a public place where anyone could see and she would hastily withdraw her hand mid-air.

'If you would prefer it, we could meet somewhere more private,' he said, reading her mind as he caught one of her hands before she could take it away and tugging her gently towards him. 'I have a flat near the office in the old Merchant City where I sometimes stay overnight. It goes back to my days as news editor on the morning paper when I was often at the office very late at night. It's in a battered old building. But no one goes there, so it's very private.'

'Yes,' she said, making the transition from public to

private meeting with a psychological ease she would have found impossible only a week ago.

The flat was on the top floor of an early nineteenth-century building near the Sheriff Court and was reached by several flights of stone stairs worn down in the middle. But beyond its unprepossessing approach and behind a front door of solid oak, contemporary furniture in the clean-cut Scandinavian style and a pale beige carpet that ran throughout the flat enhanced the bright, airy spaciousness of high-ceilinged rooms. The living room had a pleasant view over the Clyde and was hung with several paintings of Scottish seaside resorts originally commissioned by the London and North Eastern Railway company. Matching built-in cupboards, a refrigerator and a second black and white television set continued the modern look in the kitchen.

It was by the soft lighting skilfully diffused around the living room and the glow of an electric fire which looked like live coal that Edwina began to talk about her life before her marriage. Encouraged by his newspaperman's skill at drawing people out, she recalled her mother's put-downs and her struggle to get her father's attention. She remembered her days at the Mary Erskine School in Queen Street, Edinburgh. She told him about summer holidays in Elie and her life as a model. And she talked about her marriage and all the times she had wished Diana Watson dead. And when the clock in the hall struck half past five, she stopped talking and got up and went home to her children.

She was becoming used to their intimacy — the way their hands brushed as easily as if they had being doing so for years and his lips pressed casually on her forehead when they met and parted, the way she had started to save up things to tell him. Everything about him – the curl of his lips when he smiled, the way he threw his head back when he laughed, how his eyes seemed deeper blue when he was listening intently – was becoming so familiar to her.

Then one day towards the end of January in 1961, when the darkest days of winter were beginning to recede, Drew Hamilton at last let go of his wariness about his boss's wife and told her about himself . . .

'I was born into the newspaper business,' said Drew. 'My father was a printer on the *Globe* and his father had been a printer with Outram's before that. Everyone in the family assumed I would follow them. But I had other ideas and when I left school at fourteen I became a copy boy on the *Globe*, running errands for the news editor and the reporters. I learned my trade by watching how they worked, how they talked to people on the telephone, made contacts and played those contacts. But not for long. The war broke out after I'd been there only six months. A lot of senior reporters were called up, leaving the paper short staffed. So I was still only fourteen when I got my chance as a junior reporter. I was writing stories about kids not much younger than myself being evacuated from Glasgow to places as far apart as Ayr and Aberdeen. Three quarters of them had drifted back by Christmas and had to be re-evacuated when the heavy bombing started in 1941. We knew Glasgow, like the big industrial English cities, was a German target. But Clydebank got the worst of it. I was there when it was blitzed. I saw the conflagration and the charred and mangled bodies of the dead. I heard the screams of the dying. And I was covered in glory with huge front-page bylines and a pay rise at the end of it. I was sixteen years old when the utter randomness of life and death made its mark on me — how the bad luck to be in the wrong place at the wrong time meant death and the good luck meant you stayed alive to go on playing the game. I'd been lucky in Clydebank. I knew I needed to be lucky all my life. I decided I would make my luck.'

Edwina sat up on on the edge of her chair in response to the gusto of his story. Unlike her spoiled husband, who had been born privileged, this man had had to make his own way in life, and the virility and sheer swashbuckling style of his approach to life struck a chord deep within her.

'I was in the right place helping out on the news desk when a woman rang up and said a German plane had crashed not far from her home and a German officer with his parachute had been found suffering from a broken ankle and taken to hospital in Glasgow,' he said. 'When I found out which hospital it was I raced up there and discovered the man was giving his name as Horn. You develop an instinct about stories and when someone is telling the truth or a pack of lies. This was a bit obvious. Horn didn't sound a likely name for a German officer. It was late on a Monday night and I should have met a girl I had stood up on Saturday night hours ago. But a newspaperman's social life is a very unreliable calendar and the job always comes first. I hung about the hospital. Not long after eleven I learned that Officer Horn

was Hitler's deputy, Rudolf Hess, who had crash landed his
Messerschmitt 110.

'I raced to the nearest phone box to ring the news desk.
They said 10 Downing Street had just put out an official
statement that the man was Hess. The story of my hospital
vigil was front-page news the next day.'

Watching his face animated by memory, Edwina realised
the difference between this man and her husband: Drew
moved and made the things he wanted happen while Max
simply sat and waited for them to come to him, and when
they didn't he whimpered.

'I stayed lucky for the next two years throughout the
blackout in Glasgow. In 1943 when I was eighteen I was
called up and made my luck by talking my way into a
place in the army's propaganda machine. After Normandy
I got attached to the Information Section that dealt with
war correspondents and I travelled with the correspondents,
accompanying the 51st Highland Division that victoriously
swept across the Rhine on the night of 23 March 1945.

'When I got back to Glasgow after the war I married the
girl I had stood up for Rudolf Hess. By the time I celebrated
my twenty-first birthday the next year and was officially
adult, I already had a son and there was another baby on
the way and I was the chief reporter on the evening paper.

'Slum clearance was the big postwar story in Glasgow —
that and the beginning of the end of the heavy engineering
industries which had made it the Second City of the Empire.
As the slums were demolished and the people moved out to
peripheral housing estates like Easterhouse and Drumchapel,

the city began to decline. Its imperial greatness now belonged to the past but it had yet to find a new role.

'As chief reporter, I got all the best jobs and was better paid than men a lot older than myself. But I had breathed the air of foreign parts and mixed with correspondents, and I knew I wanted to be a correspondent and see the world at the company's expense.

'So I wrote to James Rutherford and told him that in light of the way America was going to have to prop up Europe on the postwar road to recovery, Globe Publishing ought to have a bureau in Washington and I was the man to open it.

'A week later I was at my desk in the reporters' room when I got a call from his secretary summoning me up to his office immediately.

'Reporters are notoriously scruffily dressed people and photographers are even worse. But I'd mixed with the correspondents and I saw they were always meticulously dressed. Which is as it should be because you don't know who you're going to be sent to interview next.

'So I was wearing an extremely decent blue suit, which my eagle-eyed employer commented on the moment I was ushered into his eyrie and the door closed behind me.

'"You've got it all wrong, Hamilton" was the first thing he said to me. "Where on earth's your news sense? Washington isn't the place to be in the aftermath of the war.'

'Well, I wasn't letting that go and myself down by not standing my ground. So I argued with him, pointing out that America had emerged from the war as a superpower, the guardian of the free world, and it wasn't enough simply to have an office in New York. The *Globe* needed to be where the decisions were made.'

'"Well, I'm most certainly not setting you up in a plush office in Washington," said James. "Besides, journalists in Washington don't do any work as you and I know it. They don't go out looking for stories. They sit on their backsides waiting for the White House or State Department press offices to tell them what's news. You'll get fat and lazy there and your talents will never be properly developed. And you'll get the idea that being a correspondent is a ticket to an easy life. If you want to be a correspondent, you can go where the action really is."'

'I looked at him and waited.

'"You've got a young family and another one on the way,"' he said. '"I think you and your wife should discuss what I can offer you because you'll be going into another war zone. Not the kind of war you've been used to, but the kind we'll see more of now that the atomic bomb has effectively outlawed war as we've known it. Terrorism and guerilla warfare are now the tactics of our time, and the future, and it's happening right now in Palestine. You can go to Jerusalem."'

'My wife, who'd been expecting me to get a job in the New York office if I didn't get Washington, was horrified. But I wanted to go, and when we talked it over she agreed that I couldn't expect to get the plum jobs right at the start, but once I came back from Jerusalem I'd be better placed for a good posting abroad. My son was six months old and she was three months pregnant with my daughter. She was very brave and loyal.

'I arrived in Jerusalem on 20 July 1946 and booked into the King David Hotel, where all the press stayed. On 22 July the British Army had arranged a press facility trip out of town, but I was so hungover I slept in and missed the bus. I was in my room when a wing of the hotel was blown up by the terrorist group, Irgun Zvai Leumi, led by Menachem Begin. Forty-two people were killed, fifty-two were missing and fifty-three were injured. And I'd made a brilliant start to my career as a foreign correspondent. I'd made my luck even when I had a hangover!'

And now as she sat with her hands clasped round her knees, Edwina felt she was in the front row of the cinema – right there with him on the Big Story as the flak flew and missiles came out of nowhere to cut off lives in their prime and sentence others to long years of handicap and suffering. Drew's story was the real thing and she could feel it happening now – not long ago or detached as even the best of James's recollections and information had been.

'For the next two years I virtually commuted between Glasgow and Jerusalem until the State of Israel was born in May 1948. I was often there for months at a time and built quite a network of contacts in the guerilla groups and the Haganah, which was the unofficial and illegal Jewish army. They blew up railway lines and they wanted the British out, but they never indulged in terrorist tactics like Irgun and the Stern Gang.

'I watched the Haganah immigrant ship, *Exodus*, packed with five thousand Jews, being turned away by the British at Haifa. Some of the wretches had started their journey in

America and been on the high seas for five months. I'd never thought much about having a homeland, a place where I belonged, before that. The ugly streets of Glasgow seemed the most beautiful in the world when I got back that time.

'The company twice paid for my wife and children to fly out to join me on holiday in Cyprus when I was in Palestine.

'When it was over I was made news editor of the evening paper. I was only twenty-three, the youngest news editor in the business. But I was restless behind a desk, sending other people out on stories when I wanted to be out myself, but not in Scotland. I wanted more of the world.

'"You need executive experience," said James when I complained and threatened to take off for Fleet Street. He paid me a Fleet Street salary to keep me in Glasgow and made me foreign news editor of the *Daily Globe* before my twenty-fourth birthday in 1949. That suited me much better because I could get a proper handle on foreign news. But when the Korean War broke out in 1950 I refused to stay at home any longer. I was there for two years till your husband somehow managed to persuade his father to pull me back and I had one helluva fight to get back for the finish. But James backed me, much to his son's fury.

'After that I cruised round the Far East for a bit, filing stories for all the papers in the Globe group. When I finally got back James summoned me to the seventh floor.

'"I want to make you editor of the *Evening Globe*," he said. And just as I was about to express my joy and satisfaction at this accolade, he promptly took it away. "But first you need to round off your education. I want you to be diary editor for a spell."

'"But that's a pansy's job. In fact it's not a proper job at all for a newspaperman," I protested before I nearly choked. "Oh, you don't need to do any work," said James. "Get your staff to do it. But I want you to move around a bit in society, get to know a few people you'll find useful later."'

Now she remembered what Max had said about Drew wanting to be one of the people he wrote about — and she wondered if it was true or had merely been inspired by jealousy.

'Well, you can imagine, every newspaperman and woman in Glasgow thought there'd been a great falling out between James and myself,' said Drew. 'The golden blue-eyed boy was on his way out. I heard the stories as fast as people put them about. I also got a lot of job offers, which James heard about even faster. I didn't want any of the jobs but they were a great encouragement to James to keep putting up my salary while I swanned through the London social scene. I lost count of the number of deb parties I got invited to or gatecrashed and I was almost trampled underfoot in the bunfights for a cup of tea at the garden parties at Buckingham Palace. And when my diary spell was over I confounded all the prophets who said it was all over for the golden, blue-eyed boy when I became editor of the *Evening Globe*.

'Since then I've been a visiting fireman, thoroughly enjoying running my own show at home but able to take to the road when the story's big enough — like the troubles in Cyprus and the grand Anglo-French disaster at Suez. It keeps my eye in globally and stops me from becoming too parochial in outlook.

'I also get the pick of the free trips – correction, facility trips, as the hosts like to describe them – organised by governments and airlines to countries all over the world. They're a real swan, but useful for background information.

'I think I've got the balance about right now. But I've met men who never do, who spend their whole lives chasing wars, rushing from one world trouble spot to the next. So often what they're really doing is running away from problems they don't want to face at home. So they become foreign correspondents or travel writers. But I know of no more pleasant way to run away from problems. One of the great joys of the correspondent's life is the camaraderie – being able to drop into any city or town in the world and immediately belong because you meet up at once with people doing what you're doing, people with your background, people you've met in other towns in other wars and trouble spots. And you all put up at the same hotel. It was the King David in Jerusalem and the Ledra Palace in Nicosia. If the whiff of gun smoke makes you nervous you need never leave the hotel because you can always pick up enough of the story from colleagues or people like the night porter at the Ledra Palace, who was the source of a good ninety per cent of the stories which got into the British press about the troubles in Cyprus.'

Now his expression had darkened and she was sensing a hint of loneliness before he said, 'Of course there's a price to pay. For me it was that I wasn't around as I now wish I had been when my children were very small. They still regard me as something of a stranger and I've never been able to make up for the closeness I missed out on in their early years. Sometimes I feel it's my children and their mother who're the family unit and I'm merely the lodger who pays the bills because I have a room there. And yet my home means more to me now than it ever did. I realise how fortunate I am to have a home and a family and country I can call my own. This world's full of people who don't enjoy such fortune. And the more I see of the world the more I think that perhaps the greatest lack is to have no homeland to call your own. It's an alien condition and gives rise to the most profound and dangerous rootlessness.

'But I'm becoming too philosophical. What I'm trying to say is, there's a price to pay for everything. You make your choices, you pay. And if you're lucky or make your luck well enough, you stay alive and live as you want to. Because we *are* lucky to be alive. Life is the greatest gift we get, though for millions it becomes a burden from their earliest years. But we owe it to ourselves to live it as fully as we can whilst it's ours because we don't get the gift again . . . Am I making any sense?'

'I could listen to you for ever,' she said, taking his hand between her own.

CHAPTER NINE

T he road through the south-western suburbs was slushy in the blackness of the January night. Drew reached for the radio switch in his new Jaguar and tuned in to the chimes of Big Ben and the nine o'clock news on the BBC Home Service. In Washington John Fitzgerald Kennedy had been inaugurated as the thirty-fifth President of the United States. The Queen had met Archbishop Makarios in Cyprus and the Russian Orthodox Church had been elected to the World Council of Churches at a meeting in New Delhi. Tomorrow's headlines would be full of talk about the new American presidency heralding a new era. But American politics apart, it had been a slow news day.

His hands were steady on the wheel, his eyes alert on the road and his ears to any unexpected news on the radio, but his mind was brimming with his blossoming friendship with Edwina Rutherford.

Of course he'd known for years about Max and Diana and the marriage James had arranged for his idiot son to an innocent girl less than half his age. Everyone in the higher executive reaches at Globe Newspaper Publishing knew about it, though they were far too concerned about their careers for it to be the subject of open discussion.

Drew hated Max for several reasons. Two of them were that Max had been born rich and privileged (Drew believed inherited wealth was immoral and should be legislated against) and had then squandered the opportunities of his birthright. The third and motivating one was that Max had tried to put the brakes on his career as a foreign correspondent.

'He's jealous. Just because he failed to make the most of his own chances he doesn't want me to succeed,' he'd told his wife in the early days of his career. 'Every time I go abroad he goes whingeing to his father and the board that the *Daily Globe* is not a national newspaper and they can't afford to keep sending me abroad and why don't they just take Reuter and rewrite it in the office.

'If he knew a bit more about the company he'd know that his father thinks national and wants the *Globe* built up into a British national daily.

'If Max'd had to fight for every chance as I've had to, he wouldn't have thrown them away. Now it's too late for him. And he hates to see someone succeed where he failed.'

What had turned rivalry into bitter hostility had been Max's attempts to prevent Drew attending the signing of the armistice at Panmunjon at the end of the Korean War.

'He's gone too far this time,' Drew told his wife. 'There's an indisputable case for a series of pieces about the postwar picture in the Far East. He hasn't got a tiny toe to stand on yet he's out there trying to sabotage me.'

James had resoundingly smacked down his son, but from then on Drew had set his sights on getting Max's job and one day taking over the company.

He saw himself as James's spiritual son and natural heir. They shared the same entrepreneurial spirit and the same passionate belief that it was news — not advertising or the meddling ways of accountants or James's idiot offspring — that sold newspapers.

'You're more like my son than my own flesh and blood,' James had once remarked. 'You're carving the career both he and I would have liked him to have, but he never made the most of the chances I gave him.'

Of course there had been a price to pay for success. Drew's marriage had been sacrificed from the beginning. He had quite simply never given it a chance. There had been times when he resolved to devote more time to his wife and children. Then the big story would break. There would be a terrorist outrage in the Middle East, a war would erupt in some godforsaken spot and America and the Soviet Union would be backing opposing sides. And the adrenalin would flow, sweeping aside all considerations except getting there and getting the story back to the office in time to catch the first edition. No other thrill could match it.

'You're a good provider but not much else,' she'd once said to him bitterly.

It was shortly after he'd bought the big detached house in Seamill on the Firth of Clyde looking out to Arran. Safe, beautiful Seamill so far away from the world's troubled places. That was why he bought it. The more he'd seen of the world the more he appreciated the safety of his own country and the importance of a home in a planet full of refugees and people who had no home.

But it had been too late to save his marriage in any real sense by that time. So he lived in a beautiful house by the sea with his family but he had no home. There was no one with whom he belonged . . .

A wry smile spread over his face as he left the city behind and headed homeward across open country. Sleety rain which had followed the snow was now battering the windscreen, but he was warmly and comfortably cocooned in his company Jaguar, and as the news finished he switched to music on the Light Programme.

The most desirable women had thrown themselves at Max Rutherford because he was rich and privileged. They always did when a man had enough money and social position, irrespective of his age and character. Drew had seen it in his diary days – and resented it even more than he resented all the other privileges of the rich and famous.

But things were changing. The editorship of the company flagship, the *Daily Globe*, was now within his reach. So was the prospect of Edwina Rutherford becoming his mistress . . .

CHAPTER TEN

For the next week Edwina thought constantly about Drew — not in the self-centred way she had done before, simply as the confidant for her troubles for whom she saved up things to tell. Now she thought about the man and his achievements, the thrust of his ambition and the way he looked at the world, forever seeking new opportunities and challenges and mountains to climb. Apart from James Rutherford he was the most exciting man she had ever met. She skipped through the days at the prospect of seeing him again and got to the flat before him for their next meeting.

For once the bedroom door on to the hall, normally closed, was slightly ajar.

She looked at her watch. It was exactly 3.24. Perhaps if she was quick!

As her fingers reached for the handle she noted the door was no more than an inch open. She must be careful to leave it that way.

Unconsciously she tiptoed as she pushed the door open — and was promptly arrested by the sumptuousness of walls covered in a strong, clear shade of green silk. Sunlight was filtering through a window dressed in cream silk curtains hung on a brass rod and falling on a large double bed whose fitted cover and upholstered head matched the walls. A small mahogany table in lovely faded tones stood by the bed, bearing a lamp with an intricate gilt base, a telephone, a small cabinet with drawers and a copy of *The Thirty-Nine Steps*. Two handsome winged armchairs in a complementary shade of green flanked the fireside and there was a television set on a desk in a corner. Though the neatly honed masculine elegance of the room was striking, Edwina felt completely comfortable in it as she stood taking it all in.

Then she noticed that the top drawer of the small cabinet on the mahogany table was slightly open. It was two steps away, on the side of the bed nearer the door. She moved towards it and narrowed her eyes to peer into the drawer, but she couldn't quite see inside. She tugged it gently right open. It contained a packet of male contraceptives.

A bolt of jealousy like a flash of sheet lightning shot through her. So this was what her friend, her confidant, the man she trusted, got up to! So this was why this room was far superior to the rest of the flat and why so much care and money had obviously been lavished on it! She felt betrayed. She slammed the drawer and the bedroom door shut behind her and strode to the living room.

She was trembling now. He would be here any minute and she needed to calm down. She took several deep breaths and stared out the window at the dark stormy waters of the river.

Then slowly as she went on gazing out it dawned on her

she was being very selfish. For weeks now she had been trying to convince herself that Drew was merely her friend and there never would or could be anything else between them. Whenever her instincts had veered towards attraction to him she had shut them off, denying them. Now she realised that in denying her needs she had also been denying his. Though his marriage might be over in every real sense, he still had needs as a man.

She heard his key in the door.

'Anyone home?' he called as he opened it, and it sounded just like they lived together.

She hesitated for a fraction of a second before she answered, 'I'm in the living room.'

She stood still as a rock with her back to the window, her lips pressed close together, as he entered the room.

'Oh, there you are. Sorry I'm late. There was a slight panic over the Stop Press in the last edition,' he said, his arms wrapped round a brown paper carrier.

As their eyes met she knew it had been none of her business who this gorgeous, handsome man, who had offered her his friendship, invited to share his elegant bedroom; and she had no right to go snooping around it uninvited. But from now on it *was* her business — because she didn't want him to share that bed and that room with anyone else but her.

She watched his hands as he carefully placed the carrier on a table.

'That's better,' he said, his eyes meeting hers again.

She held his gaze for a moment and her lips pursed into a thin line.

Then she walked purposefully towards him and placed her arms round his neck.

'Make love to me,' she said.

CHAPTER ELEVEN

I will fight for you, Drew Hamilton. I will kill for you. Because you are my life. And without you I am nothing. I was in a long unconscious sleep before I met you. Before you I didn't know what it was like to be alive. But you brought me alive. And when you know what it is to be alive, there's no going back to death. It's impossible.

As winter drifted into the spring of 1961 and the days at last grew longer, Edwina often thought these things after they had made love in that wonderful masculine bedroom lined in green silk with an old mahogany table in gorgeous faded colours beside the bed. But when she returned home to her children and their exuberance filled her world she told herself she was dreaming an impossible dream. She was thirty-one years old and she was having the first real grown-up love affair in her life. That was the beginning and end of it, the way it had to be. They were both married and had children and responsibilities. Except . . . she was beginning to wish there was a way for them . . .

'My wife and I have led quite separate lives for years,' he said on a gorgeous June afternoon when the sun was beaming bright blonde light into the green bedroom. Edwina looked surprised because he hardly mentioned his wife. 'She's going to start teacher training, after the school holidays. Now that the children are well into their teens she wants to be independent and have her own career.'

'That's very enterprising of her,' said Edwina carefully, wondering why he was suddenly telling her this.

'I don't know if it will work, but I hope so,' he said.

She wasn't sure what he meant so she said nothing. And they sat in bed silently as he drew slowly on a cigarette. At last he said, 'I'm telling you this because I want you to know there's at least hope for us. I know what we have isn't enough for you.' He placed an arm along her shoulders and held her eyes with his. 'It isn't for me either. But it's all we can have, perhaps for a very long time. We're beggars in love, Edwina. And I want you to know I mind as much as I sense you do and I wish it could be different and I wish we had more.'

If he had gone down on his knees and said he loved her a thousand times, she could not have felt more loved than she did at that moment. She placed her arms around his neck and then they were smothering each other in kisses and she could not see him for her tears. So often he had seemed detached and comfortably able to compartmentalise his life, and he said so little about his feelings no matter how carefully or delicately she had approached the subject.

'I'll fight for you, Drew Hamilton. I'll never let us be parted. I'll never let anyone come between us.' She spoke the words at last when they had made love again and the sunlight was slightly lower in the room. Her passion for him was giving her a strength she never knew she possessed. She could feel it powering her limbs, coursing through her whole body till it reached every cell and flooded the farthest reaches of her soul.

'I may need you to do that one day' was all he said. But there was an unfathomable look in his eyes which she would never forget.

It was nearly seven before she reached Kirklee Terrace and found James waiting for her in the family sitting-room with Marietta and Keith.

'I thought you had tea with the children,' he said gruffly.

'Usually I do. But the traffic was particularly heavy tonight,' she said lightly. Love had given her the confidence to lie glibly to a man she had once held in awe. 'And what brings you round here without warning?' she asked as Marietta took hold of one hand and dragged her towards a colouring book spread open on the floor.

'Do you think Dolly should have a pink or a purple blouse?' she asked as Edwina dropped into a big easy chair by the hearth and the colouring book.

'Well, as she's wearing a blue skirt, perhaps a pink blouse might be nice.'

'Yes,' said Marietta, getting down on her knees and reaching for a pink crayon.

'I'm here because we need to talk and I did try telephoning you several times this afternoon,' said James as Keith jumped down from his knee and scampered towards his mother's lap.

'Have you been a good boy today?' she asked as he cuddled into her.

'I'm always a good boy,' he assured her solemnly.

'Well, I'm here, let's talk,' said Edwina to James.

'Shortly,' said James with a look that said it was time the children were in bed.

But Edwina played with them and answered their endless questions for twenty minutes before she took them up to bed.

When she had kissed them goodnight and freshened up, she breezed downstairs in a bright blue silk kaftan she'd bought that morning. And when she'd poured large scotches for James and herself she sank gracefully into her favourite easy chair, looked at her father-in-law and said, 'I think having a title suits you. You look like a lord.' She raised her glass. '*Slainte*, Lord Kilmacolm.'

'You're in good spirits even before you touch a drop,' said James, a critical note in his voice.

'Why not?' She shrugged. 'I have a beautiful home, two beautiful children and an utterly adorable father-in-law. What more could I ask for?'

'A better husband,' said James, catching her off guard.

'I'm surprised to hear you say that,' she said, realising James had something serious to say.

'I've told him to go to Lagg and stay there till he comes to his senses. He's not having anything to do with running the business until he does,' said James.

'What's he done?' asked Edwina, trying to sound interested.

'It's not what he's done. It's what he wants.'

'Which is?'

'A divorce.'

'He's not getting one,' said Edwina without any of her former conviction.

'That's what I hoped and expected you'd say,' James replied, the tension easing from his voice. 'He came to see me today asking me to talk to you about it. He'd obviously been put up to it by that fancy woman of his who's now set her sights on becoming Lady Kilmacolm after I'm gone.'

'I know,' said Edwina, but there was unashamed, glorious hope soaring in her heart. Though he was as fit and spry as ever her father-in-law was now eighty-two and he could not last for ever. Perhaps divorce *would* be possible. Perhaps on this day the very first gentle breezes of change which would enable her to make a life with Drew were beginning to blow gently. 'And I'm glad you know and at last it's come out into the open,' she continued as if there was no chance of change. 'It's been horrible for me this past year the way she's been making it so obvious but nothing was being said.'

'I know it's been difficult for you,' said James, leaning forward confidentially in his chair. 'But she's dropped him before – that's the way it is with her – and when he tells her she's got no chance of becoming Lady Kilmacolm I'm sure she'll drop him again.

'My son has been divorced twice and each time it's caused me a great deal of pain. But at least he had no children by his previous marriages. Now he has and he cannot continue to behave as recklessly as he has in the past. He has responsibilities to his children and he's going to stand by them. There's going to be no divorce, I told him. And I've ordered him out of the office.'

James took a long, slow draught of his drink and eased back in his chair. 'My son is a terrible disappointment to me,' he sighed. 'I've given him everything and he's had every business opportunity a man could wish for — and many would give all their teeth for, not just the back ones — and he's thrown them all away.'

'Except you never let him do what he wanted,' said Edwina.

'And what was that?' barked James.

'He wanted to be a foreign correspondent.'

'Oh, yes, I admit that was one of his fancies as a young man. But as heir to Globe Publishing he had to learn the whole business. I couldn't have him going off and getting locked into one specialist area of it.'

'It wasn't a fancy,' said Edwina. 'It was what he wanted. With all his heart. He's told me so himself.'

James fell silent for a moment and Edwina noticed his Adam's apple wobble before he said, 'If a man has his heart truly set on something he'll find a way to do it.'

'If he has extraordinary determination,' agreed Edwina. 'But not everyone is made like that. Sometimes people become fatally discouraged. And I think that happened to Max.'

She was amazed at the compassion she now felt for her husband. But that was what loving and being loved by Drew had done for her this very day and now she felt compassion for everyone for whom love had failed, as it had from the beginning for Max.

James stayed to supper and trawled over the news just like old times. The Queen had been in Glasgow that day, visiting slums in the Gorbals. But James was far more interested in Iraq claiming Kuwait in the wake of Britain abandoning its Protectorate status, the recent defeat of the far Right in the elections to the French National Assembly and the space race between the United States and the Soviet Union.

'The Americans have been desperate since the Russian cosmonaut Yuri Gagarin became the first man in space in April. President Kennedy has given orders the Americans must put the first man on the moon,' he told Edwina.

It was late when he left and almost midnight as she was getting into bed when the telephone in her room rang.

'Edwina?'

'Yes.' She was startled to recognise Drew's voice.

'Edwina, I thought you'd want to know. There's been a road accident on Arran just beyond Whiting Bay — a head-on collision between a lorry and the sports car Max was driving. He was thrown clear and is perfectly all right apart from a few bruises. But his passenger was killed outright. It was Diana Watson.'

'Oh, I am sorry, so sorry. He'll never get over that. Never.'

'Would you like me to come over?'

'Thank you, but no. I expect James will be here in a minute. Does he know?'

'Alex Regan's trying to reach him now. Are *you* all right, Edwina?'

'Oh, I'll be fine,' she said, her voice suddenly breaking. And when she put down the phone she wept for her husband and his lost, dead lover and everyone who had lost in love and lost in life like Max because they didn't have the courage and determination to stand up and do what they wanted. And she wept for Drew at Clydebank in the blitz and in the ruins of the King David Hotel in Jerusalem and in all the places where he had watched the dead and the dying — and lived. And she thought about what he had said about making your luck and staying alive and living to the full because you never knew when it could be snatched away . . . and you could never get it back. And she thought again about Max on the road to Lagg — his going-home road, as he called it — going to the one house he called home. And she wept for their lost happiness and how they had never been able to reach each other.

And when she had shed her tears and her eyes were all swollen and tired she looked in the mirror . . . and her reflection reminded her she had never felt more alive . . .

CHAPTER TWELVE

'I've spoken to James.'

Alex Regan's balding head peered round the door of the executive entertainment suite on the seventh floor.

'What did he say?' asked Drew, prowling with a sturdy glass of Glenmorangie.

'That his idiot son is lucky he didn't kill himself.'

'Very lucky.'

'I liked Diana. She was a lovely lady,' said Alex, crossing the room to the sideboard where the bottle of malt whisky stood beside a wooden tray holding several glasses.

The night sky was a deep violent purple, the darkest it ever got in the long light of the Scottish midsummer. In another couple of hours, by three o'clock, it would be bright and a new day would be in the making.

'Max could be a long time getting over this. She really was the love of his life,' said Alex solemnly, coming to rest at Max's side.

'Uh, huh,' said Drew noncommitally.

They stood in silence, clutching their tumblers, sharing the view of the city lights that fanned out in every direction.

'I wonder what he'll do,' Alex said eventually.

'The stringer in Arran will file a story about the accident,' said Drew as if Alex had not spoken. 'We'll have pictures by the afternoon. I think I'll put them on the front page.'

'But I thought there was a ruling about no publicity for the family.' The older man looked dubiously at Drew.

'In the past perhaps,' said Drew. 'But times change and rules are there to be broken. Besides, such as the rule was, it applied only in life. Now we have a death on our hands. There's bound to be a fatal-accident inquiry, possibly charges of reckless or careless driving, perhaps even manslaughter . . .' He gave Alex a meaningful look.

It was already starting to get light when he walked the short distance from the office to his flat to catnap and enjoy the newfangled shower he had just installed in his bathroom, before another working day began at seven o'clock.

When he let himself into the flat he stood for ages gazing out over the Clyde towards the southern suburbs, watching the street lamps go out as day reclaimed the city.

It was not just his latest sports car Max Rutherford had written off in killing his mistress. Psychologically he had finally written himself off, effectively killing himself.

Drew breathed deeply and his chest broadened as hope brightened with the morning light. He could be chairman and chief executive of Globe Newspaper Publishing yet . . .

CHAPTER THIRTEEN

Seven months later on the February day in 1962 when Lieutenant Colonel John Glenn became the first American to orbit the earth, Drew Hamilton was made editor of the *Daily Globe* at the age of thirty-seven. He led the paper with the space story the next day. He also ran features explaining the importance of the United States catching up on the Soviet Union in the space race.

As winter yielded to spring and rolled into summer he often led the paper with foreign news or news which originated in London. On a sensational summer night the Prime Minister, Harold Macmillan, fired seven of his Cabinet colleagues. Telstar, the first communications satellite, went into orbit, Marilyn Monroe died in mysterious circumstances; a young South African lawyer, Nelson Mandela, was sent to prison for five years, and for several dark days in October the world stood on the brink of nuclear war until the Russian leader Khrushchev agreed to remove missiles based in Cuba and return them to the Soviet Union. Drew wrote banner headlines for them all and projected each story in the simple tabloid language and style his readers understood.

But 1962 paled into insignificance almost as soon as the vintage news year of 1963 was born. As Beatlemania swept Britain, a young Russian, Valentina Tereshkova, became the first woman to soar into space, the Pope died and an armed gang who stopped and robbed a Royal Mail train at a remote spot in Buckinghamshire got away with £1 million in a crime that became known as the Great Train Robbery. But the biggest story of all, which shook the country's faith in the ruling classes, was the Profumo Affair. The ramifications of War Minister John Profumo's denial and later admission of lying to the House of Commons over his affair with a call girl, Christine Keeler, who was also sleeping with the Russian military attaché, Captain Eugene Ivanov, sent previously declining newspaper circulations soaring for months and months.

'We are not a Scottish newspaper, but a national newspaper published in Scotland,' was Drew's constant message to his staff, and 1963 was the year to prove it. But readers also looked to the *Daily Globe* to take up their causes and support their interests in a way that newspapers emanating from London, or their northern editions published in Manchester, could not. Drew did not let them down.

When Dr Richard Beeching, the chairman of British Railways, announced plans to close over one hundred rural railway stations and five hundred miles of railway line in remote regions of Scotland, Drew sent reporters all over the country to investigate the consequenes of the threatened closures on lives, jobs and the way of life of people in out-of-the-way places. The biggest fears were for the lines which ran north and west out of Inverness to Wick and Thurso and Kyle of Lochalsh and the West Highland Line to Oban and Fort William and Mallaig.

He also attacked the government's lack of investment in Highland roads, saying that if the railway lines were closed money must be spent on widening the network of A-roads which often amounted to no more than single tracks with passing places — lay-bys where one vehicle could wait to let an oncoming vehicle past — at all too infrequent intervals.

But his heart was where the big news was, and there was no end to it in 1963.

'We keep saying there can't be anything more sensational to happen this year, but there is,' Drew said to Edwina early in November. 'There's just no end to the big news this year. I wonder what it will be next.'

Two weeks later around six o'clock he was in his shirt sleeves in the middle of the newsroom when the news editor came hurtling across the floor.

'President Kennedy's been assassinated in Dallas,' he said, thrusting forward the Reuter's wire.

Drew raised his eyes to the big clock with black Roman numerals which glared from a pillar in the middle of the room, a constant reminder of deadlines.

It was exactly five minutes past six. They had thirty-two minutes to catch the first edition.

'We've got a new front-page lead,' he said quietly to the night editor, handing him the wire.

Like the smell of greasepaint and the roar of the crowd, the challenge and excitement of a big story to tell with a deadline minutes away was sending the adrenalin coursing through his veins.

Reporters, subeditors, everyone in the office was hauled off whatever they were working on to tell the story of the triumph and tragedy of the brief presidency of John Fitzgerald Kennedy and the legend of the new Camelot at the White House.

They made the front page in the first edition. By the time the last edition hit the news stands in Glasgow the next morning it was almost the only story in the paper.

By noon a memo on all *Daily Globe* editorial noticeboards said:

> I would like to thank everyone involved for the tremendous effort which went into this morning's paper.
>
> We can handle the big stories better than any of the so-called nationals coming out of London, and today we proved it.
>
> We printed 30,000 extra copies of the paper last night and the circulation department tell me it has been a complete sell-out.
>
> Drew Hamilton, Editor

But as always there was a price to pay. The gorgeous afternoons of love quickly came to an end as he built his name and reputation as a national daily editor. The paper was everything and he was often there fifteen hours a day. And with his flat being close to the office, he was often in just after nine thirty in the morning — a good hour before most daily editors arrived at their desks. Sometimes he took the evening off and dined discreetly with Edwina, but he was constantly watching the clock, and then the first editions of other newspapers had to be read around midnight. She hated leaving his flat in the middle of the night. It made her feel cheap; so occasionally she stayed overnight. But it was awkward and the deception had to be so elaborate and risky and somehow the children always managed to make some reference to it when James called.

The relationship was becoming increasingly fractured and heading downhill when, four days after the Kennedy assassination, at the every end of November, he rang her early one morning.

'What are you doing this weekend?' he asked.

'I haven't thought about it.'

'I know it's short notice. But would you like to spend it with me?'

'Where?'

'Inverlochy Castle.'

'That sounds a lovely idea,' said Edwina, who had once stayed with Max at the luxurious hotel in the shadow of Ben Nevis.

He heard the happiness in her voice and swallowed. 'Does that mean yes?'

'Yes.'

CHAPTER FOURTEEN

'You never want their sympathy. Give me their hatred, their anger, their resentment, their anguish, their jealousy, their fear, their burning desire to see me dead – but their sympathy never. Because their sympathy is death,' said Drew, talking to Edwina about his relationship with his senior executives. 'And they are poised, ready to douse you in sympathy if they think you've made a mistake and made the wrong story the front-page lead.

'It's torture and a tremendous assault on your confidence. Maybe you haven't been quite sure which story to lead on. When the first editions come up around midnight, you look to see if anyone else has used the same lead. If no one has, you think well perhaps they'll change their minds through the night. But they don't. You listen to the morning news on radio. They're hardly mentioning the story you've led on. Your last hope is, the first edition of the evening paper will choose the same lead. They don't. When the departmental heads start arriving in your office for the morning conference, they scent blood. They know you've done it wrong and they're poised for a kill. One of them asks how you are with a smile on his lips and murder in his eyes. "Fine," you say with your everyday nonchalant smile.

'You sit down at your desk and ask the news editor what's on his schedule.

'It's over and you haven't cracked and a new day full of new opportunities to make the world forget what you did wrong yesterday has begun.

'That's how I live and sometimes suffer.'

'Life or death,' said Edwina.

'It can be,' said Drew. 'You don't want to get it wrong too often.'

They were strolling arm in arm in the grounds of Inverlochy Castle Hotel on Saturday afternoon. Though patches of mist lurked in the shadows of the Ben Nevis foothills, the day was warm and sunny and the trees were still ablaze with the lovely red and amber of autumn.

But the days were short in November. Soon the light would begin to fade and the day would be gone. They had only just arrived last night in their separate ways for discretion's sake and already the time was fleeing.

There had been so much catching up to do on ordinary newsy things — the little mundane exchanges of bits of information that were the bread and butter of a relationship — that there had been no chance to talk as she felt they needed. About important things. About the future. About where they were going.

Since Diana Watson's death Max had plunged headlong into an endless round of boozing and womanising and had virtually moved out of Kirklee Terrace into his own flat in

Crown Gardens, where he took his women. Edwina hardly saw him except when he came, by arrangement, to see the children.

An affair with Drew was no longer what she wanted. Perhaps it never had been. Perhaps even at the very beginning of their friendship, unconsciously at least, she had wanted to be with him for the rest of her life. But it had taken the hiatuses in the relationship caused by his appointment as editor for her to realise it. His promotion had pointed up the weaknesses and limitations in their discreet affair, which had become almost impossible now.

In light of Max's conduct she could not see how James could oppose a divorce now. But where had Drew and his wife got to? She needed to know.

Yet she had sensed him eluding her emotionally from the moment he had met her at Fort William railway station last night, endlessly spinning out the newsy smaller talk, skilfully evading even her most delicate probing.

She looked up at the head held proudly in the clean mountain air and the aura of a mane which permeated the modest length of his hair and for a terrible moment she thought: I'm losing you. We're losing each other not because there's anyone else. We're drifting apart by default, because we don't see each other and the love of your life is your newspaper.

'One day I'll fight for you, Drew Hamilton.' She remembered one day voicing what she so often thought after they had made love in the afternoon.

'One day I may need you to fight that fight, Edwina,' he

had answered, making her name sound like the most beautiful sound in the world.

She sensed that the time might be soon when she would have to tackle James's achings for dynasty, which, with the effective demise of Max, were now focused more than ever on her six-year-old son. But Drew was James's favourite, the son he would have chosen if given a choice. She snuggled up close against his rough tweed jacket and felt confident it could all be managed somehow even though the way might be long.

But Drew remained evasive and noncommittal when, over roast guinea fowl and a sturdy warming Nuits St Georges in the discreet elegance of the hotel's dining room that evening, she delicately inquired about his wife's plans.

'Yes, Cathy's in her third year of teacher training now,' he said. 'This time next year she'll have a job and be a woman of independent means,' he added, smiling. 'Which seems to be what women want these days. We're running a series about it in the paper next week.'

And they were back talking about the paper and the news and her precious chance had gone again.

And he eluded her, too, in bed that night. There was something mechanical about his lovemaking, as if his soul had gone away.

What is it? What's wrong? she wanted to cry out. But she didn't want a row. The time was too precious. She wanted to be happy again with him as they used to be. And she told herself it was all because they hardly saw each other any more and you couldn't switch on the magic just like that.

But they were close again on Sunday night, their last night

together until goodness knew when. She couldn't go on living like this.

Lying in his arms, she felt at last they could talk as they needed to when he ran his fingers through her hair and said, 'Brave Edwina. Dear, brave, lovely Edwina. You have meant so much to me for so long now . . .'

She seemed to hear a warning note in his beautiful words.

'You make that sound like you were saying goodbye,' she murmured, looking up at him.

'A word I hope I will never say to you of all women,' he whispered, his eyes holding hers.

And then they were back together, joyously closer than they had ever been, as if they had never been parted by his blasted newspaper and yet stronger, closer now that they had overcome their alienation.

And in the morning she felt younger, confident and alive and reinvigorated as if she had bathed in dew . . .

The blanched skeletons of trees hundreds of years old rise like ghostly statues from the peat bogs on Rannoch Moor — remnants of the great Caledonian Forest where bear and wild boar, wolf and brigand roamed. Corralled to the west and south by the glowering towers of Glencoe and the Black Mount and to the north by the Grampian Mountains, its desolation is apocalyptic when storm clouds gather. But the sun was shedding a gentle amber light on the heather and the mountains were deep, mysterious blue as the train bound for Glasgow left Spean Bridge and began its long traverse

of the moor. The mellowness of the late November day on
the harsh terrain found an echo in Edwina's own spirits,
reminding her of the tranquillity love brought to the wild,
bitter landscape of Drew Hamilton's soul.

Last night they had loved each other with a passion she
had never known before. It had been wild and untrammelled
and she had met face to face the fury which drove him to
wealth and fame and power – and the deprivation and the
longing to be loved and needed and to belong. He had seemed
to give her everything of himself last night and hold nothing
back, as if he had wanted to imprint all of himself on her
memory for ever.

'I will fight for you, Drew Hamilton. I will kill for you.
Because you are my life. And without you I am nothing. I
was in a long unconscious sleep before I met you. Before you
I did not know what it was like to be alive. But you gave
me life, brought me alive. And when you know what it is
to be alive, there is no going back to death. It is impossible.'
She had said it all, every word of it, last night as they had
bound their troth to each other in every real way.

And it was still brimming in her soul as the sun clouded
over and the train abandoned the moor . . .

James was waiting in the family sitting room when Edwina
got back to Kirklee Terrace.

'Don't tell me Max wants a divorce to marry one of his
floozies,' she sighed, rolling her eyes towards the ceiling as
she dropped into her favourite easy chair and lit a cigarette.
'It's what I expect when I come home to find you here.' The

way he had of barging in without warning and lying in wait was beginning to annoy her intensely. She felt her privacy was being invaded. 'Now who wants to be my husband's wife and the next Lady Kilmacolm?'

'Didn't Drew tell you her name's Elsie MacLelland?'

The question froze the air between them.

James was sitting with his back to the light facing her.

There was no escape from his interrogator's gaze.

'Didn't he mention it over the weekend you've just spent with him?'

Her cheeks felt like molten lava.

She started to choke on the smoke from her cigarette.

'Edwina, you will not be seeing Drew Hamilton again. Your affair with him is at an end. Did he not make that plain to you at the weekend?'

'I don't know what you're talking about,' she managed.

'I'm talking about the affair which until recently you had the good sense and grace to conduct discreetly. But being seen leaving the *Daily Globe* editor's flat by sub-editors on their way home in the middle of the night is neither discreet nor seemly behaviour. The fact that my son now knows about your affair is irrelevant. The point is that I will not have him publicly cuckolded.'

'But how do you know . . . anything . . .?'

'I wouldn't be much of a newspaper proprietor if I didn't know what my staff and family get up to.'

Edwina was staring at him, gripping the arms of her chair to try to stop herself shaking.

'I am not an unreasonable man. I am I hope a man of the

world and I know what goes on, even if with my Presbyterian background I don't approve of it. I don't think a decent married woman, particularly if she is a mother, should be having anything to do with men other than her husband and the father of her children. But I know my son has not been the ideal husband. And I'm very fond both of you and Drew, whom I regard also as a kind of son. But loyalty to family is stronger than feelings for the people you adopt spiritually or by marriage, and I will not allow my own son to be a laughing stock, with people sniggering behind his back.

'Drew has a family and future to think of. He's a sensible man whose upward path in the company is something both he and I wish to continue. He was very sensible about the whole matter when I talked to him.'

'What do you mean?'

'I mean he will not be seeing you again. And my impression was that he intended to tell you so over the weekend, which had my blessing. If he has not done so I can understand. Men aren't very good at saying goodbye to women. And I believe he holds you in very deep affection. So it would not have been easy for him.'

She remembered Drew's words then. 'Brave Edwina. Dear lovely brave Edwina, you have meant so much to me for so long now . . .' He'd been saying goodbye, as instructed.

And he'd said it again at the railway station in Fort William. His eyes had been full of longing when he walked along the platform with the train till it gathered speed and when it left him behind he'd watched till she was out of his sight. She had known then that his heart was breaking, but she quickly told herself she was imagining it — and that her heart and mind were still out of focus after the sublime night they'd shared.

'One day I will fight for you, Drew Hamilton.' The words sprang up in her heart. Ever since her marriage, even before, James had been manipulating her life. But not any more! She had her children now, and with her husband boozed out of his brains most days now, he would never get the children from her. There was nothing James could do now to stop her divorcing and she would cite this Elsie MacLelland or whoever else she needed to name to get rid of her husband! She would fight that fight she had promised Drew.

'I want a divorce!' she cried.

'That's out of the question. There's been enough divorce and scandal in this family to last several generations. You and Max have children to think of. The stigma would hurt them. And I'm an old man now. I couldn't take any more of it.'

'It's my life, not yours!'

'It wouldn't make any difference. Drew certainly doesn't want a divorce.'

'Doesn't he? We'll see about that.'

'Editor's office,' Drew's secretary answered the phone.

'This is Mrs Maxwell Rutherford. I'd like to speak to Drew Hamilton.'

'One moment please.'

As Drew's secretary placed a manicured hand over the receiver, Edwina looked at the mantelpiece clock in her bedroom. It was almost half past three, which she knew was a good time to call − after lunch but before the pressure of getting out the first edition had started to build. She'd never rung Drew at the office before but urgency had sent all thought of discretion to the winds.

'I'm sorry, Mrs Rutherford. Mr Hamilton has someone with him at the moment. Can I ask him to ring you back?'

She left her number but he didn't return her call and there was no reply when she rang the flat several times quite late into the evening.

The next day she rang the office three times and left her name and number with his secretary. But none of her calls were returned and there was no answer from the flat in the evening.

On the third day she was all churned up inside and could not endure the humiliation of not having her calls returned.

She had two large scotches for lunch and chain smoked. Her nerves felt about to split every time the phone rang. She tried not to sound frantic when she answered it, but she promptly shushed every caller away, saying her mother was seriously ill and she was waiting for an urgent call.

But the call she needed to put her life right never came. She re-ran the weekend over and over in her mind, desperately trying to work out what he had really meant by every word he'd said, looking for clues she had missed. And every time she blamed herself more and more for what had happened and what she had not seen.

But she knew she needed to be calm and in control when she spoke to him. So she forced herself to nibble at an omelette for supper and chain smoked away the evening until eleven o'clock when she rang the flat.

It rang for a long time and she was about to replace the receiver when a woman answered in a husky voice, 'This is Drew Hamilton's telephone.'

Edwina opened her mouth. But her throat was dry and she could not speak. She was shaking.

'Who's calling?'

She heard the woman's voice as she held the telephone away from her like a poisonous thing.

Then she replaced it silently, shrivelling inside at the intimacy of the scene on which she had intruded. The only telephone in Drew's flat was the white ivory one on the faded mahogany table by the bed.

Her mind closed in agony and she sank on her knees to the floor.

Sleep came in nightmarish bursts, but eventually when she was exhausted it took over for a couple of hours. When she awoke the next morning her body felt heavy and listless, as if it had turned to lead in the night. Her mind was in the grip of a total paralysing blackness; she could feel nothing. The battering her confidence and self-esteem had suffered since earliest childhood had finally overwhelmed her and the door had slammed shut on the cruel, icy prison of clinical depression.

PART THREE

CHAPTER FIFTEEN

Edinburgh 1963

Sunlight streaming through high arched windows cast an ethereal light on the pale oak pews in the First Division of the Appeal Court. The public gallery was packed with the friends and business associates of Alexander Warrender QC, who at the age of forty-one was about to be installed as the youngest Supreme Court judge in Scotland.

In the stall reserved for the new judge's family, his sixteen-year-old half sister, Roseanna, noticed that the documents tied and untied with pink ribbon and the books that usually cluttered the Bench and the clerk's table had been cleared away. She noted, too, that the three high-backed leather chairs where her father, who was the senior judge, normally sat with his colleagues had been replaced by a single high chair surrounded by lower seats which would be occupied by all the other Supreme Court judges. She had been eight years old when her mother first brought her to the court to see her father and she had hardly recognised him beneath his wig and robe of crimson silk.

'Why do you have to dress up to do your job, Daddy?' she asked him when he returned to their New Town home that afternoon.

'Judges have been wearing robes for as long as kings and queens have. It's part of a long and respected tradition,' he told her.

'But the Queen doesn't wear robes when she does her job,' Roseanna came back at him. 'She wears normal clothes.'

'She wears robes on special ceremonial occasions – when she opens Parliament or installs a Knight of the Thistle or the Garter,' replied her father.

'But that's not every day,' Roseanna persisted. 'You wear your robes every day.'

'Ah, but every sitting of the Supreme Court is a special occasion.'

'There's nothing special about sending people to prison,' said Roseanna.

'But there is about going there, especially if you haven't been before,' said her father. 'Robes convey the dignity of the court and, in criminal cases, help people to understand the gravity of what they may have done.'

'But you don't look like my daddy in your robes,' said Roseanna, determined to have the last word.

Even then she knew her father was a very important man – the Lord President of the Court of Session and Lord Justice General, the most senior judge in Scotland and leader of the proudest, most exclusive elite in the land. She knew, too, that he was the latest in a distinguished legal dynasty which had sat in judgment on Scotland for generations; and because of that she was always treated in a special way by her friends and their families, especially their mothers. As she grew up she had become increasingly aware that people took very great care not to offend her. It gave her an enormous sense of power.

Now she pretended not to notice the admiring glances of many of the young advocates who were packing the aisles on either side of the public gallery and the overhead galleries in their wigs and gowns. Tossing back the mane of sun-gold hair that framed her high cheekbones and apple-green eyes, she instead favoured her father's elderly clerk with a gracious smile.

Then at ten o'clock sharp the head macer walked on to the Bench crying 'Court!' He was followed by Lord President Warrender, who took the central chair, and a procession of fifteen judges who seated themselves on either side of him according to their seniority.

When everyone was seated Lord Warrender announced he had received a letter from the Queen appointing Alexander Robertson Warrender to be a judge in the Supreme Courts of Scotland and a Senator of the College of Justice.

'Would you like this letter to be read out?' he asked his fellow judges.

They nodded and his clerk rose and read out the letter in a clear, ringing tone.

When he had finished, Lord President Warrender and the entire Bench rose.

Then the whole court rose and stood in silence.

Roseanna watched her father and half brother raise their right arms as Alexander took the Oath of Allegiance to his Sovereign and Country.

Alexander and his younger brother had been law students at Edinburgh University when their father, a widower, had married Helen, a widow, not long after the end of the war. Her half brothers, so much older than Roseanna, had always seemed more like uncles than brothers.

'I, Alexander Robertson Warrender . . .'

Now as the words of the Oath of Allegiance passed over his lips, Roseanna had the strangest sensation of him ascending, rising up towards the high astragalled windows where the sunlight played, of leaving one world behind and entering another.

Nemo Me Impune Lacessit – No One Provokes Me with Impunity. The ancient motto of the Kings of Scotland hung large over the Surpeme Courts. From this day forth other men must address Alexander Warrender with a special kind of respect. They would no longer simply ask him for what they wanted . . . they would 'make submissions' in the hope of finding favour with him. They would stand in plain black gowns when they addressed him while he sat on high, magnificently robed, looking down. He would no longer enter the court quietly by a side door. A macer would herald his entrance into court and everyone would stand while he entered and no one would sit until he did. Convicted men would stand before him in fear and trembling awaiting his decisions on their punishments. From this day forth he would personify the majesty of the law and all the mighty apparatus of the State itself would lie ready to enforce his orders. From this day forth he was a man above and apart from other men . . . just like his father and hers . . .

When Alexander had taken the oath and signed two white parchment documents on the clerk's table, his father invited him to put on his robes and take his place on the Bench.

Roseanna could not take her eyes off him as he moved slowly up the steps to the Bench and started to walk along it, shaking hands with each judge and receiving their murmured welcome. At the end he stopped and bowed first to his fellow judges, then to the court and finally to his family.

As he sat down Roseanna's gaze ran along the row of judges in their robes of crimson silk till her eyes met and held her father's. One day she was going to be the first woman to take her place on that Bench . . .

CHAPTER SIXTEEN

1968

'You're a lot later than I expected. I thought you were going to be here by lunch time or just after. It's nearly half past five. I've been so worried in case something had happened to you,' Helen Warrender remonstrated with her daughter who had just arrived at their ancestral home near St Boswells in the Borders.

'I'm sorry, Mother,' said Roseanna wearily. 'But class was late in finishing. And I was hungry when I got back to the flat so I thought I'd make a sandwich. But there wasn't any bread. So I had to go out and get some. And then the phone rang and it was Maria in a terrible state because she's just broken up with Mark. So I had to listen and then the traffic was just terrible.'

'People must have been leaving town early. The traffic isn't usually that bad in the middle of the afternoon,' said Helen sharply.

'But there are roadworks all over the place.'

Roseanna looked at her mother's slightly slanted emerald green eyes and remarkably unlined face for a woman of fifty-nine, and wondered what she'd say if she heard the truth: I was in bed till four o'clock with this gorgeous man I met at the Traverse Theatre Club last night. No, you wouldn't approve of him, Mother. He hasn't any money and his career prospects are probably zilch because he's an out-of-work actor. But he's not just GIB – good in bed – he's SIB and FIB – super and fantastic in bed. But you don't know about my secret life, Mother, and I wonder what you'd think of that – your dedicated, dutiful daughter who does so well at her law studies having a secret sex life.

Roseanna had never been able to understand why her mother, who was so elegant and attractive and had been widowed twice before she married her father, never slept with him. Though they seemed to be very good friends, Roseanna could never remember them sharing a bed. As she had discovered sex she assumed her mother was frigid – one of those women who looked attractive but didn't like it. Which was a terrible waste and a shame for her adored father because although he was fifteen years older than Helen, he was a handsome, well-set-up man who was still in his prime at seventy-four.

'Well, now that you're here, would you like a cup of tea before I show you what we've done?' asked Helen, her tone more forgiving though reproach still lingered in her eyes.

'No, Mother, I'm fine. Just lead the way,' said Roseanna, trying not to sound bored.

She followed her mother across the hall, which had

been banked with scented flowers, and up the red-carpeted staircase leading to the ballroom.

'Oh, Mother, it's beautiful,' she exclaimed, her boredom transformed into enthusiasm at the sight of magnificent urns of red and white roses set on white marble columns before gilded pier glasses. Floor to ceiling windows were draped in velvet curtains in two shades of opulent, vivid green and gilded red velour chairs had been placed around the parquet floor. And there was a white piano where the band would play by the romantic staircase to the west lawn.

'I've dreamed of this day and this night since before you were born, since the time you were conceived — here at Auchinvreck just after your father and I were married,' said Helen, her green eyes shining with pride. 'The house hadn't been well looked after and was very run down. Your father gave me carte blanche to renovate it. And I did it all for him — except the ballroom, which I did for you. Since the time I conceived you I've planned to give a ball here for your twenty-first birthday. And as I've been going around the house today supervising the work, I've hardly been able to believe that you're now twenty-one and my dream is coming true.'

Roseanna saw the tears poised at the corners of Helen's eyes and drew her mother into her arms.

'I'm going to make your dream come true this evening,' she promised.

As a small child at her mother's knee, Roseanna had thrilled at Helen's stories of how she had single-handedly run a shipyard and a shipping line in Glasgow in the 1930s after her first husband died. 'Women didn't run companies, especially all-male bastions like shipyards. I was a pioneer, way ahead of my time,' Helen had told her daughter.

But as Roseanna grew up and saw the sedate, conventional life Helen led as a judge's wife, she decided her mother was romancing — and though she may have inherited the shipyard and shipping line, the companies would really have been run by a man who tolerated the noises her mother made and then did things his way.

The ball was not starting until ten o'clock. So there was plenty of time for a catnap, and she was now beginning to feel tired after her night of love with the gorgeous stranger.

'I think I'll stretch my legs for a bit,' she said, letting go of her mother. 'Rannoch, are you going to keep me company?' she asked the black labrador, who had wandered up the staircase from the garden and was now making his way towards her across the ballroom floor.

There had been black labradors called Rannoch and Flora at Auchinvreck ever since she could remember. Each time one of the dogs died, it was replaced after a decent interval of mourning. The current Rannoch was a bouncing two-year-old whose tail was wagging furiously at the prospect of her company.

She knelt and took his head between her hands, cuddled him and let him lick her face before he led her back out into the garden.

Roseanna loved Auchinvreck far more than her parents' house in New Town, Edinburgh. She loved the scent of its magnificent cedar trees, hundreds of years old, which soared to the sky and sheltered the house. She loved its neat, orderly lawns and rosebeds where weeds were never allowed to grow. She loved the salmon river surging by and the ruins of the abbey which was just a paler, more ancient shade of pink than Auchinvreck. She loved the walled garden and the policies where she walked with her father when she wanted to get him to herself. As a little girl she had raced the dogs around the grounds and through the house till she was exhausted. And then they came and licked her face all over. She had never had to be superior to all the other girls at Auchinvreck the way she had to in Edinburgh. At Auchinvreck she had always felt truly loved for herself alone and not because of who she was.

When she had walked Rannoch along the river and thrown in sticks for him to retrieve she came to rest on a wooden bench on the main lawn in front of the house.

'I wonder what David would make of Auchinvreck,' she said to Rannoch, thinking of her last night's lover as she patted the dog's back. She wondered if she would see him again, make love to him again. Naturally, she had not suggested the idea. That would not have been cool. This was 1968, not 1928 or 1938, when her mother had been young, and girls were every bit as entitled as men to enjoy sex with strangers they might never see again. It was ridiculous that that old fool Malcolm Muggeridge had resigned as rector of Edinburgh University over plans to offer the Pill free to students. The real trouble was not sex but that the older generation were jealous. That's why they tried to make it difficult for girls to get the Pill if they weren't married.

Her hand rested on the dog's back and his soulful brown eyes met hers. She would like to see David Miller again. She had known that from the moment she woke up in his arms in the bedroom of the lovely flat in the fashionable enclave of Ramsay Gardens, next door to Edinburgh Castle, which was her parents' twenty-first birthday present to her. Together they had watched the sky fill with brilliant, wild heraldic light and the sun rise over the city and the sea and the rugged mountains that rose far away in the north. Though the Pill enabled a girl to enjoy casual sex just like a man, it didn't guarantee she would feel casual and it didn't stop her wanting just one man who would be faithful to her. But all David Miller had wanted was a one-night sex marathon and he had no idea or interest in 'who she was'. Beyond the sense of bravado she experienced when she answered her mother's questions, she had never felt more used and rejected, uncomfortable and vulnerable in her life.

Then she saw her father's Jaguar emerge from the avenue of lime trees on to the drive that curved before it opened on to gravel sweep in front of the house.

As the dog shot off to greet its master she watched the handsome, substantial figure of her father emerging from the car. His hair was now completely white, but his spine was still ramrod straight and he had lost none of his vice-regal, proconsular bearing. She jumped up and ran after the dog straight into his arms.

'I'm glad you're home, Daddy,' she said, swallowing to prevent the tears suddenly welling at her throat.

'So am I when I get a welcome like this,' he said. And

she felt safe and protected and sure again of who she was when nestling in his arms, and all the horrible feelings of a moment ago were gone.

It was after midnight and supper was being served in the ante-room when Robert Warrender invited his only daughter to take the floor for an old-fashioned waltz.

'Did your mother tell you she dreamed of this night before you were born?' he asked.

'Before I was conceived by the sound of what she said.' Roseanna loved the way her father held her when they danced. He didn't really seem like her father when she was in his arms — simply a man she adored, and flirted with, a man who could keep her in her place and over whom she could not ride roughshod, a man who was stronger than she was.

'You and Angus Brodie made a striking couple when I saw you dancing earlier,' said Robert.

'Oh, Angus is so big and cuddly you want to give him to a child for Christmas,' she said.

'I don't think you should let him hear you say that,' said Robert. 'He might not be very flattered to hear it.'

'I've already done so. Often. He always laughs. I think I'm going to devil for him when the time comes.'

'Does he know that?'

'Yes.' She nodded. 'We've often talked about it.'

'I'm glad to see you're taking such an interest in the courts already. And I'm always very pleased to see you in the Appeal Court. But you'd learn a lot more about the techniques of cross-examination if you spent more time in the courts of first instance.'

'I do, Daddy, but I always find it most interesting in your court. There's nobody more interesting to watch and listen to than you are. I feel I can learn more from you than from anyone else. Sometimes I think my life won't be long enough to learn all you can teach me.'

'Oh, my darling daughter, you flatter an old man.'

'You're not old, Daddy. You'll never be old.' When the music stopped he bowed to her. 'I want to have one of our talks, Daddy. Take me for a walk in the garden.'

'But you have guests, scores of young men who want to dance with you.'

'Please . . .' She pressed her head gently against his shoulder

'But not for long,' he said as she slipped her arm into his.

It was surprisingly warm for late in May, more like a night of high midsummer when they sat down on the terrace. A moon veiled in a chiffon of mist high in a black and starless sky was casting a platinum light on the river and only the sound of it racing about its business disturbed the silence of the night.

'I wanted to be alone with you,' said Roseanna.

'What's the problem?' he asked gently.

'That I'm missing someone I met last night and I wish was here tonight. I've not been able to stop thinking about him all evening.'

'Oh, dear,' he said. 'Is it that important so soon?'

'I would like it to be, but it wasn't to him.'

'Wasn't?'

'Oh, Daddy, you're far too clever a lawyer. I should have said "isn't". Yes I . . . we . . . did.'

'Well, times have changed since my young day. And that's maybe not a bad thing. But no one has yet invented, and I hope they never will, some magic pill or potion which can control the yearnings of the human heart.'

They sat exchanging a look of infinite understanding for a long moment before he said, 'You can tell me it's none of my business — and it isn't — except that I have a deep interest in your welfare. But are what I sometimes hear described in court in the lingua franca as "one night stands" intrinsic to your way of life?'

'Yes and no . . . It depends . . .'

'You don't need to make excuses.'

'If you like someone it's expected. You've no chance otherwise.'

'So it's harder for a girl than it was in my young day. She's got nothing to bargain with.'

'Oh, that sounds horrible, Daddy. It's not like that.'

'Relationships between men and women involve a great deal of bargaining, as anyone who has sat in judgment in the divorce court will tell you. The traditional bargain between men and women is sex in return for stability. What's happening in society is that women are losing a lot of their traditional bargaining power. But what you cannot change is a woman's need for a stable relationship. It's built into her make-up anthropologically because she has to bear and rear the next generation and she needs stability in a relationship to do so. If things go the way they seem to have started going, it will have a destabilising effect on society because what the Pill really does is make it easier for men to move on . . . Women give everything and are guaranteed nothing in return.'

'Don't say that, Daddy,' said Roseanna. There were tears in the corners of her eyes.

'I'm sorry if you've been hurt by some young man,' he said sympathetically. 'But what's happened to you is the way the world is going. It's going to grow harder, become more of a fight, for a woman to get and keep a man. Even if she loves him very deeply. That's what the Pill and so-called sexual freedom really mean for women.'

'I love you, Daddy. I always will. I'd like to marry someone just like you,' she said, reaching for his hand.

She wondered if she would ever meet a man as strong as her father. She needed a man like him, who was stronger than her. If she couldn't find him, she would never marry. But if she did, it would be a different story . . .

PART FOUR

CHAPTER SEVENTEEN

1964—7

In the discreet neighbourhood around Harley Street in the heart of London's famous medical quarter, the distinguished psychiatrist Dr Edward Carson had established a practice which specialised in the talking cure for clinical depression. He had been on Colonel Robert Warrender's staff in British Intelligence in World War Two and his connections there had provided some of his first post-war clients. Helen Macrae, a colleague's widow who suffered a serious breakdown after the end of the war, had been one of the earliest. When she recovered she married his former boss, who had become a Scottish Supreme Court judge on his return to civilian life. Maxwell Rutherford had also been one of Edward Carson's wartime colleagues, and when the latest tranquillising and sedative drugs failed to make any impact on Edwina's depression and if anything she seemed to be getting worse, James Rutherford persuaded her to give the talking cure a chance.

'You mean I just sit here and talk about myself and my life?' She looked incredulously at Dr Carson at their first meeting in the elegantly furnished flat where he ran his practice.

'That's the general idea,' he replied.

'And it will cost a lot of money?'

'The work is very highly skilled and I believe the fees are commensurate with those skills,' he replied.

'And what good is that going to do me?'

'The purpose of psychotherapy is to help a patient come to terms with what has happened to them in the past and integrate the experience so that their lives are no longer crippled by it. Most people suppress or repress unhappy experiences.' Edwina looked at him dubiously but she was curious. 'Consciously they forget them. But the pain remains unresolved and unconsciously afflicts their lives and their relationships with other people.'

'And talking about it makes it better? I've talked over and over again to my friend and I'm not any better!'

'About what you believe to be the immediate cause of your depression?

'Yes.'

'But perhaps not about the roots of it?' Edwina looked puzzled before he continued, 'The skill of the psychotherapist lies in being able to ask the right questions so the patient is guided towards the areas of their past experience that they need to examine.'

'I don't understand.'

'The root of almost all unhappiness lies in childhood,' said Dr Carson.

The spectre of her mother's words rose in her mind: 'If anyone ever gets to know what you're really like, they will not want you or like you.'

But what had *they* got to do with it? Max Rutherford and Drew Hamilton left her because they'd found out what she was really like. That she was badly flawed and unlovable? Wasn't that the truth? Her mother had been right.

'You are who you believe you are,' said Dr Carson. 'You can do what you believe you can do. Perhaps you have believed you're unworthy.'

He was beginning to make a little sense.

She looked at him with a very serious face for a long time before she said, 'I'll give it a try.'

His look was equally solemn.

'It's no easy cure,' he warned. 'It's major surgery for the emotions and the mind. The pain and anguish are likely to be excruciating. But in your case I'm cautiously optimistic. You're thirty-four, still young enough to get considerable benefit in your life out of psychotherapy. The younger you are, the easier it is. Like many things, it becomes more difficult with age. Memories are more deeply buried, harder to excavate the older a person is. But change is possible at any time in life, though the older a person gets the harder it may be for them to effect a change — and the motivation may be much less. You'll need to be very brave because the journey into yourself is the most difficult and treacherous any human being can undertake. And it takes work as well as courage.'

But Dr Carson had given her hope.

'But I have a chance and I'm in the fortunate position of being able to afford this expensive treatment,' she said. 'You've given me a hope I didn't have when I walked into this room. I'll try to be brave and do whatever I must to understand and try to get better. I want to get better. I want to change . . .'

The talking cure was slow, expensive torture. But for two years from the spring of 1964 she took the first flight to London every Tuesday morning and spent two hours talking to Dr Carson before flying home later in the day. In the beginning she strenuously resisted all his attempts to break through her defences and reach the injuries at the root of her problems and lack of self-confidence.

'I'm sick of being told I'm well defended,' she cried angrily after she'd been seeing him for six weeks. 'I *am* talking. I *am* trying to tell you about myself.'

'You're entertaining me enormously, but that's a defence. Unconsciously you're amusing me so that you can keep me away from your real problems. You keep me on volcanic soil so there's nowhere I can get a hook in and penetrate your defences,' he said. 'The purpose of your visits here is not to brighten my life, but to help you to understand yourself and hopefully to change.'

That made her think. 'I don't suppose I can help it. It's what I've been doing all my life. Entertaining people, making them laugh, keeping them away because I suppose unconsciously I believed that if I ever let them see what I was really like they wouldn't want me. And it *is* what happened. I let my husband see and, well, you know the rest . . .'

'But your husband's behaviour towards you doesn't mean you're unlovable. From what you tell me he's had his own difficulties in his relationships with his parents, which would have contributed to his need for the relationship with Diana Watson.'

After that she overcame her shame about the emotional abuse she had suffered from her mother — enough to admit to it.

'"If anyone ever finds out what you're really like they won't want you." That was all I ever heard all through my childhood,' she cried out one day.

'Whatever I did was wrong. And when I did something right, like having a success at school, she always said it was a fluke. She turned every success sour and made every pain worse. And my father had no interest in me. There was no comfort for me anywhere.' Tears salty and bitter as the Dead Sea rolled down her cheeks.

But the pain and shame at the therapeutic sessions were nothing to the toxic, festering filth they dislodged and sent welling up and surging out between the sessions like a volcano unable to contain its raging inferno.

'Tears from the underground' were what she called the harsh bitter sobs which accompanied the shedding of old grief at the pain of being belittled and humiliated. Their long, bitter howl sounded quite a different note from the clear, bright tears of anguish expressed at the time. Regurgitating old unexpressed grief could take hours; the agony could last for days and was followed by exhaustion.

But nature seemed to know just how much old grief and pain her body and soul could cope with unloading at a time. And scourging periods of grief were followed by glorious periods of harmony and wellbeing. And when she had shed a huge chunk of old pain, her whole body felt lighter, more together and more of a piece, and within herself she felt more of one whole person. Though she went on talking to Dr Carson there were many pleasant, sunny weeks when there was no major unloading. And slowly she began to get better and for the first time in her life believe she had some value in her own right and not just as someone's wife or mother . . .

'A divorce! But Edwina, my defences would be in ruins. I've achieved the perfect way of handling women − I'm simply irrevocably married to a woman who will never divorce me.' Max sat back in a fireside chair in the family sitting-room in Kirklee Terrace and roared with laughter. 'It eventually deters even the most determined of women.'

'Including Elsie MacLelland?' Edwina pinioned him with her eyes.

'Yes, including Globe Publishing's celebrated office bike.'

'Oh, what a horrible way to describe anyone.'

'Best-loved bed warmer is another name by which she's revered.'

'Poor woman,' said Edwina, pouring her husband a fresh cup of tea.

She was glad they now were friends.

'Friendship with your husband will not just benefit your children,' Dr Carson had advised Edwina. 'If you can heal the breach between you, it will help you both in your future relationships with other people.'

It had not been easy at first. The estrangement was deep and bitter, but gradually as she began to change and believe in herself for the first time in her life she was able to reach out to Max. And the insights she gained in therapy into her own conscious and unconscious motivations helped her to understand his painful relationship with his father.

'Are you serious?' he asked as she handed him the cup.

'Very.'

'Have you met someone?'

'No.' She shook her head and her dramatic dark hair danced round her face like a maypole. 'But I want to make a fresh start in life. Margaret Flaxman is retiring to Spain and she's asked me if I'd like to buy the Albion Model Agency. I would. I want to stand on my own feet and have my own money and be free again.'

'Oh, Edwina, I'm delighted you've found something you want to do. It sounds right to me and I'm sure you'll do it very well and make a great success of it. But right at this moment I can't help feeling great sadness — I don't know whether it's for what we lost or what we just never had. But it does mean something being married, and having been married, even when it's all over and gone. It's not like just . . . well, anything else. It's different.'

'Yes,' she said, looking at the handsome sculpted features

of a man she had once loved so well, and those lustrous black eyes which could still undress a woman on sight. At sixty-one, Maxwell Rutherford was an extremely attractive, sexy man.

'I stayed in love with you for a long time after it was over between us,' she said, not knowing whether or not it was true. But it seemed the right thing to say, like an expression of sympathy after a death or a funeral.

'I know,' he said. 'Sometimes I hated myself for that.'

Now her heart was flooded with incredible sadness at what they might have had if they'd tried harder with each other. But being the people they were, with the legacy of problems they had each brought to their marriage, perhaps they never stood a chance. And yet she knew that in some infinite, impossibly incalculable way they had both lost.

'Yes,' she said. 'It is different.'

'Have you said anything to Father?' he asked.

She shook her head. 'I thought I'd speak to you first.'

'Thanks,' he said, meaning it. 'I somehow don't think we'll have a problem. Father knows we'll divorce anyway after he's gone, if not before if we really want to now, but he'll want to think he still runs the family show and we need his approval.'

'Well, I never thought it would come to this,' said the Right Honourable Lord Kilmacolm, when they tackled him together the next evening. Despite his eighty-seven years James was as sharp and alert as ever with no hint of mental or physical decay about him. 'But times are changing and the best thing is that you're now friends.'

'We are. For life,' said Edwina, sensing the old man's sadness far more than his disapproval that the marriage was ending.

'You've always been my favourite daughter-in-law, Edwina,' said James. 'I hope we, too, can remain friends . . .'

'Till death us do part,' she assured him with a smile and a lump in her throat. 'You'll always be my family,' she added, reaching for his hands. It was funny how across the years and all that had divided them, she had become closer to James Rutherford than she had ever been to either of her own parents. 'Always.'

They were divorced quietly and without publicity nine months later in September 1967. Edwina got the house in Kirklee Terrace and with part of the money from her settlement bought the Albion Model Agency.

Her new life and career were just beginning . . .

CHAPTER EIGHTEEN

1968

'**Y**ou are who you believe you are. You can do what you believe you can do.'

Dr Edward Carson's words were shining brightly in Edwina's heart on the morning early in January 1968 when she took her seat behind her brand new desk in the refurbished office of the Albion Model Agency.

The office was in Exchange Place near Rogano's famous seafood restaurant and close to the big department stores in Buchanan Street and Sauchiehall Street which the agency counted among its regular clients. Both Margaret's secretary and her assistant, who did most of the bookings, had been there for years and wished to stay on with Edwina. Their collective knowledge had smoothed her takeover enormously.

Fashion had undergone a revolution since Edwina's modelling days. The formal dressing, the distinct divisions between day and evening wear, the gloves, the hats, the elegance, the aloofness, the stockings and suspenders, the whole sweet mystery in which clothes cloaked a woman's body were history now. The mini skirt was the hallmark of the Swinging Sixties, the symbol of the new sexual freedom of girls who wore see-through dresses and strode around in tights and high plastic boots. Its sensational debut at two inches above the knee in 1965, which sent the *soi-disant* guardians of public morality screaming about the declining standards of the permissive society, was soon seen as modest as hemlines soared thighwards. The micro skirt, which scarcely covered a girl's bottom, was already a familiar sight on the streets of Glasgow and London.

'It's a different world from the one I knew and it needs someone younger to run the business,' Mrs Flaxman had said on the day she handed over the keys to Edwina. 'You're the right age to make a success of it.'

She would be thirty-eight this year and she had never felt fitter mentally and physically. In her prime, she felt reminded when she caught sight of her elegant figure in a royal-blue soft wool suit in a mirror in the outer office. The hemline was a modest two inches above the knee, the length she judged right for doing business in the fashion world. Her hairstyle, too, avoided the current geometric extremes, and its glossy, healthy black length was simply cut straight above her shoulders with a neat fringe.

She was ready for the new day, the new year and the challenges of the new career in which she was determined to succeed. She also had a new name, or one which was now new to most people. She was once more Edwina Buchanan,

and the name was on her notepaper as the owner of the
Albion Model Agency.

When her secretary brought her a cup of the real coffee
she had introduced as part of the agency's new image, she
glanced through the crisp pages of the new year's diary.

She already had a healthy number of lunch dates made
with both existing clients and the picture editors from
Globe Newspaper Publishing who had got word from Lord
Kilmacolm's office that the Albion Model Agency was the
place to go whenever they needed a pretty girl to cheer
up a page.

'And you can get publicity in the papers as well which
will help your business,' James advised her when she took
him out to a thank-you lunch at the Malmaison early in
March. 'Whenever you have a story about any of the girls
getting engaged or married or just taking up some interesting
hobby, ring up the diary editors and tell them about it. I'll
have a word.'

Within days the diary editors of the daily, evening and
Sunday papers had made lunch dates with Edwina and their
switchboard extensions and direct lines were added to her list
of newspaper contacts.

Word soon got round – the sexiest, prettiest girls were on
the books of the Albion Model Agency. The business began
to expand, which often meant Edwina working late. But
the children were growing up fast – Marietta was fourteen
this year and Keith eleven – and rapidly becoming quite
independent. And there was always the housekeeper there for
them at Kirklee Terrace, which meant they never went home

to an empty house. So Edwina did not feel guilty or pressured when fashion shows kept her away from home in the evening. She had been there constantly when the children were small and now she was building her own new life and career.

She was lunching at Rogano's on a glorious day in July with the managing director of one of the large department stores and his press officer when Drew Hamilton made his entrance.

She saw him before he saw her and she knew from the way his eyes were searching the room that he was looking for her. Everyone lunched at Rogano's and she was almost surprised she had not seen him here before — unless he had stayed away deliberately, because she knew he was very happy with the work the Albion Model Agency did for the papers of which he was now editor in chief as well as editor of the Daily.

'The editor loves the photographs we get with your girls,' the Daily picture editor had told her at lunch quite recently.

She had thought about him more in the past few months since she had been in his orbit again and doing business with his people than she had done for a couple of years. But she had no idea what she felt for him now — if she felt anything at all or if she was simply playing her old familiar game of denying need. But her life was full, she was her own person — and she knew that whatever she felt when they met, it would be different because she was a different person to the one he had known.

He was different, she realised, watching those searching

eyes. The aura of suntan and mane was more golden than ever, glinting with success, endowing him with an even more buoyant air of youth than he'd had five years ago. And those Mediterranean-blue eyes now possessed the supreme confidence with women that once shone in the eyes of Max Rutherford. He had presence now, too, and it drew every eye in the room to him as he surveyed it. He was forty-three years old and the message radiating from every cell and gesture of his superbly athletic figure was that the best was yet to come.

At the instant their eyes met, all she felt was excitement at the prospect of meeting this gorgeous man.

Every eye followed him as he crossed to her table and bowed.

'My dear Edwina, your success is the talk and toast of the town, and we simply can't get enough of your girls in our papers,' he said. 'Yet how very long it seems since last we met.'

At that moment she remembered a journey she had made years ago north of Loch Kishorn and how the landscape changed from the gentle shores of the West Highlands to the rugged, rockier clime of the Far North. But it had only been when she reached Toscaig and looked back that she realised the huge extent of the change and that she had travelled from one geographical country to a completely different one.

It was only now looking at Drew Hamilton that she realised the vastness of her own changes.

'You are what you believe you are. You can do what you

believe you can do.' Dr Carson's words ringing in her head had replaced her mother's mantra inculcating disbelief. This was what she now believed in the depths of her being.

As their eyes went on holding, she knew that whatever was going on in his life right now, she could get Drew Hamilton back . . . if she wanted him . . .

CHAPTER NINETEEN

'The talks between the Czechoslovakian leader Dubček, Brezhnev and the other Eastern bloc leaders have ended with little agreement,' David Ross, the *Daily Globe*'s foreign editor, told the afternoon editorial conference.

'There's going to be trouble in Prague. The Russians have their tanks poised on the border and they're never going to let Dubček go his own way,' said Drew. 'It can't be long before the Soviet tanks roll in. And the West will do nothing because it's not in our interests. Anything else?' He looked round the departmental heads on the alert in the semicircle of chairs and settees around his desk. No one spoke. 'Right, that's it,' he said, swinging his feet off his desk as the executives rose and the red light blinked on the intercom from the chairman and chief executive's office.

'What are you doing about Richard Nixon?' demanded Lord Kilmacolm.

'Nothing right now,' said Drew, conscious of the bitterness in his voice.

'He'll probably win the Republican nomination for the American presidency next week.'

'The foreign desk have the Republican convention well under control. Richard Scott is going from New York. He'll be in Miami by the weekend.'

'So will I,' said Lord Kilmacolm. 'I'd like to see him.'

'I'll tell the desk.'

When he replaced the receiver, Drew rose from his desk and wandered towards the window. Rain was just beginning to fall and people were shooting up umbrellas in the street. He dug his hands deep into his trouser pockets and looked at the heavy rupturing clouds. In a minute it would be coming down in gallons . . . just like it did on the day he was summoned to Lord Kilmacolm's seventh-floor suite and told his affair with Edwina Rutherford was over . . .

'I will not have my son publicly humiliated and cuckolded!' Lord Kilmacolm had been adamant on that terrible afternoon. 'You either end your affair with my daughter-in-law or cease to be the editor of the Daily. And there is no other place for you in Globe Newspaper Publishing.'

James's ruthlessness was legendary.

'Like the Lord, James Rutherford giveth power but he also reserves the right to taketh it away,' a senior executive once observed to Drew. 'Especially if he thinks someone is becoming too powerful.'

His ability to strip away all editorial power struck Drew like lightning that afternoon. He was thirty-eight years old and though there was no doubt he was still young enough to get a good job in Fleet Street his career prospects in London were no longer as gilded as they had been ten years ago.

He had invested too much of his life in Globe Newspaper Publishing and he wasn't going to get the editorship of a national daily published in London.

'It was the most wonderfully clarifying moment,' he said much later to Elsie MacLelland. 'Choose to live or die. I chose what I believed was life, at least the life of my career. I had no choice in terms of my ambitions . . .'

It was also the moment he knew that blood relationship was stronger than the favourite-son status he had so carefully cultivated with his employer for over twenty years.

'The way we had been ended that day,' he also said to Elsie.

But a newspaper proprietor's inner sanctum was no place for a show of emotion.

'I'd like to see Edwina to say goodbye,' he said in a cool and utterly decisive voice on that terrible afternoon.

'By all means,' said Lord Kilmacolm. 'Take the whole weekend . . .'

. . . Except he never said 'goodbye' because women never accepted it was over with a man with whom they were in love. To them the word meant the relationship wasn't quite working as well as it might and was a signal they needed to put in more effort to make things all right again. The need for a relationship to continue on almost any terms could be pathological in women.

Edwina would never have accepted it had to be over — and she would have wrecked his career to keep it going.

Yet he sensed she knew . . . and that his heart was teeming

with unspoken, unspeakable grief. And that afterwards she would understand what he had not been able to say, and why.

He had done what he had to do — and paid the price. There was always a price to be paid.

Drew got drunk with Elsie MacLelland three nights later. She was still bitter over recently being discarded by Max, and he had taken her home to his flat. She had been in his arms in his bed when she answered the phone call he knew came from Edwina. Despite the drink he had consumed he felt wretched . . . before he lost himself in Elsie.

She had stayed in his bed for days and nights. Then he took her to bed for a week in Venice just before Christmas. When they got back the whole office knew and neither of them gave a damn.

They did each other a lot of good for six months, taking the sting out of one another's wounds and aiding their mutual recovery until Lord Kilmacolm summoned him to the seventh floor and said, 'You've been riding the office bike for long enough.

'I want you to be editor in chief over all the papers as well as editor of the daily. But I have to think about how the other editors will feel because they're both doing good jobs and I don't want to lose either of them. And they just won't stand for an ongoing relationship with Elsie.'

But the affair had run its course and they both knew it. Elsie had been very sweet and understanding. She was still woman's editor on the evening paper and as she had comforted most of the senior executives except Lord

Kilmacolm in times of infinite stress, she was probably unfireable.

Then a year ago she and Alex Regan stunned the world by announcing their engagement.

'But why?' Drew wanted to know. 'I thought you were anti marriage.'

'Security,' she admitted. 'It takes a lot of energy to live as I've done, and men don't want you when you're older. There's always someone younger coming up. Just look round the talent in the reporters' room. It's full of girls who'll take their chance, and good luck to them. I've got to look to the future. But I'll still be there for you. Still your pal.'

He had been best man at her wedding.

Not long afterwards his wife had asked for a divorce.

'I've met someone,' she said. He was the headmaster of the school where she taught and had been a widower for several years.

After the divorce he had sold his flat in the Merchant City and moved into a much grander apartment in Crown Gardens, not far from the flat where Max Rutherford entertained women at all hours of the night and day.

Now all the trappings of power and success for which he had longed as a fourteen-year-old copy boy watching James Rutherford arriving at the office in his chauffeured Rolls-Royce were his. Now he, too, was chauffeur driven to the office and home at night – in a Jaguar – and had a fine home in the West End where he had employed an interor designer to create the ambience he desired. Now he, too, could have any woman he wanted. And like all men who are successful with women, he let them do the running. But there hadn't been anyone important, though some had tried hard enough. And when the paper had been put to bed at night and he at last rolled home in his chauffeured car there was no one waiting for him in his magnificent West End flat . . .

It was after midnight and the next morning's papers, which had not long been sent up by car from the office, were strewn around the drawing-room fireplace in Drew's flat as he reached for the telephone.

'Back bench,' said a man's voice.

'John Reynolds,' said Drew.

'John Reynolds,' said the night editor when the phone was passed to him.

'I can't see anything to worry us in the first editions,' said Drew. 'Looks like a quiet night.'

'And there's nothing new coming up on the wires.'

'Good. I'm not in the mood for much excitement tonight,' said Drew. 'Well, I'll see you tomorrow, John. Goodnight.'

When he replaced the receiver he poured a large brandy and dialled a number he had not rung for years.

'Hello,' said a woman's sleepy voice.

'Edwina?'

'Yes.'

'Drew Hamilton.' He had known from the look in her lunch-time eyes that she could be there for him again. And his spirits had soared as he went on holding her eyes. It was then that he knew how much he had lost. But that price had been paid yesterday and was over and gone. And now at the sound of her voice in the night his soul soared again and today was a new day and everything was possible once more. 'If you're willing, we could try again . . .'

CHAPTER TWENTY

'What kind of a Dickensian offer is that?' she laughed. 'It sounds like the spectre of something dragged out of *David Copperfield*. Is that the best you can do, Drew Hamilton?'

'When I've seen the paper to bed, I'm a spent force these days,' he sighed.

'You're making whatever you have in mind more unattractive by the minute.'

But they were laughing now and their laughter was dissolving the years and the time apart and the pain and alienation – and every hurtful thing that divided them under the sun.

'You're a different woman, Edwina,' he said when they had cancelled their existing dates and met for lunch at the Malmaison the next day.

Lunch was safe. It could be business – the Albion Model Agency did an awful lot of work for Globe Newspaper Publishing – and they could walk away from each other with no loss of face.

'I think we're both different people,' she said.

'Which means that if we decide we like each other we can start from scratch . . . with no nasty stuff from the past . . .'

She heard the question in his voice, saw uncertainty for the first time in his eyes.

She knew enough from her time in therapy to realise that pain from the past had to be let go — or else it crippled and destroyed the present and the future. But she wasn't sure how much she could put the theory into practice with Drew. It would depend on how strong, how healed she had become, and the only way to find out was to try to get close to him again.

'Let's see what happens,' she said.

Everything was different now. Their marriages were behind them and they were single people free to meet and be seen together without the need for discretion and deception — though in the beginning they dined quietly well away from places where they were known as they tried to find out about each other again and re-establish their links. And there was so much to find out about the years between.

She sympathised with his sadness over the final ending of his marriage and the breakdown in his relationship with his adult children, whom he hardly saw. She listened for endless hours to his obsession with newspapers, which was greater than ever.

'Newspapers are my true mistress,' he said when she finally got out of him that it was Elsie MacLelland who had answered her call.

'The office bike,' she said without bitterness or rancour.

'Elsie's a good pal,' he said, standing up for the woman who had been so loyal to him.

'I was using the common parlance in which I've heard her talked about. I wasn't being pejorative,' she said with a dignified smile.

But she encouraged him to talk about other women with whom he had enjoyed relationships and slipped easily into the role of confidante. The new, recovered Edwina wanted to understand her man because she was never going to lose him again.

And she told him about her own sadness at her divorce, about her children, and how she bought and was building her business. But she never told him about her recovery from clinical depression because people were funny about mental illness and afraid of it. And though she was certain she would never be depressed again, she did not want him to know because he might think there was a risk it could happen again. Besides, people needed secrets and she was never going to give all of herself to another human being again.

'But there's a mystery about you now there never was before,' he said one Saturday when they had driven up towards Lake of Menteith for lunch.

'And that makes life more interesting for you,' the new, recovered Edwina said with a confidence that would have been utterly alien to the old.

'I have to admit it does,' he said.

They became lovers again that afternoon at a quiet country inn he knew not far away.

Suddenly, though it had been a long time on its way, the time was right to love again.

She had managed to live without a man's love for so long, and her life was so busy and full, her time so occupied, that she had almost ceased to be aware of her own needs. But afterwards the length of her deprivation seemed appalling. It was not good to be as alone as she had been for so long, letting no one near her. Emotionally she had withered and become a skeleton.

'I've become very good at denying I need what I may not be able to have,' she whispered, looking up at him.

'Yes,' he said. 'I noticed. But now you can have — all you want . . .'

The last shreds of her fear of intimacy fled away as he took her once more in his arms and made her his again.

After that things changed again. They started going away for weekends and he became a regular visitor to Kirklee Terrace, though he never stayed overnight.

'Do you like Drew Hamilton a lot, Mummy?' Marietta, who would soon be fifteen, narrowed her eyes and fixed them on her mother over the breakfast table on a Saturday morning.

'Yes, I do like him a lot,' Edwina answered honestly.

'Do you think you'll marry him?'

'He hasn't asked me.'

'But if he did?'

'You and Keith would be the first to know.'

'But what if we didn't like him?'

'I could never marry anyone you and Keith didn't like. So, young lady, tell me, do you like Drew Hamilton?'

'I don't know.'

But Drew got along well with her children and especially Keith, who at not quite twelve was already very interested in the news and ever ready to discuss it and air his strongly held opinions on everything from an unknown Australian called Rupert Murdoch taking over the *News of the World* and the first flight of Concorde to Golda Meir's election as Prime Minister of Israel and Neil Armstrong becoming the first man to set foot on the moon.

Edwina had now met Drew's adult son and daughter, who had been coaxed out to separate Saturday lunches. And she was confident that when she married Drew they would all weld together into one big, comfortable extended family.

She was sure marriage was not far from his mind the weekend they flew by helicopter to the Ardnamurchan peninsula on the west coast to see a house, advertised in the *Sunday Globe*, which was what he had been seeking for a long time.

It was a clear day in the west and the sun was glinting on the deep blue mountains and islands that rose up out of the ocean. The deep penetration of the land by the sea all along the coast was striking from the air as she slipped her arm into his and rested her head against his shoulder. She could not remember when she had last felt so protected. It was wonderful to have an independent business life but even more wonderful to be part of a loving couple.

The Ardnamurchan peninsula jutted for seventeen miles

into the Atlantic Ocean. At its end, twenty-three miles farther west than Land's End, a lighthouse tower of grey granite stood 118 feet high atop a 60-foot cliff on the edge of a wild, bleak moor.

Round the corner away from the moor the house on which Drew had set his eye stood looking out over the sunny, sheltered white-shell sands of Sanna Bay. Beyond, the ocean rolled free for over three thousand miles.

'Oh, it's beautiful,' cried Edwina when they landed and the helicopter blades had come to a standstill and the calling of the grey seals and the gulls filled the soft, sweet air.

For a minute they stood side by side looking at the handsome whitewashed house with its window frames painted pale blue like the crofters' cottages. It was much bigger than either the house where her parents had taken her on holiday to Elie as a child or Max's place in Lagg. But Edwina had always been happy in whitewashed houses with blue-painted window frames and she knew that here she would be happiest of all.

'Let's go see inside,' said Drew, taking her hand and leading her through the garden where wild orchids, meadow-sweet and wild thyme grew.

The rooms were lit by brilliant sunshine and gorgeously furnished in cane and chintz with lots of pretty rugs scattered on wood floors, and there was central heating and an Aga in the kitchen. Edwina saw the future here. Here their families would visit and old wounds in relationships would be healed. She would give him back the family life he had lost and make up for the years he regretted. She would cook enormous meals for them. And they would dine on the terrace in the long, long light of the summer evenings and gather round glowing peat fires in the eternal darkness of the Scottish winter. Here they would make love to the rhythm of the ocean and she would bind him to her in a million ways so he would never want to leave her.

The house came furnished right down to the last teaspoon and they talked about it when they lunched on the terrace on the sandwiches and white wine they had brought in a cool-bag and looked out to the small isles of Rhum and Eigg rising out of the deep blue sea.

'Like it?' he asked, his eyes holding hers.

'I love it.'

That night they stayed at the luxurious Glenborrodale Hotel, which nestled on the wooded southern shore of the peninsula where the helicopter dropped them in the afternoon. The next day he drove a hired Mini along the narrow winding road to the west to give the house a second inspection.

'Well, do you think we'll be happy here?' he asked.

'Very, very happy,' she said, placing her arms around his neck.

But he never said a word about marriage either then or when he completed the purchase of the house or on any of the weekends when they helicoptered in.

As time went by she realised it simply was not on his agenda . . . and she was going to have to do something about it . . .

CHAPTER TWENTY-ONE

'But why ruin a perfectly good relationship by getting married?' asked Drew wearily.

'Because I feel it *is* less than perfectly good,' said Edwina.

'It was until you dragged marriage into it,' he retorted, pacing up and down the family sitting room in Kirklee Terrace. 'What's wrong with the way we are or have been? We have our separate homes where we lead the separate working lives we both want, but the whole world knows we're together. We're respected and accepted. This is 1971. People don't need to be married the way they used to be. And marriages break up, and you and I both know how very painful that is.'

'Our relationship breaks up today if we're not getting married, and *that's* going to be extremely painful,' she said.

For the past two years, ever since he had bought the house in Ardnamurchan, she had tried every kind of sweet talk, persuasion and cajolery to lead him gently into marriage. And it had failed. She had allowed him to grow far too comfortable without getting married. He had his own flat in Crown Gardens to go home to when he was late at the office or wanted to read the papers at midnight and she might have gone to bed because she had an early appointment in the morning. But he stayed with her or they helicoptered to Ardnamurchan for weekends or high days and holidays. It was the perfect bachelor life and she had let it go on for far too long.

'What if I'm unfaithful?' he suggested.

'I hope you'd have no cause to be, but it wouldn't be the end of the world and I'm sure we'd get over it.' Her eyes pinioned his with a look that said she would brook no nonsense.

'Ah, by the sound that, you think that being unfaithful is just a one-night stand. What if it was serious? What if I fell passionately in love?'

'I hope that wouldn't happen,' she said. But she neither sounded nor felt quite as confident as she had done a moment ago. Wasn't that why she wanted to be married? So she was better protected if that dreadful thing ever happened and it was harder for him to leave her. She was now forty-one and though she easily passed for ten years younger, she knew time would increasingly be less and less on her side. She knew, too, that marriage in itself guaranteed nothing except legal rights. Financially she didn't need any of them and was never likely to need them. She revelled in her financial independence and the power it gave her over her own life. She could not live now without being a person in her own right and would never again be content simply to be someone's wife or mother. And yet she wanted to be this man's wife; it was more important than anything now. And nothing else was good enough for their relationship. For all her years in psychotherapy, she wasn't sure she understood her own motives. All she knew was that marriage was the only thing that was right for them now, and in some strange way being a part of someone else would complement and enhance her independence.

'If the day ever came when you no longer wished to live with me, I'd no longer wish to live with you. There'd be no point in holding you if your heart belonged to someone else.' She spoke the words quietly, with dignity, and knew every single one of them was a lie.

So did he.

'You don't mean that,' he scoffed. 'But you're so smart these days, Edwina. You absolutely fascinate me more and more.'

She kept up the dignity and the solemn eyes. 'If that was what you wanted I'd let you walk away from me.'

'It would break your heart.'

'We're right for each other,' she said, maintaining her cool, dignified mien, but there was a lump in her throat and tears behind her eyes.

The way they lived suited him perfectly. He had all the advantages of marriage without any of the disadvantages. It wasn't that he had any objections to marrying Edwina; it was just that he had no wish to get married again. Why were women so insistent upon it, especially when, like he and Edwina, they didn't plan to have a family? So there was no need to think about the benefits legitimacy conferred on a child.

He loved Edwina. He had been faithful to her since they

got back together. She was his woman and that was it and he hadn't looked at any other. She had no need to worry.

But what if he did? Marriage, a piece of paper which said he was her husband and she was his wife, would not stop him falling in love.

But he knew she meant what she said — they would part if they didn't get married. He looked at her solemn eyes and her brave, determined expression. They had known each other for a long time now and been through so much and their families got on so well. She was more precious to him than anyone and he didn't want to live without her now — or return to the loneliness of a turnover of women in his life but no one to whom he belonged.

They belonged, he and and Edwina, and if marriage was the only way of keeping her . . .

'Well, perhaps it's not such a bad idea,' he said grudgingly.

They were married four weeks later in Dowanhill Parish Church in the presence of their families and close friends, including Lord Kilmacolm who, at Edwina's insistence, had used his power and influence and the fact that he was the son of a Presbyterian minister to get her the church wedding she felt she must have this time.

Afterwards they were photographed on the steps of the church. When the pictures had been taken she looked up into the eyes of her new husband. She had fought hard for her second chance at love and marriage. This time there would be no Diana Watson stealing her man. This time she would fight the best fight to keep him . . .

BOOK TWO

ANOTHER WOMAN
IN LOVE

PART ONE

CHAPTER TWENTY-TWO

1972

Social

Lord Brodie of Craigendhu

Lady Helen Warrender

*The engagement is announced and the marriage will
take place shortly of Lord Brodie of Craigendhu,
Inverness-shire, and Lady Helen Warrender, widow
of the late Viscount Warrender of Auchinvreck, of
Moray Place, Edinburgh.*

Roseanna Warrender lifted her head from the social pages of
The Scotsman and was starting to close the paper when a
headline on another page caught her attention.

LORD BRODIE OF CRAIGENDHU TO WED
LORD PRESIDENT'S WIDOW

Lord Brodie of Craigendhu, whose long anti-hanging campaign was instrumental in leading to the abolition of the

death penalty, is to marry Lady Helen Warrender, widow
of the late Lord President of the Court of Session and Lord
Justice General, Viscount Warrender of Auchinvreck.

Lord Brodie, himself a widower whose wife died in a
tragic shooting accident on the grouse moors near his estate
in 1967 . . .

Roseanna skimmed the story, taking in details she already
knew until she came to a paragraph which said:

It will be Lady Warrender's fourth marriage and her third
to a leading Edinburgh lawyer.

As the widow of the late Glasgow shipbuilding and
shipping magnate, Harry Dunlop, she caused a sensation
in legal circles in 1930 when she hired John Brodie, then
a young advocate, to defend a shipyard worker accused
of murder.

At the time it was Poor Law practice for a person
accused of murder to be defended free by King's Counsel.
But the then Mrs Dunlop obtained permission from the
Faculty of Advocates to hire Mr Brodie, at the time a
junior counsel, at her own expense.

The subsequent acquittal of the accused saw the
start of the rise of Lord Brodie's spectacular career at
the Bar . . .

'You never told me you once hired your fiancé to defend a
shipyard worker on a murder charge,' said Roseanna when

her radiant mother and Lord Brodie, fresh from their photocall on the steps of the house in Moray Place, came into the drawing room. 'You kept pretty quiet about that.'

'Our little secret.' Helen giggled girlishly at her future husband.

Roseanna lowered her eyelids, unable to go on watching them. She could not stand the way her mother had gone all silly and giggly since she had decided to marry Lord Brodie. At sixty-three she was behaving like sixteen. Lord Brodie had always impressed her as a real sobersides to the point of dour. She had devilled for his son, Angus, when she was training for the Bar, to which she had recently been called, and Lord Brodie had always seemed to have his nose buried in his legal books any time she called at the house in Heriot Row. Now at the age of seventy-two he seemed to have taken complete leave of his senses, and she was embarrassed by the way he and her mother were forever holding hands and looking into each other's eyes. Her mother had never behaved like that with her father, and though she was pleased that Helen was finding someone to take away the loneliness she had endured since he died suddenly two years ago, their conduct was discomfiting.

'Have you decided when you're getting married?' she asked when Lord Brodie had thankfully taken himself off to meet one of his cronies at the Cockburn Club for lunch.

'The ninth of October and you, I hope, are going to be my bridesmaid.'

'Of course, Mother,' said Roseanna, thinking what a relief it would be when the lovebirds were married. Perhaps they'd settle down. She was sitting with her back to the light and could see every line and wrinkle on her mother's face — though she had to admit there were hardly any, and she hoped *she* looked as good at sixty-three. 'But tell me about the sensational murder trial, Mother. You and your fiancé have got me really intrigued,' she added, determined to find out about it now that she had her mother to herself.

'I'd like a sherry,' said Helen, strolling to the drinks table. 'How about you?'

'A dry martini,' said Roseanna, sensing her mother's slight uneasiness.

When she had poured the drinks and handed her daughter the martini, Helen sat down.

'Well, Mother . . .' said Roseanna, thinking it more and more curious that Helen had never mentioned the murder trial in all the stories she had told her daughter. 'You've told me all about your first husband, Harry Dunlop, and your second husband, the advocate Henry Macrae whom you met on a yacht during Clyde Yachting Fortnight shortly after you were widowed for the first time, and Father who you also met on the same yacht on the same day. But you've never told me about Lord Brodie. And as he's going to be your next husband I'd like to hear about him.'

'I've often told you that I met John and Henry Macrae and your father all on the same day,' said Helen, patting her skirt, then smoothing her hair as Roseanna heard the brittle, defensive note in her mother's voice. 'My solicitors, Campbell and Aitken, gave an annual party on board their yacht, the

Monadliath, during Clyde Yachting Fortnight. And in 1930 they invited me.

'It wasn't long after my first husband had died. I was still in mourning and trying to come to terms with running the businesses, and I almost didn't go. But a friend persuaded me that what I needed was a day out. The place was hoaching with the Edinburgh advocates that Campbell and Aitken employed in the High Court.

'Photography was your father's hobby even in those days and he took a picture of me with all the members of the Edinburgh Bar on board the yacht. John Brodie sent me a copy which I had framed. And it was sitting on my desk the day a young trade-union leader called Graeme Wilson — better known to you as a Labour Cabinet minister — came to ask me to get a lawyer to defend Robbie McMenemy, a young shipyard worker charged with a murder Graeme was sure he didn't commit.'

Though she had only recently been called to the Bar, Roseanna had often accompanied senior lawyers to interviews and was used to listening to people tell their stories — and to how they looked as they told them. What struck her now was that either her mother had long rehearsed this story or she was carefully editing every word before it passed her lips. There was something too well chosen about her words, which told Roseanna her mother was putting a best face on a story which had not happened in quite the way she was telling it.

'I'd heard that John Brodie was the brightest and the best young advocate there was — '

'But he was just a junior counsel, and under the Poor Law men on murder charges were supposed to be defended by a Queen's Counsel,' Roseanna interrupted.

'And a pretty makeshift system it was, according to Graeme,' retorted Helen. 'Graeme had come to me asking for the best, and the best was what he was going to get – '

'But he was still only a junior counsel.' Roseanna rammed her point home.

'He was the man Graeme and I wanted,' said Helen and Roseanna glimpsed the steel in her mother's character as she had never seen it quite so nakedly before. 'After the case was over we kept in touch and he often took me to dinner when he was at the High Court in Glasgow . . .'

'And that was it?' Roseanna saw her mother faltering. She sat up closer to the edge of the chair and invisibly began to slide from the role of daughter into one of inquisitor.

'Not quite,' said Helen, getting up and teetering across the room in her high heels to replenish her sherry.

When she sat down again her eyes held Roseanna's for several moments before she said, 'Well, as John and I are now finally getting married, I suppose I might as well tell you. It was always my intention to tell you one day . . .'

She took a sip of her sherry and sat back in her chair as Roseanna focused her eyes intently on her mother's, which had taken on a faraway look.

'There was also a girl on the yacht on the day we met. Her name was Grace Mitchell. Her father was the Lord President and it was obvious even then that she had set her cap at John Brodie. She did her best to keep me out of even being photographed with the members of the Edinburgh Bar.

'Anyway, after Robbie McMenemy's trial, when I dined with John I realised he was most certainly not in love with her. Gradually John and I fell in love, but before we became lovers Grace Mitchell in her desperation to marry him had seduced him and got herself pregnant. It only happened once — '

'How do you know?'

'Because John himself told me.'

'He would say that.'

'I believe him,' said Helen. 'But if you'll stop interrupting' — Helen sounded cross — 'and let me tell my story. Anyway, John was forced to marry her by her father, who threatened to destroy his career otherwise. So we parted, and within months Grace Mitchell had a miscarriage and lost the baby.

'I didn't know this until several years later when I met Henry Macrae in the street outside my office in Glasgow and he asked me to tea. I felt very bitter and angry when he told me. But by this time John had a daughter and his son had just been born.'

'Angus?'

'Yes.' Helen paused and Roseanna sensed her mother's pain at the memory. 'Well . . . gradually Henry and I became friends and we got married in 1935.'

'Wait a minute, Mother,' Roseanna interrupted. 'You're going a bit too fast. You haven't said anything about falling in love.'

'It wasn't the same as it had been with John, but we

were good friends,' said Helen, and Roseanna sensed a boring compromise.

'So how did you feel when you started seeing John Brodie again once you came to live in Edinburgh?' she asked.

'It was all right, perfectly civilised. We were both married then.'

'And just what difference did that make to the way you felt?' asked Roseanna.

'Then the war came and we were all in London,' said Helen as if she hadn't heard the question. 'Henry and John were both in British Intelligence working for a unit headed by your father which operated out of a country house in Hertfordshire.

'Henry used to go away a lot on dangerous missions behind enemy lines. One time he was so long overdue in returning – it was over two months – that even your father was convinced he'd been killed. John's marriage was already over in every real sense. We were both alone in wartime London and the spark was kindled again between us. But Henry came back – '

'Did he find out about you and John?'

'There were no admissions by anyone. But he tacitly knew. Everyone knew what was going on, but none of us talked about it. Then he was killed just after D-Day. He died in John's arms two days after the Normandy landings.'

'So the way was really clear for you and John Brodie now?'

Helen shook her head. 'He still had a wife in Edinburgh. As the end of the war approached, he talked about getting divorced. It was what he wanted — I know he really did — but Grace refused. And once again we parted . . .'

'So then you married Father on the rebound,' said Roseanna cynically.

'It wasn't like that,' said Helen. 'I'm going to have another sherry. How's your drink?' she asked, getting up.

'I'm fine,' said Roseanna, who had hardly touched her martini. But now, sensing something ominous, she took a sip.

'John and I had talked a lot about having a family when we discussed divorce. It was what we both wanted . . .'

Sunlight was playing on the flowers banking the fireplace and a blackbird soared high in the sky over the trees in the gardens of Moray Place, but Roseanna was only aware that her mother was swallowing hard.

'When John came back from Edinburgh after Christmas and the New Year of 1945 he told me Grace had refused to divorce him. But there was no going back for me. I was already pregnant — '

'Pregnant!'

'Yes. I had been looking forward to seeing him because I believed it was what he wanted as much as I did. Or he had done. But everything had changed when he was in Edinburgh. And now he simply wanted away from me . . . I didn't . . . I couldn't tell him . . . We'd met in the American Bar at the Savoy and till the day I die I'll never forget him just walking away from me . . .'

'What happened to the baby?'

'Your brother, John's son, was born at Rustington in

August 1945, the day the Japanese surrendered . . . He was stillborn . . .'

Now the air brimmed with silence as Roseanna stared open mouthed at the strange woman sitting opposite her . . .

'Baby . . . Thomas Randolph Macrae . . . is buried in Rustington and to this day fresh white flowers are laid on his little grave . . . He was born dead . . . He had been alive when he was inside me . . . He had lived within me . . . But he was born dead!'

Roseanna watched tears stream down the strange woman's face.

'By the end of the war I'd lost everything. My husband, my lover, my baby. Most of all my baby. That was the end. There was nothing left for me. I lost the will to live. One day the housekeeper I'd hired to look after me in Rustington and her husband found me half submerged in the incoming tide.

'I was ill for a long time and I was looked after in a nursing home near Arundel where I was under the care of Dr Edward Carson, who had been on your father's staff in British Intelligence during the war.

'Your father had been made a High Court judge just after the war and seconded to run a Commission of Inquiry into Scottish Affairs. It meant he had to be in London for several months in the spring of 1946 to interview Scottish Members of Parliament. He hadn't been long widowed himself and he'd written to me from Edinburgh. My solicitor in London forwarded the letter and after I replied he came and had tea with me one afternoon in Arundel – '

'Did you tell him about you and John Brodie and – '

'Oh, I told him everything . . . everything . . . before I had any idea he wanted to marry me. I even took him to your brother's grave.

'It was after that he asked me to marry him and gave me the new life I needed and the baby I longed for. Oh, Roseanna, I longed for you — '

'You mean you longed for a replacement for John Brodie's son. It wasn't me you wanted,' Roseanna heard her voice crying out at this strange woman who was robbing her of her identity.

'Oh, but it was, it was. You were more important than anything, than anyone. Why, I left your father — '

'You did what?' Roseanna's voice demanded.

Helen took a gulp of your sherry. 'It was you I wanted, Roseanna, not baby Thomas. Whatever you may think of me, and I can see it's not a very great deal, I loved you for your own sake. Perhaps one day when you have children of your own you'll understand. I've loved you from the beginning. But I've been aware, once you began to grow up and became so enamoured with the law, I enjoyed neither the respect nor affection in which you held your father.

'But I think you should know the whole story. Your father was very good to me and, as you know, we were always good friends — great friends. Robert Warrender was the best friend I ever had. But it was not one way. I was as loyal to him as he was to me.

'As you were growing up I knew you wondered why we never slept together. I could see it in your eyes. You never asked, though sometimes you tried to tiptoe round the matter with your questions.

'What we had was the accommodation we reached for your sake after your were born.

'I left your father when I'd been married to him for seven months and I was six months pregnant with you. The reason I left him was because I discovered he had relationships with men.'

'*I do not believe you!*' Roseanna shouted at the strange woman. 'And I will not listen to another word of your sordid story. You have taken leave of your senses! You have gone mad!' But she was mesmerised by the story the strange woman was telling and she did not move.

'Your father often worked late in his library on his judgments and sometimes he spent the night in the little room off it where there was a bed.

'But I was concerned that he never seemed to come to bed at all. One night I woke around one o'clock to find I was alone. I went downstairs to the library but as I reached the door I heard voices so I knew there was someone with him. My fingers were on the handle when I remembered I was in my dressing gown and your father would be most affronted if I appeared before his guest.

'I went back upstairs and waited. To stop myself falling asleep I didn't go to bed but sat in a chair. But I must have dozed off because it was after three when I woke up again. I heard noises in the hall. I dashed from the room. When I got to the first floor I saw through the balusters that your father was locked in a passionate embrace with a young advocate who was in the habit of calling on him. His name was Robert McLeish and he's now a judge in the English High Court.'

Roseanna watched the earnesty of the strange woman's face. Her words no longer sounded quite so well chosen and she knew that every word of the shocking story was true.

'Relations between men were illegal in those days, but there was your father, appointed to uphold the law, indulging in a horrible illegal practice. But that wasn't the end of my discoveries that night.

'When he'd closed the door behind Robert McLeish I dashed downstairs and confronted him in the library. But there was no shame, no regret, no apology. I've never in my life seen such self-possession as your father showed that night. He was so utterly matter of fact. It was simply the way he was — bisexual — and there was nothing he felt he had to apologise for.'

'And what else did you discover?'

'That your father and my second husband, Henry Macrae, had had a long-standing relationship before I married Henry. It had been broken off when we married but was resumed in wartime London when John and I became lovers again. Later your father married me because he'd given his word to Henry that he would. Henry and I had been happy for a few years. He'd been desperate to be normal, which I think was why he married me. And he felt he'd become normal. He remained fond of me. Before D-Day he had a premonition he was going to die and he made Robert promise to marry me and take care of me. So now you know all there is to know.'

But even in her shocked state Roseanna did not think so.

'Have you told your fiancé about his baby?' she asked, a sneer in her voice.

'I told him twenty years ago in this very room.' Helen sipped her sherry and Roseanna heard the rehearsed, well-chosen ring back in the words. 'The Lord President, Lord Carlyle, had collapsed and died suddenly on the golf course at Muirfield.

'John was then the Lord Advocate in the Labour government and the tradition was that the Lord Advocate automatically became Lord President when the job came up.

'But as your father pointed out, if the newspapers ever got hold of the story about my baby, there'd be a terrible scandal which would bring the whole legal profession in Scotland into terrible disrepute.

'Between us, your father and I decided it was best that I told Graeme Wilson, who was then the Secretary of State for Scotland, about it so that he and the Prime Minister could decide what it was best to do. So I told Graeme, and the Prime Minister decided your father was a more suitable candidate for Lord President than John was.'

'But who told John Brodie?'

'He heard it first from Graeme, who was forced to give the reason why the Prime Minister felt he couldn't give the job to John.'

'So you took your revenge on him.'

'That was not how your father and I saw it.'

'But that's what it was. Admit it.'

'I had suffered a great deal – '

'So you harboured a great big grudge for years against

John Brodie. And when you saw your chance, you took your revenge.'

'It was a long time ago,' said the strange woman, lowering her eyelids.

'And what did John Brodie have to say about discovering you'd had his baby and never told him?'

'Don't be so hard, Roseanna. One day — '

'What did he say about your carefully timed announcement to make sure he never got the job he wanted?'

'We talked in this very room, and with your father's permission we went to Rustington together and I took him to our son's grave.'

Helen paused and sipped her sherry before she said, 'But after all the pain some good came out of it . . . Because it was after that John devoted his life to getting the death penalty abolished and saving the lives of men in memory of the son whose life had been taken at birth. Time heals, Roseanna.'

'That's what you'd like to think now that it's all turning out so smugly right for you! But you've just told me that my whole life and everything I believed about myself and parents is a lie. A big horrible lie. Find yourself another bridesmaid!' she cried, getting up and throwing the martini she had hardly touched in her mother's face.

'Yes, it's all true,' said Angus Brodie sympathetically. 'My father told me about it after Mother's fatal accident.'

'But it makes my life a lie. I'm not the person I've believed I was all my life — and neither are my parents,' said Roseanna.

They were sipping wine in the sitting room of her flat in Ramsay Gardens on the evening of the day after Helen's revelations about her past, with the blazing heraldic colours of the setting sun making dappled patterns on the walls.

'And you and I have a half brother buried down in the south of England. Have you ever been to his grave?' she asked.

'No.'

'Were you never curious?'

'Not really.'

'I suppose it's different for men,' she said slowly. As the shock of her mother's revelations began to wear off, she was conscious of a gnawing, aching emptiness, a horrible void inside her.

'Though I knew nothing about my half brother as a child, I lived with my parents' unhappiness,' said Angus. 'Mother was very unhappy.'

'Because of my mother?'

'Because of Father's involvement with your mother. They were both in it. It does take two.'

'And yet you never held it against me,' said Roseanna, looking up at this big cuddly bear of a man. 'You've always been so nice to me and kind to me and you let me devil for you. And there's never been a harsh or unkind word out of you.'

'I've never had any reason to feel other than very well disposed towards you,' he assured her.

'Dear Angus,' she said, patting his hand. 'You've always been like an extra brother.'

'The most unjust thing about all of it was that my mother died just when she was happy at last,' said Angus. 'She'd found someone else and asked Father for a divorce.'

'What?'

'Yes, our next-door neighbour at Craigendhu, Viscount Grampian, who hadn't long been widowed.'

'And what exactly happened?'

'She was in the butts on the glorious twelfth at the start of the grouse-shooting season and jumped up at the wrong moment when she saw a snake coming in her direction and straight into the line of fire intended for a game bird. She was rushed to hospital in Inverness. My father was with her when she died. Apparently she forgave him on her deathbed. He always said only her willpower kept her alive till he got there.'

'What do you think now of your father marrying my mother?'

'It's their lives. What we're talking about is the past. Life has to go on.'

'But didn't your father hate my mother for what she'd done? She really took her revenge on him when he was reaching the top of his career.'

'He didn't talk to me about it until after my mother died. By then at least he was quite philosophical about it. He said his failure to get the top job pointed up the utter vanity of his existence. And he really did find a new purpose in his campaign for the abolition of the death penalty, which he'd been opposed to all his life. He'd never have had so much time to do that if he'd

become Lord President. So he turned something bad into
something good.'

'I hate my mother,' said Roseanna. 'I've never liked her
very much since I started to grow up — maybe because all
the time I somehow unconsciously knew that she was false.
It was all lies that she had wanted me so much and how
happy she was when I was born. She wanted her precious
son back and I was just a substitute.'

Suddenly the tears she'd been holding back since yesterday
came tumbling down, drenching Angus Brodie's green tweed
jacket as he held her in his arms.

'And do you know what I hate her for most of all?'
she cried.

'Perhaps for having been born?' suggested Angus, trying to
humour her.

'I hate her most of all for what she said about my father.
She didn't need to tell me that. But she wanted to drag him
down, make out he was even worse than she is.'

'I think you're being a bit unfair to her — '

'She's not fair to anyone. The only person she ever thinks
about is herself.'

'But lots of men are bisexual,' he said. 'It's not a crime.'

'It was then!'

'People do what they have to do to survive,' said Angus.

'I hate her and I'm not going to her wedding.'

Warm September sunlight filtering through stained-glass
windows was warming the ancient stone walls of the chapel
at Auchinvreck.

Daddy, where are you? Are you somewhere here? Seated in the front pew, Roseanna raised her eyes from the communion table towards the lights of the angels in the windows high behind.

It over two years now since the June day when leading members of the Bench and Bar had packed the chapel for her father's funeral service and his body was lowered into its last resting place in the vault beneath.

'Oh, Daddy, I still miss you. So much,' she whispered. 'But sometimes when I walk in the garden like we used to, you seem to be there, speaking to me in a funny silent way. I can almost feel you reaching for me, as if you were still there.

'But I didn't find you in the garden today. You weren't there. So I've come here looking for you.

'Please don't go from me, Daddy. I need to see you . . . to know you're still there. Because it's all being taken away from me. *Everything* we had, everything I believed about you and me has been taken away.

'Just tell me you're still there, that you haven't changed, that I can still find you when I need to.

'Don't leave me . . . don't go away from me now, Daddy, please don't go . . . not now . . .'

She sat there for ages, watching the shadows the cedars were making on the walls as they swayed elegantly in the autumn breeze that was freshening the afternoon air.

'Always be nice to your clients. People in trouble with the law have enough problems without snooty advocates making them feel worse. Men and women don't cease to be human because they may have broken the law or have to resort to the law. In fact, they're more human, more vulnerable, more in need of being treated decently by other people, especially those who deign to represent them.' She smiled as she remembered her father's list of 'alwayses' which he used to recite to her regularly like a favourite story that a child asks to be read again and again.

'Always remember solicitors like briefs returned promptly . . .

'Always appear confident. Never let a judge see you uncertain or nervous. Always look as if you expect him to give you what you're asking for. And most of the time you'll get it . . .'

'Oh, Daddy, Daddy, you understood so much about people . . . you were so wise . . .' The tears flowed powerfully and unrestrained. 'It doesn't seem like two years since you went away. Because you didn't really. I know you're still here, even if you're hiding from me today.'

She remembered her mother's tears behind her veil as his coffin was lowered.

'Your father was the best friend I ever found in a man,' her mother had said after the funeral. 'He gave me a new life and identity when I was lost and alone. One day we'll meet again. We're just going our separate ways for a bit and we'll meet up again . . . as we always have done . . .'

And now what about John Brodie getting in the way? But her father had known all about John Brodie and her dead half brother before he had married her mother.

Though she sat for a long time watching the shadows of the trees and the lights of the angels, her father did not seem to be there this afternoon. Maybe he didn't like the chapel. Maybe he was busy, sitting in heavenly judgment.

But when she rose at last and left the chapel and walked out into the warm sunshine she had a powerful sense that it was his wish she should attend her mother's wedding . . .

'Well, it was a very nice service,' said Angus.

'And you thoroughly enjoyed yourself,' said Roseanna, still slightly taken aback by the radiance of Angus's demeanour at the wedding of her mother to his father.

'And why shouldn't I be celebrating now I have you officially as my sister?'

They were sharing a bottle of wine in the flat in Ramsay Gardens on the evening after the wedding.

'And good luck to bride and groom,' he added, raising his glass. 'May they make the best of however many years are left to them.'

'Oh, Angus, your generosity of spirit towards our parents puts me to shame.'

'I can understand how you feel,' he said. 'It's all come as a bit of a shock to you. But it's easier for me because I've known about them for a long time.

'I also know my father was particularly touched that you went to the wedding. He really wanted you to be there.'

'That's nice.'

'Apparently when you were a baby he once carried you in his arms and you howled your head off and he's been desperate to make his peace with you ever since.'

'That's nice,' she said again. And it would be nice to have

Angus as her brother — he was so much nearer to her own age than her half brothers. And she had told herself that life went on and she would make the effort to get on with everyone and be nice to her mother.

But an axe had been taken to her identity and her past and she wasn't able to help the terrible feelings she had about it . . .

CHAPTER TWENTY-THREE

'Always appear confident. Never let a judge see you're uncertain or nervous. Look as if you expect him to give you what you're asking for. And most of the time you'll get it.'

Her father's words, spoken so often when she was growing up and in love with the idea of becoming an advocate, filled Roseanna's mind without bringing her any comfort as she waited to make her court debut. For years she had dreamed of the day she would stand up in her wig and gown and address a judge.

She had felt like a different person on the umpteen occasions she had put on her wig and gown and studied her reflection in her bedroom mirror — calmer, cooler, no longer a prey to her emotions, a rational being who handled the mighty instrument of the law with the greatest care.

'Of course you'll be nervous the first time you get up in court,' her half brother Alexander, who had succeeded his father as Lord President, had counselled her in his library last night. 'Everyone *is*, when it comes to the bit. But remember the judge knows that — he once stood where you'll be standing, he's not going to make life difficult for you.'

But she still had to go through the ordeal on her own. Now she sat at the Bar of Court Four, hands trembling, stomach churning, waiting for an elderly judge to invite her to address him. But there was something else troubling her — that after all the years of dreaming of this day she didn't want to be here at all.

The judge sat on high in his crimson robes between white coupled Corinthian columns which enhanced the appearance of the judgment seat. And he seemed to be intent on writing for ever in a large notepad.

Her eyes rested anxiously on his deeply gnarled forehead. Then at last he looked up.

'Miss Warrender.' He had a thin high-pitched voice.

As she rose her throat felt dry and rough as sandpaper. She pressed her fingers hard on the desk to stop her hands shaking. She ached for a sip from the decanter of water but knew she dared not touch it. It didn't matter that the judge, Lord Cross, was her godfather. He could still ask her anything.

'My Lord.' Her voice sounded encouragingly normal. 'This case is a dispute between the Stirling Motor Traction Company, whose business includes the provision of hired cars and chauffeur services, and the Lowland Wool Company of Alloa, a firm of textile manufacturers. I appear for the pursuer, and my learned friend, Mr Irvine, appears for the defendant. The case is set down for hearing next week and will take a day. My learned friend is seeking leave to amend a motion which I will be opposing.'

'I see,' said the judge, looking at the young man in wig and gown already on his feet at Roseanna's side. 'Mr Irvine, what do you have to say?'

Roseanna sat down and reached for the decanter of water as Ewan Irvine addressed the judge. The water seemed to make an awful noise as she poured a little into a glass. It tasted slightly warm but as it trickled over her tonsils it felt like the sweetest water she had ever tasted.

'Miss Warrender,' the judge addressed Roseanna, who was instantly back on her feet. 'Are you raising any objection to the amendment?'

'No, My Lord. I will simply be opposing the entire motion,' she said, suddenly feeling more confident. She sat down again.

'The motion may be amended,' said Lord Cross. 'Em, Miss Warrender.' Roseanna shot back on to her feet. 'You say the case will take a day.'

'Yes, My Lord.'

'Do you mean it will last for a whole day or that it will be finshed within a day?' asked the judge.

Her half brother, the Lord President, had not prepared her for this question.

She hesitated for a moment, then said, 'I believe the former, My Lord.'

'It doesn't matter.' Lord Cross's deeply lined face broke into a smile. 'May I congratulate you on an accomplished debut, Miss Warrender. You have made a confident start to what I am sure will be a promising career.'

'Thank you, My Lord,' said Roseanna, bowing before she left the Bar and the court.

'Well, that wasn't so bad,' said Ewan Irvine when they stepped into the flagstoned corridor.

'No,' she agreed. But still it was no longer where she wanted to be.

Yet she persevered, and because of who she was she got a lot more opportunities than most tyro advocates in their first year at the Bar. But she was determined to prove she was worth them. She researched her cases thoroughly and her attention to detail was meticulous. She visited the scenes of accidents, went down mines, inspected shops and factories and fully acquainted herself with the technical terms used by any profession involved in a civil case. She also got chances, which were much rarer for a woman, at the criminal Bar and word soon spread that the presence of an attractive, sympathetic young woman at pre-trial interviews with clients encouraged them to talk about their family background and could open up areas of conversation and information which would simply never occur in a man-to-man situation.

She was still learning techniques of cross-examination, and whenever she had a free moment she haunted the public benches watching senior counsel at work. Sometimes, too, she sat in the First Division Appeal Court watching her half brother preside. But nothing was what it had been or seemed any more, and to her own disgust more often than not instead of listening to the cases she found herself wondering if he, too, was secretly bi-sexual as their father had been.

More and more the courts seemed to her to embody the Walter Mitty aspect of Edinburgh — a place which was the opposite of what it pretended and aspired to be, which used the mask of the Edinburgh Festival to pose as an international centre of culture while it was really a stiflingly provincial town that would not give a penny to support a struggling local artist. A place where genteel poverty hid behind net curtains and people went without proper food and shoe repairs so they could say they were paying for their children's education.

'All that makes it a very human place,' said Angus without a hint of apology when he had listened to yet another tirade from Roseanna on the ills, the evils and the faults of the city and the law courts.

They were sipping wine in her sitting room in Ramsay Gardens and the papers were full of the news that President Nixon was refusing to hand over the White House tapes to the Senate Committee investigating the Watergate affair.

'It's all much worse in Washington,' he said, giving her a jovial smile.

'You don't understand what I'm saying, Angus,' she said. 'I'm saying that I'm leaving Edinburgh and I have no wish to go on practising at the Bar. I want to make a new life somewhere else.'

CHAPTER TWENTY-FOUR

'Douglas and I had an escort of seals when we went for a swim this morning,' said Marietta. 'They encircled us and their big soft eyes were full of questions. It was lovely.'

'And they looked quite sad when we left them behind in the water,' said Douglas.

'You should have invited them back for lunch,' Keith put in. 'I'm sure Mother wouldn't have minded a few extra friendly faces,' he added, winking at Edwina.

'And they'd have been welcome to a glass of wine,' she replied, smiling at her tall son.

Though Keith and Marietta and Drew's son Douglas, and his daughter Catriona, were all regular visitors to the house at Ardnamurchan, it was not often they were all there together, which made this gathering round the family lunch table very special.

It was exactly the kind of gathering Edwina had dreamed of when she married Drew and vowed she would put their two broken family lives together into one bigger and much happier whole. And it was working out. Their adult children all got along very well both in their individual relationships and as a group.

'The seals who swim in Scottish waters prefer a dram of whisky to a glass of wine for lunch,' said Drew, smiling at her across the big round table.

She saw the happiness shining in his eyes and knew what he was thinking.

'You've given me back my children,' he'd often said to her since their marriage. 'I hardly saw them when they were small because I was away so much chasing wars around the world. We became estranged by default, because I wasn't there for them. It was the saddest part of the price I paid for success.

'But you've changed all that. Now they want to be near me and I have a place in their lives again. And all because I married you.'

She knew she was binding him to her with the ties of family life, all the time strengthening the bonds between them and aware of the need constantly to renew them. They both led such busy separate working lives that the time they shared was very precious and important in building their life together.

'Who's for bread pudding?' she asked, raising her voice above the chatter, which had moved on from the seals to the subject of walking to the lighthouse in the afternoon.

'Yes, please,' they chorused before she had the chance to offer them a choice from the other desserts she had prepared. But she knew they liked her bread pudding best. And looking at their happy, animated faces, it seemed as if they'd been one family all their lives.

'I am rooted in you. But you know that,' said Drew, his arm around Edwina's shoulders as they walked apart from their children across the moor towards the lighthouse. 'Rooted in a way I never thought I could be in anyone. And I never was until I married you.'

'And just you see it stays that way,' she said, looking up at him and laughing.

'It's being married, isn't it?' he said. 'Because it wasn't like this when we were unmarried and I don't suppose it would be like this now with our families if we'd remained unmarried.'

'Are you saying you have no regrets about marrying me?' she quizzed, giving him a teasing look, but he heard the serious note in her voice.

'Not yet,' he replied, taking her in his arms. 'because I haven't met anyone else I want to marry.'

'And you know you're free to go when you do.' She looked up at him boldly, confidently.

'And you know you're talking rubbish — one because I hate getting married. And two and more importantly,' — he pressed his lips against her forehead — 'because I love you and want to spend the rest of my life with you even if you decide we'd be better unmarried again.'

'Fat chance.'

'But I'll tell you what I do regret,' he said, casting an anxious eye around the moor.

'Yes?'

'Right now I regret we didn't leave the kids at home because I can't do what I want to do to you with them around.'

'We could lose them,' she whispered, feeling very sure of him.

PART TWO

CHAPTER TWENTY-FIVE

November 1973

'Susan Small's press officer says she can't tell me anything about Princess Anne's wedding dress because she doesn't know. And the first anyone, including her, will know what it's like will be on the wedding day.' Roseanna sighed wearily.

'Well, have you got any contacts in the rag trade, the people making the dress, who've seen the design or a bit of it? Or have any of your top-notch pals who get their clothes from London couturiers like Norman Hartnell got an in anywhere, or a whisper?' asked Ian Russell, features editor of the *Daily Globe*.

'I don't have any top-notch pals, as you put it, who get their clothes at Hartnell. They buy Miss Selfridge, and Mary Quant and Bibi and Frank Usher, and get their lingerie at Marks and Sparks like everyone else,' she retorted, her patience beginning to wear thin.

'But you were hired for your contacts, the people you knew

in the right places,' said Ian. 'The editor said so himself. You must know someone.'

'I don't know anyone who'll tell me what the dress is like because it really *is* a secret. And it's true what that press officer says. I've looked at the cuttings and nobody ever knows beforehand what a royal wedding dress will look like,' she said.

'But we haven't had a royal wedding since the Queen was married in 1947,' said Ian. 'That's a generation ago. Times change. And I know the editor's been counting on you to bring in lots of big society scoops.'

'The editor doesn't like me because I was wished on him by Lord Kilmacolm who just happens to know my stepfather who put in a word,' said Roseanna grimly. 'So I get all the rotten jobs that have no chance of getting into the paper just to prove I'm no good. So the editor can turn round and say to Lord Kilmacolm, "I told you so. She's no good. She can't do the job." I was warned by my stepfather before I came here. He said the editor wasn't very keen on people like me, but I had to get started so nothing would put me off.'

'I'm afraid Drew Hamilton's got a thing about people starting at the bottom either on a local paper or as a copy boy like he did himself,' Ian explained. 'He doesn't think anyone's a real pro unless they've been a foot-in-the-door reporter. He doesn't much go for the idea of graduate training even when people come straight from university. And I'm afraid he finds it harder still when someone's thrown up a promising career in another profession. He feels that person may simply throw away chances that other people have to fight for.'

'But I want to make a career in journalism and I'm not being given a chance,' protested Roseanna, seeing the broad frame of Drew Hamilton, shirt sleeves rolled up above his elbows, emerge from his office and cross the big editorial floor to where the back bench were putting the first edition together. 'I'm going to go and see him. As soon as he's finished talking to the night editor and goes back into his office I'm going in there after him.'

'He won't like that,' warned Ian. 'Apart from his secretary, you know how he uses the praetorian guard of the deputy and associate editors to distance himself from people.'

'I don't much like the way I'm being treated,' said Roseanna determinedly.

'Be fair,' said Ian. 'I try my best. Why don't you sit down and write a story angled on the secrecy about the royal wedding dress?

'You could point out that though we've been through the 1960s and times and fashions have changed it's no change at the Palace and they're as tight-lipped as ever about the wedding dress. Use that as your angle and then work up a piece about the guests, personal and official, the coach she'll drive to her wedding in, and all the work that has to be done behind the scenes arranging the seating in the Abbey and the protocol. And then you end by saying but of course the whole thing is that the royals are just getting in a bit of practice for the wedding of the Prince of Wales. How about that? Don't say I don't try. I think we could get that in the paper.

'Drew really does want some light stuff. There's been so

much heavy news what with Watergate going on most of the year and seeming to get worse with every revelation about what Nixon's been getting up to in the White House. And the Yom Kippur War last month. He really does want to get some lighter relief into the paper.'

'Yes, I'll do it. But I see he's heading back to his office —'

'It's not a good idea, Roseanna.'

'It's my chance,' she said, sliding off the edge of Ian's desk and taking quick high-heeled steps across the big room.

'You can't go in there,' she heard the dragon who sat on guard outside Drew's office call as she closed the door of his inner sanctum.

The editor was sitting at a large leather-topped mahogany desk apparently studying a dummy of tomorrow's paper. He did not look up or seem aware of her presence.

After the hurly-burly of the big floor outside there was an unnatural, almost eerie calm about the room at the heart of the editorial operation, graciously furnished with settees and a glass-fronted bookcase, and walls hung with memorable front pages in frames.

Her eyes fell on the powerful manicured hands holding a large black pencil over the dummy. She noticed the prominent, well-developed arm muscles, that a button of his pale pink shirt was open revealing a sliver of smooth suntanned skin and that in close-up the golden mane was mellowed by straying grey hairs which were beginning to turn it a pale antique shade. It had a silky quality and she wondered what it felt like to touch.

She decided to sit down on one of the chairs which stood at right angles to the editor's desk.

He seemed to notice the movement so close to him and looked at her with an expression that was unfathomable except for its naked hostility.

'What can I do for you?' he asked.

'You can make much better use of my talent on the paper,' she said in the confident tone in which she had addressed Supreme Court judges.

'My impression is that both Ian Russell and the woman's editor, Ann Robertson, put a great deal of effort into trying to make the best use of your talent. Are you telling me it's otherwise?'

She knew enough about newspaper politics not to criticise executives he had appointed.

'No. But I can't get anything into the paper.'

'And whose fault do you think that is?'

She saw the trap and smartly sidestepped, but she felt the ground slip a little.

'I feel I could be given work, at least sometimes, which had more of chance of getting into the paper.'

'Do you mean the kind of work entrusted to senior, experienced journalists?'

The ground was slipping further and becoming dangerous now. Mentally she quickly recomposed herself.

'I know I haven't as yet got much experience – '

'I wasn't aware you had any at all before a place was

found for you on my staff,' he said, rending the air with sarcasm.

'But I can only learn by experience, if I'm given the chance — '

'You're given chances every day of your life by my executives. It's not their responsibility if owing to your complete lack of experience you're unable to make the most of them. If you're unhappy with the work you're given here I suggest you take yourself off and gain some experience on a local weekly.

'We don't have time to train people on the *Globe*. We expect them to arrive with at least some experience unless they start, as I did, as a copy boy.

'By working on a local paper you'll learn that even the most boring and dreary pieces of information can be turned into a story. A sale of work, a flower show. You'll learn that. And when you *have* learned I don't think you'll wish to take up an editor's time complaining that the jobs you're given aren't interesting because you'll know that what you're really saying is you're not up to it. So you'll not give him cause to think you're not worth a place on his staff.

'Now, unless you have some other matter you wish to raise with me, I have a paper to get out.'

She had never felt so humiliated in the whole of her life. At least when a judge put her down he was polite and the rebuke was cloaked in coded diplomatic language. But this man, this monster Drew Hamilton, was brutal.

'"I don't want you on this newspaper. Why don't you

go somewhere else and learn your job, you ignorant bitch," that's what he more or less said,' she told Ian Russell in the pub across the road from the office afterwards.

'I did try to warn you,' he said. 'This is not the law or the polite society of Edinburgh you're in any more. You're in the rough, tough world of Glasgow newspapers now. It's people like me who are supposed to get kicked by the editor. Part of my job is to protect you, and he knows that. You broke the rules. So you've got hurt.'

'I'm only trying to work for the paper,' she said forlornly.

'So are a lot of other people,' said Ian gently. 'People have to work very hard to get their chance of a job on the *Globe*. They have to serve apprenticeships on local papers first. They don't learn their business on the *Globe* because there isn't time to teach them. It's very competitive.'

'Are you saying that other people as well as the editor resent me being on the staff?'

'I think a few possibly wish they'd had your luck in getting a staff job so readily,' he said carefully. 'But no one resents you. You've made friends in the time you've been here. People want to be helpful.'

'Thanks,' she said. 'What's that?' she asked, pointing to his almost empty glass.

'A Bell's.'

She rose and walked to the bar, which was not yet crowded, and got him a large Bell's and a martini for herself.

'Why did you leave the Bar?' he asked when she sat

down again. 'That's what puzzles a lot of people. With your connections you must have been set for a glittering career despite the male dominance.'

'It was going to be too easy,' she carefully lied. She had got used to people asking this question so she knew the right answer. 'I wanted a challenge and I wanted to do something different. There are enough lawyers in my family.'

'But you could probably have made history and been the first woman to sit on the Scottish Supreme Court Bench.'

'But I wouldn't have earned it,' she said. 'I would have been given it. At least I'll earn my success in journalism. Nobody, least of all Mr Drew Hamilton, is going to give it to me.'

'That's the spirit,' said Ian heartily. 'Hang in there. You never know what tomorrow will bring. That's the thing about newspapers. No matter what went wrong today, tomorrow's another day to start all over again.'

But she was still burning with humiliation when she got home to Edinburgh.

How dare Drew Hamilton speak to her and treat her the way he'd done? She was the daughter of the last Lord President of the Court of Session and the Lord Justice General of Scotland, the most important judge in the land, and the half sister of the present one. And he didn't give a damn — the jumped-up Glasgow keelie!

And then at last when she'd scoffed two more martinis the tears came scalding and salty.

She had nowhere else to go. Her past was rubbish. She was not the person she'd believed herself to be. She'd left the

Bar and the polite society of the legal elite behind. Now she had to make it on her own with no influence except what it had taken to get a job on the *Globe* without any experience. When she had undressed and soothed and cosseted herself in a warm scented bath, she slipped a white satin negligee over her shoulders and and sat before her dressing table gazing at her slightly slanted green eyes which people said were so like her mother's.

In this calmer state other echoes and memories of Drew Hamilton's inner sanctum began to drift across her mind. This man had power. Not the cloaked and robed stately power her father and brother enjoyed to sit on high in judgment and hand down their decisions to send the convicted to languish in prison or grant their pleas for clemency. Drew's power was raw and naked. He worked in his shirt sleeves in a big room where men smoked and swore, but he could get his thoughts and his way of looking at the world on to people's breakfast tables and into their work places. People argued and discussed his opinions and other opinions he allowed into his papers in their offices and after work in the pubs. He could ask or send reporters to ask questions of any public figure or institution. He could question the rights and wrongs of the way the country was run, investigate and publicise wrongdoing and misdemeanours and send corrupt officials scurrying for cover and their lawyers.

Drew Hamilton probably had more power and influence than her father or brother. And it was a faster, aggressive real power with ordinary people. What he decided today people talked about tomorrow. Drew had instant, intoxicating power.

The smile spread slowly from her eyes over her high cheekbones to her full, sensual lips until it lit her whole face.

There had never been anything she couldn't do when she set her mind to it.

She was going to make her mark in journalism . . . and make Drew Hamilton fall in love with her . . .

CHAPTER TWENTY-SIX

'Your Princess Anne piece works very well and I'll be using it in Thursday's paper,' Ann Robertson, the women's editor, told Roseanna two days later. 'Just a couple of queries. Could you make a bit more of Janice Wainwright, the actual designer at Susan Small who's created the dress? We don't know what it will be like, but we can speculate on the kind of work Janice Wainwright and Susan Small do. And make a bit more of the task of designing and making the dress going to a ready-to-wear house and the couturiers' noses being out of joint. Just a couple of pars.'

Roseanna looked at the slim, neat figure of the older woman, who by the day was losing the battle not to look well over forty, and hoped she never had her job – stuck on women's topics and excluded from editorial conferences. Her job title might impress the outside world but she was not the proper executive she wanted to be in the male-dominated newspaper world. Besides, Roseanna's sights were set on becoming a foreign correspondent.

'Will do,' she said, pleased to be getting a piece into the paper.

'Not quite yet,' said Ian Russell, grinning broadly as he emerged from the morning conference and plonked his girth on Roseanna's desk. 'Here's your big chance,' he added, his grin getting broader by the second.

'What?'

Ian glanced up at the big clock, which could be seen from every corner of the room, then back at Roseanna.

'In three minutes from now, at exactly noon, a statement will be issued by a firm of Edinburgh solicitors called Henderson and Macphail on behalf of the Supreme Court judge, Lord Scott,' he said. 'It will confirm that he is living apart from his wife and will be seeking a divorce. The statement will say that no one else is involved.

'We, however, know differently. We have photographs of him on holiday at Majorca this summer with Lady Rose Anderson, the young widow of the late Lord Anderson, who died a year ago, just six months after taking her as his second wife.'

'Rose Marie Mackenzie, the actress?'

'That's the lady. Lord Anderson was one of the trustees of the Central Theatre Company where she was doing a season in rep and she swept the poor old widower off his feet – and into an early grave by the look of it.'

'He was old enough to be her grandfather,' said Roseanna.

'Correct. She was twenty-six and he was sixty-nine. There's not quite such a big difference in ages between her and Lord Scott. He's only fifty-six and she's now twenty-eight.

'Anyway, as well as the happy holiday snaps, we've got

pictures of his car parked outside her home in the Borders and the pair of them emerging hand in hand from the house. We also have pictures of him leaving the grieving widow's house in Ann Street in Edinburgh at four in the morning.'

'Do you want me to try to get an interview with her?'

David shook his head and Roseanna felt disappointed. 'Nope. We've got people doorstepping Ann Street and the Borders.

'What the editor wants you to do — and this request comes straight from the man himself — is to interview Lady Scott and get her to spill the beans.'

'But she's my godmother!'

'Exactly. The editor knew you'd be well placed to get inside the front door when the competition's still on the doorstep. It's your big chance, Roseanna, the one you've been hoping and waiting for.'

'But . . . that's not fair.'

'But that's newspapers. And it's your chance — the one you've been going on about!'

Not *this*, she thought. But she had learned enough not to say any more.

'Now what the editor wants you to do,' Ian went on, seeming to take particular pleasure that this was a Drew Hamilton special request as Roseanna reached for her notebook, 'is a blow-by-blow account of what's been going on from Lady Scott's point of view. How long has she known about it? How did she find out? What did he say? Has the old devil been creeping into her bed when he got back home in the middle of the night? Her side

of the story in full glorious Technicolor detail as only you
can get it.

'Bob Salter will be here in a minute. He's going with you.
He's one of our best photographers and he knows the ropes.
Listen to him. He knows how to play it, and he's a good
team player. Sometimes the picture is more important than
the story. In this case the story is more important than the
picture. We've plenty of stock pictures of Lady Scott. Bob
knows that and he'll support you all the way to get the story.
Trust him.'

Roseanna had only worked with Bob Salter once before
because he tended to go out only to the biggest and most
important stories. But he had once gone with her to a
fashion show given by Albion Model Agency because Drew
Hamilton's wife owned the agency.

It came back to her now as the black-bearded photographer crossed the room, reminding her she must pick his
brains about Drew's wife.

Ian was just finishing the briefing when Bob reached
her desk.

As she gathered up her bag and put on her coat, she
knew this was the big chance she had demanded from Drew
Hamilton. But she didn't want this one, which took her back
face to face with the world which had betrayed her, which
she had run away from and never wanted to see again.

Dick Place, which nestled in the heart of the genteel and
leafy Grange district of south Edinburgh, was still the same
cloistered avenue Roseanna remembered from childhood —

where people who lived in large detached houses lifted up their eyes to the Pentland Hills from behind the high walls, silver birch and copper beech trees that ensured their deep secluded privacy. The area hoached with the legal elite who found the New Town claustrophobic and wanted to bring up their families in houses with gardens over which fresh hill air blew.

'Everyone seems to be here,' said Bob Salter, adding his old Ford to the line of Press cars parked on one side of the street.

When she got out Roseanna saw the motley crew of men and women amassed outside her godmother's home and felt nauseated.

'Doorstepping' was not what she had gone into journalism to do.

'Now you've got your note to slip through the door.' The photographer looked at her anxiously as he adjusted the cameras hung round his neck.

'Hot in my hand,' said Roseanna, whose uneasiness about getting Lady Scott to talk to her was heightening by the minute.

Between them they had composed a brief letter: 'Dear Lady Scott, I know you're not talking to the hordes camped on your doorstep, but I hope you are all right and I would like to see you. Love, Roseanna.'

'Does she know what you do these days?' Bob had asked.

'I've no idea,' said Roseanna. 'But my mother may have told her.'

'The thing is to get inside the house and then explain what your business is.'

'Yes.'

'She'll probably be glad to see a friendly face,' he said, reading Roseanna's uncomfortable thoughts as they made their way towards the hordes at the high black wrought-iron gate to Lady Scott's home.

'Excuse us,' said Bob, leading the way through them.

'She's not talking to anyone,' said one of the photographers.

Bob shrugged. 'You know what it's like. The office want us to go through the motions.'

'Who's the dolly bird?' called another, nodding towards Roseanna.

'New reporter,' said Bob. 'Will introduce after we get the door slammed in our faces.'

'Nice legs.'

I'm not his or anybody else's dolly bird, Roseanna wanted to scream when they got inside the gate and Bob closed it behind her. Dolly bird! Men used to call her 'My learned friend'.

Bob rang the bell, which still had the same high tinkling sound Roseanna remembered.

There was no answer, nor the sound of any movement within.

'I'll ring the bell again and you can put your note through the door,' said Bob.

'She won't want to talk to me.'

'You don't know that for sure. Let's see what happens. If she comes to the door, get your foot inside. Fast.'

He rang the bell again and Roseanna pushed her note through the brass letter box.

'She's there in the hall,' whispered Roseanna, suddenly feeling excited. 'I saw her legs when I pushed the note in.'

'Be ready to move,' said Bob.

There was a clanking of chains and the door opened between two and three inches.

'Roseanna, what on earth are you doing here?' asked a middle-aged woman with greying hair, narrow lips and a high thin voice.

'Lady Scott, I need to talk to you.'

'Roseanna, if you have become one of those terrible news people as, from what your mother tells me, you appear to have done . . .'

A black labrador appeared from behind Lady Scott and pushed his nose out the door.

'Oh, Schehallion,' cried Roseanna, taking the dog's head in her hands.

The animal pushed the door open wider to greet her and in the kerfuffle Roseanna and Bob got inside the house.

'You're quite right to keep people out,' said Bob, firmly closing the door as if he was doing Lady Scott a big favour.

'Oh, really, this is an outrage. Really, Roseanna, I can't talk to you. I don't know *what* your mother or your late father would think.'

'Lady Scott, believe me, I wouldn't be here if I didn't think I could help you. It must be awful having all those reporters camped round your gate at a time like this,' said Roseanna. Suddenly all the lines in which Bob Salter had carefully rehearsed her on the road from Glasgow were flowing from her lips. 'The reason I'm here, and the editor of the *Daily Globe* particularly wanted me to come and see you, is because I know you. And if you talk to me the others will go away because they'll know they're wasting their time. Believe me, I'm here to protect you from those terrible hordes.'

Lady Scott looked dubiously at her goddaughter but said, 'Well, I suppose you had better come through,' and led the way to the drawing room as Bob winked at Roseanna.

The room had hardly changed in twenty years. Two large china dalmatians still sat on either side of a blazing log fire and lithographs of Old Edinburgh still studded the walls. The greenish carpet looked the same though the pile was less ebullient and so did most of the rugs, but the bright blue and primrose-yellow chintz curtains matching the settee and chairs around the fire were new and gave the room a much more cheerful look than Roseanna remembered.

Lady Scott sat in the chair with her back to the window, so Roseanna, facing her, could not see every line and wrinkle as clearly as she would like to have done. Bob sat on the settee like a referee.

'I hope you're not going to try to take any pictures,' Lady Scott reproved as he laid his cameras beside him.

'If I was I'd be keeping these round my neck, not laying them down,' he reassured her.

'This really is disgraceful, Roseanna, the way the newspapers are carrying on,' said Lady Scott.

'But it's only in response to the statement your husband made today.'

'What is there to say? My husband and I have had a very good marriage, but now we have decided it is time to go our separate ways and lead our own lives. There really is no more to it and I can't think what all the fuss is about.'

The spectre of pretence, of all that had hurt her in the appalling hypocrisy of Edinburgh and the way people pretended things were one way when they really were exactly the opposite seemed to rise up with this woman's words. Everything had to be respectable — at any cost. Respectability was even more important than its twin pillar of religion. Her life, everything she had believed herself to be, had been a lie — told in the name of respectability.

At that moment, as Lady Scott blabbed on about her supremely happy marriage, Roseanna decided to strike back. She would get the story and force this ridiculous old hypocrite to tell the truth.

'I'm sorry you appear to know so little about your husband,' she said in the old confident voice in which she used to address judges.

'I beg your pardon.' Lady Scott flushed with indignation.

'Lady Scott, we have photographs of your husband on holiday in Majorca with Lord Anderson's widow, Rose Marie Mackenzie, the actress. We also have photographs of them at her home in the Borders and of Lord Scott leaving her home in Ann Street in the middle of the night.

'Even as we speak there are more reporters and photographers camped outside Lady Anderson's homes than there are at your front door.

'Rose Marie Mackenzie is an actress used to dealing with the Press. If you think she's saying nothing to them, I fear you may be very much mistaken.'

'But my husband and I agreed that his statement would be all.'

'But did Rose Marie Mackenzie, Lady Scott?'

'My husband said . . . and I have no reason not to believe . . .'

'Lady Scott, I know Rose Marie Mackenzie and I know how very ambitous she is. Before she married Lord Anderson she was never able to get the big parts she wanted, especially in television. Believe me, she's not going to miss out on the publicity and career opportunities of getting a judge to leave his wife and run off with her.'

Roseanna had never met Rose Marie Mackenzie and knew nothing about her ambitions or otherwise. But Lady Scott now stood for everything she hated and detested in the legal Establishment world she had abandoned. And seeing her squirm was the most delicious revenge against them all. As her drive to squeeze the woman's story out of her gained momentumn, she simply couldn't stop.

'He's been unfaithful before,' said Lady Scott. 'But it was never anything serious . . . never anything like this.'

'When was that, Lady Scott. And with whom?'

'Oh, it was when we lived in the New Town . . . but it wasn't important . . .'

'Just preparation for this,' encouraged Roseanna, refusing to let her victim go.

'Oh, the women didn't mean anything to him — '

'How do you know that?'

'Well, well . . . they didn't care for him either . . . they were . . . professional . . .'

'So he went with prostitutes? Where? In the street? Leith Walk?'

'He . . . em . . . used . . . to visit Dora Noyce's house in Danube Street . . .'

'Along with all the drunken sailors?'

'He wasn't the only High Court judge who went there,' said Lady Scott, suddenly pulling herself up in her chair. 'Why do you think the police never closed Mrs Noyce down? She got taken to court every now and again, but she was never closed down because she'd done too many favours for men in high places who wished to continue using her services. Where else would they have gone?'

'When did he take up with Rose Marie Mackenzie?'

'Oh, that woman was trying to lure him into her bed while her husband, Lord Anderson, was still alive. She's a shameless hussy!'

There was now no stopping Lady Scott, and when the interview was over she posed for a photograph holding a picture of the departed husband she said she wanted back.

Roseanna and Bob left by a side gate and sneaked round by Grange Loan and Kilgraston Road to get back to the car and avoid the hordes at the gates.

'You'll get the front page and the centre spread in tomorrow's paper,' Bob said after Roseanna had phoned her story over to Glasgow. 'Congratulations. You've shown them you're a real pro.'

CHAPTER TWENTY-SEVEN

'All good interviews are acts of betrayal because they involve getting the trust of a person to the point where they forget they're being interviewed and feel they're talking to a friend,' said Drew Hamilton, prowling his inner sanctum with a cup of coffee. 'So they say things they should never admit to a journalist and perhaps not even to a friend.

'You certainly had the advantage that your godmother was predisposed to trust you, Roseanna, but it's still a very remarkable coup to have got her to admit her husband consorted with a brothelkeeper.'

'Thank you,' she said.

Drew Hamilton in the morning when the sun was streaming through his office windows and the *Daily Globe* had seven pages of a sensational scoop that left its rivals panting and reeling was a different man to the one who had so cruelly dismissed and humiliated her two evenings ago.

But she knew she was different, too. The girl who had been yearning for her big chance had taken it and made her success his. And everything in the world and even the air between them was different now.

'As you of all people will appreciate, we had a very heavy legal on this last night,' he said. 'The libel lawyers were here for some time.'

He paused at his desk and a wickedly satisfied smile spread over his face as he looked again at the front-page banner headline:

THE JUDGE AND THE BROTHELKEEPER

Lady Scott talks about husband's friendship with prostitute
Exclusive
By Roseanna Warrender

Lady Scott, wife of the Supreme Court judge, Lord Scott, talked yesterday about his friendship with Edinburgh brothelkeeper Dora Noyce.
Lord Scott . . .

Photographs of Mrs Noyce and Lady Anderson appeared on both the front and inside pages.

'We've known for years that Mrs Noyce numbered High Court judges among her clients, but we never expected the wife of one of them to come out with it in a way we could print,' said Drew.

'Friendship is such a wonderful non-libellous word. It's like comfort and confidante. So long as you don't use the words lover and mistress you can tell the story and let readers draw their own conclusions.'

Roseanna was noting intently how his hair appeared to

be a stronger, bolder shade of gold and his eyes seemed bluer than a summer sea in the morning sunshine.

'How do your family feel about your exclusive? Have you heard from them this morning?'

'My family are in no position to talk,' said Roseanna. 'But that's not a story I'm prepared to write for the paper. At least not until after they're all dead.'

'Curiouser and curiouser,' said Drew, raising one eyebrow.

'My father was bisexual and my mother bore her present husband's illegitimate son just after the war, before she married my father and nearly two years before I was born,' she suddenly blurted out. 'The reason my father married her was because he gave his word to do so to her second husband, who had been his lover for many years.'

'Lord Scott is obviously a very dull fellow indeed compared to your family,' said Drew, placing his coffee cup on his desk and fixing her eyes with his own.

'And that's not all of it. My half brother, Lord Brodie's baby son, was stillborn, but Mother didn't tell him about the baby until he was in line to become Lord President and then she and my father decided to tell the Secretary of State for Scotland so Lord Brodie couldn't get the job and my father did.'

'Lord Scott's a bloody bore compared to your family.'

'I didn't know any of this until quite recently when my mother took Lord Brodie as her fourth husband. Marriage suddenly brought on a confessional mood. She probably felt a lot better for it, but she ruined my life because she ruined my past. She destroyed everything I'd believed about myself and the person I believed I was.

'I don't know if you can understand this, but that's the reason why I left the Bar and why it's so important for me to make a success of journalism.

'The truth is that getting Lady Scott to talk to me yesterday felt like an act of revenge. I was able to expose the appalling hypocrisy of their lives.'

'I hope I can understand something at least of your motivation,' he said in an altered, more serious tone. 'I'm sorry if I misunderstood your motives the other evening. And I can assure you that so long as I have anything to do with this paper you'll be given every encouragement to develop your career. You've made a stunning start!'

Their eyes met and held in a look of mutual admiration. She had had no idea she was going to tell him about her family background. But the moment had seemed right, she was glad she'd told him and, she sensed, so was he. There was a powerful communication between them now. She would work hard for him, get the scoops and the big revealing interviews he wanted.

She had found her new life . . . and her new man . . .

'It's Scotland's oil.'

Drew switched off the radio in the chauffeur-driven Jaguar taking him home. If he heard another Scottish Nationalist politician talking through his glengarry he wouldn't let another line be written about them in any Globe newspaper.

He sat back in the cushioned leather comfort and closed his eyes. He was going home early, it was only half past ten. It had been a quiet night. The first editions of tomorrow's papers would not be up for another hour.

He was forty-eight years old, at the pinnacle of his editorial career. Until Lord Kilmacolm promoted him to the higher echelons of management — and he was no longer sure he wanted to swap editorial power for anything else — he had done it all. There were no new challenges or mountains to climb, no new avenues to explore.

He realised now that was what had been missing from his life for so long. Until today. And it was only today, when he found his new purpose, that he realised what had been missing.

Now his *raison d'être* would be to create a bright new editorial star in Roseanna Warrender, who had given him her success to make his own. Now he would be her mentor. He would fashion and shape her in his own image and pass on to her all he knew. She was ready and eager and waiting to be his pupil. And she would be his finest creation.

As the car crawled cautiously westwards in the November evening fog, a sense of youth and renewal coursed through his veins like rising sap. And his spirits brimmed with pure clear joy.

BOOK THREE

TWO WOMEN
IN LOVE

To every thing there is a season, and a time
to every purpose under the heaven.
Ecclesiastes Chapter 3, Verse I

PART ONE

PART ONE

CHAPTER TWENTY-EIGHT

May 1974

'A Scottish parliament would mean the country would be torn by civil war within three years,' Max Rutherford's husky, whisky-soaked voice was telling guests at the lunch table in the directors' dining room on the seventh-floor executive suite of Globe Newspaper Publishing. 'The Scots are incapable of governing themselves. Just look at the literally bloody mess they made of it on their own. They need the civilising influence of the English.'

'Come on, Max, you know you're not being serious,' said Ross MacPartland, the recently elected Scottish Nationalist Member of Parliament for Strathhunter and Westering Cairn.

'I'm being very serious,' said Max. 'The people of Edinburgh and Glasgow hate each other, the people in Inverness want to put Aberdeen to the sword and vice versa, and the Highlanders and the Lowlanders long to take skean dhus to each other's throats. And so it goes on.

'Put two Scots together and the most natural, instinctive thing for them is to fight each other to the death. Not simply bang you're dead, but a real gladiatorial contest – an arm and a leg hanging off and they're still going at it, claiming victory in the fatal mauling they've inflicted on each other.

'The conditions for civil war are there just beneath the surface. I know people who regard Scotland as the Balkan State north of the border.'

'I've never heard such arrant nonsense in my life,' protested Ross MacPartland. 'The people of Scotland are a united but dispossessed people. The growth of the National Party has been explosive these past three years. There's been nothing like it in United Kingdom politics since people flocked to join Sinn Fein before the Irish secession.'

'Here, here,' echoed Alex Regan.

'Yes,' said Max. 'And I can see the spectre of Belfast on the streets of Glasgow and Edinburgh.'

'Ah, if only the Scots could be like the Jews and help each other more,' sighed Lord Kilmacolm, trying to cool things from the top of the table.

'Well, what did you make of all that?' Drew Hamilton asked Roseanna as they took the lift back down to the editorial floor when the lunch ended promptly, as boardroom lunches always did, at half past two.

'Fascinating,' she said, smiling up at him, her green eyes brilliant with admiration. 'Lord Kilmacolm seems more like a well-preserved seventy than ninety-five. You don't think you're speaking to an old man.'

'The boss isn't old mentally because he still has things

to do, challenges to meet, mountains to climb,' said Drew. 'He started these lunches about twenty years ago as a good way for his executives to meet people from public life and get the drift of what they were thinking on an off-the-record basis.

'They were fairly occasional in the beginning but as there's so much turmoil now on the Scottish political scene they've become more regular. They used to be all-male occasions, but the boss never misses a trick. And he's decided it's more relaxed if he adds a sprinkling of women.'

'The other woman, Elsie someone,' said Roseanna. 'Is she Alex Regan's wife?'

'For several years now. Elsie was a very good journalist and still does some magazine work,' said Drew. 'The boss likes to ask her along because she knows the company and oils the wheels.'

'Interesting,' murmured Roseanna.

'Anyway, as you enjoyed yourself and obviously impressed the boss, watch out. You're a marked woman now for these occasions and you'll be asked again.'

'I hope so,' said Roseanna as they stepped from the lift on to the editorial floor and went their separate ways.

She was still walking on air as she crossed the big editorial room towards her desk. It was six months now since her interview with Lady Scott had launched her on the path to editorial stardom. Since then she'd done high-profile interviews with leading public figures in Scotland, the Conservative Prime Minister Edward Heath at the height of the miners' strike which had cost him the general election, and the new Labour Prime Minister Harold Wilson. She'd also sent graphic reports from the streets of Belfast and interviewed the Protestant leader Ian Paisley. And when she felt strongly about something she wrote opinion pieces which sometimes caused enormous controversy – like the one in which she said Scotland needed a parliament to balance the untrammelled power the judiciary had enjoyed since the Union in 1707, and Scots law was outdated and should never have been left in place.

'Controversy is the lifeblood of a newspaper,' Drew had told her when the letters of protest rolled in and the *Globe* switchboard was jammed with the howls of lawyers sensitive about the extent of their power being revealed. 'Well done.'

A lot of reporters and writers complained about their copy being mauled and cut by the subeditors, but Roseanna didn't have that problem. Her copy was personally subbed by the editor, who invariably improved it. And she was learning from him all the time.

Drew was teaching her everything he knew about newspapers, and she was an eager and willing student, seizing upon and storing for future use every word that came from his lips. His reasons for his decisions on news values and for fashioning the paper in the way he did were the daily bread for which she constantly hungered.

The hands on the big clock were at twenty-five minutes to three when she sat down at her desk. Her purchase of a flat in Kensington Road should have been completed by now and she would be able to get the keys from the solicitors later in the afternoon.

It was the autumn before she got the flat in Kensington Road exactly as she wanted it. As she had sold most of the furniture in Ramsay Gardens along with the apartment, she was able to start from scratch assembling the French repro, drapes, soft furnishings and Chinese rugs she blended to create an elegant retreat from the hectic newspaper world.

The flat, which looked out on an avenue gracefully lined by trees, was almost exactly halfway between Edwina Hamilton's home in Kirklee Terrace and the bachelor apartment in Crown Gardens to which her husband still returned at night when he was very late at the office.

For Roseanna its purchase marked the final cutting of her ties to Edinburgh which began when she left the Bar. Though she remained on polite visiting terms with her family, she no longer thought of Edinburgh or Auchinvreck in the Borders as home. She belonged to Glasgow now, and as she surveyed the sitting room with its gentle lighting, she wondered how long it would be before Drew Hamilton dropped easily into one of the gorgeous big fireside chairs and she poured him a late evening malt whisky from the tantalus standing on a small table by the window . . .

CHAPTER TWENTY-NINE

'Features,' Roseanna answered the telephone on her desk.

'Oh, Roseanna, Mr Hamilton would like to see you,' said the dragon who guarded the inner sanctum.

'Now?'

'Five minutes. Half past six. Give you time to powder your nose,' the dragon twittered. She was positively friendly these days.

'Right,' said Roseanna in an equally friendly voice.

Power was an uncertain affair for the dragon. As secretary to the editor and editor in chief, she knew every confidential thing about everybody; executives needed to treat her with extreme circumspection and she could and did make life hell for any junior secretary who crossed her. But her true status was simply that of an adjunct to the power holder and as such she was in far greater danger of being used and abused in an ambitious community where secretaries were among the most used and abused inhabitants. More than once in her life she had been mistaken about the love and friendship of a journalist, who had simply wanted her to copy from the office files documents that would assist the upwardly mobile passage of his career. Roseanna felt sorry for her.

'Drinkies?' Ian Russell raised an eyebrow as she put down the phone.

'Drinkies,' she said, getting up from her desk. 'And it's about time you and I had drinkies,' she added, aware that people had noticed she now had drinks with the editor on a regular basis around half past six and of the need to keep the good will of executives and colleagues despite her special relationship and rapidly developing star status. 'Better still, why don't I buy you lunch?'

'I like the sound of that.'

'Shall we make a date tomorrow?'

'I'll bring my diary into the office tomorrow specially for you,' he laughed.

She knew everyone including Ian thought she was already sleeping with Drew. But not yet. Not maybe for a long while yet — not until I'm sure he's crazy about me, she silently told her reflection in the cloakroom mirror.

She dressed for him all the time now. When she was deciding what to wear in the mornings, the most important question was: how much would it incite Drew and send his temperature soaring to boiling point with longing to rip it off? Though hemlines had plunged in the 1970s and the mini was dead, Roseanna wore short or split skirts which gave him tantalising glimpses of her very good legs, and dresses that encouraged male awareness of her figure.

Blouses and sweaters with buttons were magic for after six thirty because a couple of buttons studiously fastened during

the day could be undone. Sweaters, too, had the added bonus
of clinging like skin, like the V-neck black cashmere she was
wearing this evening atop a black wool skirt split gorgeously
high up her left thigh.

She took a spray of Miss Dior from her bag and sprayed
it strategically between her breasts, on her throat and
wrists, behind earlobes and knees. She threw back her
mane of sungold hair and her emerald eyes smiled at their
reflection.

Drew Hamilton would go apoplectic trying to keep his
hands off her this evening . . .

'I've got a job for you,' said Drew, pouring Glenlivet into
glasses on a mahogany cabinet in his office.

'I'd be very disappointed if you no longer had,' she said
flirtatiously as their eyes met.

'Would you now.'

Their fingers brushed as he handed her a glass. She loved
it when that happened and the rustle and whisper of intrigue
filled the air between them.

'What's it about?' she asked, her voice low, her eyes
intense and serious as she slid on to a settee and swung her
legs sideways so that the split in her skirt became a chasm
exposing acres of black-nylon-clad thigh at a deliciously erotic
angle to the chair on to which Drew eased.

His earnest, businesslike expression reminded her of her
father's refusal to be diverted by her playfulness when he
had something on his mind. Drew was strong in the way
her father had been, stronger than she was despite her wilful

and determined ways. He possessed the kind of strength in which her security had been rooted since childhood. She knew she was driving him mad, but he was master of his desires. He had a time and a place for making love in his crowded schedule, but it was not the early evening in his office when his mind was set on other things. She respected and admired his discipline and control because she felt safe knowing she couldn't deflect him from his purpose. But she loved the challenge of tempting him, of testing him, of pitting her will against his and trying to seduce him from his purpose.

'You met Sir Douglas Campbell at lunch upstairs last week,' he said.

'The industrialist who was recently selected as Tory candidate in the marginal Glen Blair and Auchtertoun seat? Yes.'

'He's violently anti Edward Heath, who he reckons needs to be replaced as leader of the Conservatives because he lost them the last election and will probably lose them the next one, which could be announced any day now.'

'He won't say that if he wants to get into Parliament — or afterwards. Once elected, they all become regular party men representing their own interests and not those of their constituents,' said Roseanna.

'I want you to get him to tell you what he thinks about Edward Heath before the election even starts.'

'On the record?'

'Correct.'

He's never going to criticise Heath on the record, Roseanna

wanted to say – but immediately knew better. There was no such word as never in Drew's vocabulary – there was always a chance, a first time, a moment to break the rules and do it differently.

'I'll get on to his Press office first thing in the morning,' she said.

'That won't be necessary,' said Drew. 'Alastair Pearson, the political editor, has arranged an appointment for you at Sir Douglas's splendid office by Blythswood Square at ten o'clock tomorrow morning.'

'That was thoughtful,' said Roseanna, impressed but her breath momentarily taken away by the precise organisation. But that was how Drew Hamilton did it.

'All you have to do is charm him into sharing his heartfelt opinions of the Tory leadership with you,' said Drew, his eyes holding hers beadily over the rim of his glass. He was challenging her to bring home the bacon and he would turn it into a feast. And she could hardly wait.

'After I've sat in the office till midnight reading up his cuttings,' she said, watching Drew's obvious delight as she swung her legs gloriously into the air before she got up. 'This is what makes working for you so exciting, Mr Hamilton – never knowing what's going to happen or where one's going next.'

'And you love every minute of it,' he said, getting up.

They stood facing each other for a moment before he took her hands in his.

It was the first time they had touched without the contact being 'accidental'. She felt as if she'd been struck by emotional lightning. The effect was more powerful than anything in her wildest, most erotic dreams of him. She felt she would melt, dissolve, implode, explode, go on fire and soar off into outer space all at once.

'Don't you.' His voice was lower, his eyes brilliant with a thousand desires they had never revealed to her before.

'Yes,' she whispered breathlessly.

'Kirklee Terrace or Crown Gardens, sir?' the chauffeur asked as the Jaguar pulled out of the office garage into the late evening traffic.

In the back Drew closed his eyes and was silent for a moment before he said, 'Kirklee Terrace.'

He needed to go home to his wife tonight.

He needed to make love to her to get some grip on his mind and emotions. He loved Edwina; he was rooted and anchored in her as he had been in no other human being in all his adult life. And she had been in his life for so long now — over twenty years in good and in bad times. When their relationship had been brutally severed, it had felt like an amputation. But they had got back together and somehow become the stronger because of what they'd been through, and what they had had grown deeper and closer since their marriage.

And yet it had been going on for six months now, this explosive, unexpressed, throttled affair with his young editorial star. He was telling her all, imparting to her everything he knew. But he would do it so much better if he made love to her. And she knew it even more than he did.

It was in her eyes, her gestures, the way she moved across the office and his room. She wanted him as much as he wanted her. It was the way nature had made for a man and woman to communicate, but society, marriage and the human psyche so often inhibited this vital means of communication. Oh, it didn't need to be involving. It was just part of the job, the work, the passing on of information . . .

Except it was more than that with Roseanna Warrender. It was not like the camaraderie he'd shared with Elsie MacLelland. He was already involved emotionally with Roseanna. He admired her spirit, the way she had courageously rejected the privileged background she was born into to make her chance on her own merit in an alien world. He saw himself and his own values reflected in her man's spirit in a woman's body. She believed in and stood for the principles and all he believed in and stood for. He wondered how much longer he could hold out and hold her off.

Perhaps Edwina would save him from the storm . . .

CHAPTER THIRTY

The head office of Campbell Chemical and Petroleum Industries was a gleaming palace of reflective shaded glass just off Blythswood Square.

Its marbled, pillared atrium embellished with palm trees and tropical plants exuded the coming IT age, but its commissionaires in splendid brass-buttoned granite-grey uniforms trimmed with dusky Bank of England pink were redolent of a more leisurely era.

'Take the lift to the third floor where you will be met,' one of them told Roseanna when, immaculate in a black wool suit that stunningly fitted her figure and her make-up fresh as dew, she presented herself at the reception desk five minutes before her appointment with Sir Douglas Campbell.

'Sir Douglas has had to deal with an emergency this morning, so I'm afraid it will be slightly after ten before we go upstairs to see him,' the company Press officer, who had a shining bald head, announced when he greeted her at the lift. 'Would you like a cup of coffee? We serve the real thing.'

That had been nearly two hours ago.

It was now eight minutes to twelve, and Roseanna and the Press officer had only just been summoned to Sir Douglas's suite on the fourteenth floor.

'He does get a bit caught up in things and it can be difficult to get to him. But when you do he'll be all yours and you'll have his undivided attention,' said the Press officer, pacing nervously as they waited in the secretary's office. 'I think you'll agree he's been worth waiting for.'

Roseanna pulled a sympathetic, pitying smile and thought: I'll write about this.

Then three harassed-looking executives in grey suits emerged from the great man's office as a telephone rang on the secretary's desk.

'You can go in now,' she said to the Press officer when she put down the phone.

As they crossed the threshold Roseanna was immediately struck by the stark masculinity of Sir Douglas's inner sanctum. There was an unrepentant naked aggression about the blend of black leather seating, chrome and glass tabling and walls hung with modern art.

Despite his mundane overall grey appearance as he bustled round from his desk to greet her, Roseanna sensed a kingsize ego.

'Come, let's sit over here,' he said, pointing to a low glass table over which two black leather settees faced each other. But he made no apology for keeping her waiting.

'I'll just switch this on if you don't mind,' said Roseanna, taking a tape recorder from her bag and placing it on the table as the Press officer steered her to the settee facing

Sir Douglas. Not many reporters yet used tape recorders and Drew believed there was no substitute for fast shorthand or a first-rate short-term memory so you could write it all down when the interview was over. But Roseanna liked the back-up of a tape recorder and the chance it provided to listen again not just to what a person said but how they said it.

'Go ahead,' said Sir Douglas affably. He had married for the second time two years ago — his previous secretary who, the newspaper cuttings hinted, had been his mistress for eighteen years and was twenty years his junior. The cuttings also hinted he had been a bit of a womaniser in the years after his divorce from his first wife. Roseanna decided that with his dull, lifeless grey hair, slightly hollow cheeks and scrawny neck, he was certainly unattractive and unprepossessing enough to be one and he had the money to pay for it. She suspected that like a lot of captains of industry he had serious psychological problems and the reason he had kept her waiting for two hours was either to impress or intimidate. She already disliked him intensely and was going to enjoy leading him on to hang himself with his own tongue.

'You're going to be even busier than ever once the general election is called,' she said softly, giving him a huge masking smile intended to make him think she fancied him.

'We'll manage,' he said pompously as Roseanna pressed a thumb against her blouse to switch on the small tape recorder concealed in her bra to record what he said after the one on the table had been switched off and he thought he was simply 'chatting' to her.

'Have you spent much time in the constituency since you were chosen as the parliamentary candidate?' she asked.

'Not as much as I'd like, but I hope to be there a lot more from this weekend. And of course once the general election's announced it will be a twenty-five-hour-a-day job. Well, almost.' He grinned and looked even more unprepossessing.

What is it like to be as unattractive as you are to women, she wanted to ask. Do you know they only go with you for your money? She said, 'The constituency party were split over choosing you as their candidate. Half wanted the local councillor, James Thorburn. How much does that open division still bother you?'

'It's in the past. It's healed.' He shrugged and she thought maybe his personality was not as unattractive as his looks.

'All happy families now?'

'All accommodating families, which is what I think most families are,' he said. 'We're learning to live and get along with each other reasonably amicably.'

'Your car is here,' Sir Douglas's secretary called from the door.

'Oh, my goodness, is it that time?' he said, looking at his watch and getting up. 'My dear Miss Warrender, I have a lunch appointment with your brother, the Lord President, which I'm sure you'll understand I can't possibly break even to enjoy your own charming company.

'Come and have lunch with me tomorrow at Milngavie and I'll talk to you then,' he said.

Then he shot off.

* * *

Sir Douglas Campbell's principal home was a handsome nineteenth-century grey stone mansion which stood in six hundred acres of woodland and pasture in the shadow of the Kilpatrick Hills.

As he had decided to dispense with the services of the company Press officer for the lunch, Roseanna drove her Mini on her own out through the city's northern suburbs and the upsnoot districts of Bearsden and Milngavie.

Sir Douglas was walking in the grounds with a black labrador which reminded her of Rannoch when she pulled up outside the house.

'Ah, Miss Warrender, what excellent time you keep,' he said, looking at his watch as she patted the dog which was wagging its tail enthusiastically.

'You're making me nervous, Sir Douglas,' she said carefully, pressing her thumb against her breast to switch on the concealed tape recorder.

He looked at her with slightly raised eyebrows without saying anything.

'I see you looking at your watch exactly as you did about this time yesterday and I wonder if you're about to shoot off to lunch with someone else,' she said, smiling flirtatiously.

'Ah, that was yesterday,' he said in the same way Drew Hamilton did and she found herself warming to him.

Everyone from Drew downwards had teased her mercilessly about Sir Douglas walking out on her.

'Except in foot-in-the-door cases where it may only be possible to snatch a few words, you do *not* let interviewees walk out on you before you get the story,'

Drew had said, handing her a large malt in his office last evening.

'But I tell you, he just went . . . off . . .' She knew she sounded hopelessly wet and saw the laughter in his eyes.

'Got the ball and chain as well as your notebook with you today I trust,' he'd remarked as he passed her desk this morning.

But Sir Douglas seemed a different and more attractive man away from his glass palace in the city, and the overpowering masculinity of his office could have belonged to a different man to this one, whose home was beautifully wood panelled and furnished with antiques.

As a butler served a roast beef lunch with vegetables culled this morning from the extensive greenhouses which flourished on the estate, Sir Douglas ranged freely over his view of the Scottish political scene into the tape recorder she had placed on the table.

But she waited until lunch was over, they were sitting by the flower-banked fireplace in the drawing room and she had switched off her official tape recorder and put it reassuringly away before she said, 'Do you honestly believe the Conservatives stand any chance of winning the next election with Edward Heath as leader?'

'I was wondering when you were going to ask me that,' he said. 'And the short answer is no.'

'And what's the long one?' she asked, meeting his gaze with the same rapt expression she had worn throughout lunch.

'Perhaps some other time,' he evaded.

'I know my brother feels they'll lose,' she persisted. 'Didn't the pair of you get round to discussing it at lunch yesterday?'

'We did indeed discuss the question of the Tory leadership,' he said. 'Between ourselves.'

'He wanted to go into Parliament himself at one time, like so many Edinburgh lawyers,' she said as if she hadn't noticed he was evading her. 'But life took another turn when he became a judge.'

'Sensible man.'

She wandered round and to and from the subject of his feelings for the next fifteen minutes till the coffee pot was empty and he got up sharply.

Her heart nearly missed a beat because she thought the interview was over and her chance gone. She'd got nothing but the party line, which was as dull and boring as cricket and would never get into the paper.

'I feel like some fresh air,' he said. 'Fancy a stroll before you head back to town?'

'What a good idea,' she said, jumping up.

The sun was breaking through the cloud in the west as the labrador joined them on a walk round the policies.

'Your brother said you hadn't been a journalist for long. Just a year and how sorry your family had been when you gave up the law, but they understood that you wanted to do something different and were proud of you.'

'That was nice of him — and surprising.'

'Why surprising?'

'I wouldn't have thought they'd have liked everything I've written,' she said honestly.

'Ah, Lord Scott and his paramour did give them one or two bad moments, I gather, but your mother came brilliantly to the rescue by pointing out you were only exposing the truth.'

'Well, she didn't tell *me* that.'

They had come to a lake across which two estate workers were rowing a boat.

'So, Roseanna Warrender, brightest rising star journalist in the Globe Newspaper Publishing empire, you've been sent here to get me to say what I think about Ted Heath – '

'I – ' Roseanna swallowed.

'Look, I've known a lot of journalists,' he said. 'I've known Lord Kilmacolm and his son, Max, for years. I've also known your editor, Drew Hamilton, for a long time. And I know how you work – and how a pretty young girl journalist can get a public man to talk himself out of office by saying things he should never say to her.'

Roseanna lowered her eyelids, unable to look at him. This man knew far too much about the tricks of the trade than was good for her.

She pursed her lips. Drew wanted this Tory twit to shoot his mouth off about Ted Heath and she was going to make him do it.

'But I've now met you twice before today,' the Tory twit was saying,' and I had a long chat with your brother about you yesterday, and I'm satisfied you can be trusted – '

'But – '

'But nothing,' he interrupted. 'We'll talk on a lobby basis. I'll tell you what I think of Ted Heath and you can use the information but you can't attribute it to me and officially the interview never took place.'

'That's no good,' she said, shaking her head.

'All right, I'll make you a better offer,' he said. 'I'll talk and you can use it, but afterwards I'll deny it and say you misquoted me.'

'I can't agree to that,' said Roseanna.

Sir Douglas looked at the hills for a moment.

'Might it be possible that a misunderstanding could arise about what was said on and off the record?' he inquired.

She quickly took her cue.

'That does sometimes happens,' she said cautiously.

'Well, I think Ted Heath should have resigned in February after he lost us the last election. I'm absolutely certain he'll lose us the next election and he should be replaced.'

He launched into such a tirade against the Tory leader that Roseanna wondered if he had been imbibing vitriol at lunch instead of a vintage Nuits St Georges.

The story and the ensuing furore made front-page banner headlines the next day.

Shortly after noon the Press officer for Campbell Chemical and Petroleum Industries issued a brief statement to the press:

Sir Douglas Campbell stands by every word he is quoted as saying in his interview with Miss Roseanna Warrender of the *Daily Globe*.

Unfortunately, he thought he was talking off the record.

He will be making no further statement about the matter.

'So we've all won,' said Drew to Roseanna over an after-six drink in the inner sanctum. 'Douglas has been able to get a public airing for his views on Ted Heath and we got a front-page story. And we're standing by the fact that the interview was on the record and the old fool knew all along that it was.

'Sir Douglas isn't a bad old stick. And besides you had your hidden tape recorder.

'Now, young woman, I don't care what you thought you were doing this evening. But I'm taking you to dinner.'

CHAPTER THIRTY-ONE

The Malmaison was full of the usual crowd who thronged to its fashionable tables in the evening – the prosperous bourgoisie who lived in the West End and had their villas in Helensburgh and Rhu and down the Firth of Clyde coast.

Drew's table, which he used regularly in the evenings, was number ten in a discreet corner where he could talk newspapers to a colleague or sweet everything and nothing to his wife or feminine companion.

The atmosphere was smoky, gossipy and watchful, and Roseanna loved it from the moment they entered and the head waiter performed somersaults in salaams.

From the moment she had decided to make Drew Hamilton hers, she had been determined this would be no secret affair and there would no clandestine trysts. Everything would be in the open from the start. Initially people would acknowledge their professional work partnership. So that when they went out as a couple the world would recognise that the editor and editor in chief of the *Daily Globe* was stepping out with his star writer. The idea that they belonged together would be planted in the world's mind right from the beginning.

Though their first dinner date had been a long time on the cards, she had not anticipated it would be this evening. So although her black wool sweater dress put her figure in lights there wasn't a damn thing she could do about her cleavage short of taking off her dress and sitting down to dinner in her delicious black lace lingerie.

But that was the only minor blemish in her world as she surveyed the scene from the table of the editor in chief of Globe Newspaper Publishing and he ordered Cliquot champagne. With her golden hair tumbling on to her shoulders she was acutely conscious she was the cynosure of every eye in the room. It reminded her of a day when she was sixteen years old and her brother had been installed as a Supreme Court judge and she had sat in the box reserved for the judge's family pretending not to notice the admiring glances of the young advocates in their wigs and gowns and had favoured her father's elderly chief clerk with the kind of smile she now bestowed on the wine waiter. But the young advocates had known who she was. The diners at the Malmaison could only wonder and be intrigued, an added excitement to her first dinner date with Drew.

She thrust back her head and her golden hair danced like a maypole as Drew raised his champagne glass to hers and asked, 'Does it seem a long time now since you went to work in a wig and gown?'

'A lifetime,' she murmured as their fingers touched around the edges of their glasses and her eyes met his.

'And since you came to us?'

There was an intimacy about the way he said the words

with his eyes holding hers, making them sound like a calling — as if there had always been a place for her with him.

'I can hardly remember any life before this,' she murmured.

At that moment she was filled with a powerful and acute sense of belonging, a sense of home that had been missing from her life for a long time, she knew now . . . probably since her father died four years ago but certainly since her mother's revelations about the past. One sunny September day she had quite simply been robbed of nothing less than her identity. She had been an emotional and psychological wanderer and belonged nowhere ever since. And it was only now as she gazed into this man's eyes that she realised what had been missing from her life . . . and how great had been the psychological injuries and the robbery of her roots and identity — what and whom she had believed herself to be.

She had not expected to be feeling this or suddenly to be so overwhelmed by emotion. It brought a lump to her throat.

She was acutely aware now, too, that she was already deeply emotionally involved with this man . . . before they had done more than hold eyes and touch hands.

She felt she needed to step back for a moment, to gain emotional space from her discovery.

Then a waiter conveniently hovered for their orders and by the time Drew had advised her on the menu and she had chosen sole bonne femme she had recovered her equilibrium.

'Have you always worked on the *Globe*?' she asked him brightly.

'Yes, I'm a one-newspaper man,' he assured her.

And then he told her about his own career and his early days in the Middle East as a foreign correspondent in the late 1940s just after the war, and she listened with the rapt expression which she had perfected at interviews — but she had never listened to anyone tell their story with more rapt attention than she did to this man.

And as she listened she knew he was her life, she *needed* him to be her life, and she wanted no other man. When she had sat before her mirror and vowed to make him fall in love with her, she had not reckoned on falling in love herself. It was a shock and she felt quite stunned and vulnerable. But her heart lifted with a joy that seemed to have its roots in a long time ago . . .

Oh, why, Roseanna Warrender, do you so intoxicate my soul that sometimes I even think I'm in love with you? What is it about your emerald eyes that hint of the Orient and your way of moving that reminds me of the ballet? And the way you dress that drives me to wild fantasies and imaginings? Why do you haunt my dreams, obsess my mind so that when I leave the office at night I can't wait for the next day to come so that I can see you and be with you again?

The terrible thing is that I think it's your soul I want to possess. Your body wouldn't be enough for me. And why? Do I see my younger self, the person I once was and lost along the way a long time ago, in you? Is that the reason why? Is that what your heart holds for mine?

And I am so proud to be seen with you here this evening.

I'm the envy of every man. See. Look now. They can't keep their eyes off you.

These were the welter of thoughts and emotions causing chaos in his soul when he said, 'I know why you're such a good interviewer. It's because you make a person feel your life depends on listening to their story.'

'Oh, I've learned so much listening to you,' she said. 'Sometimes I feel I've learned everything I know from you. And there are days when I feel the whole of my life won't be long enough to listen to the story you can tell me.'

At that moment he knew he would become her captive.

The candles were burning low on their table and the restaurant was emptying when they rose to leave.

Outside the late evening air was still mild, but it was September and the autumn season of the beginning of the dying was upon them.

Yet she had never felt more alive, more aware of life and all its infinite possibilities than at this moment when she stepped into the back of his chauffeured limousine. She never wanted to die.

But she knew she needed to be more determined in her purpose and more careful now she was in love with him. She must not risk becoming a victim because she was in love.

He took her to her front door in Kensington Road and walked with her up the stairs to her first-floor flat.

'Thank you for a very nice evening,' he said. 'I don't remember when I enjoyed myself so enormously.'

'Thank you,' she said, looking up at him.

'I wonder where we go from here?'

She held his eyes in hers for a long moment before she whispered, 'Perhaps not anywhere.'

'Why is that?'

'Because of what's the saddest thing for me.'

'Which is?'

'That you are not mine to love and pleasure.'

He let the car go when he emerged into the street again. He watched it set off towards Great Western Road and waved his chauffeur goodnight before he turned his own steps in the same direction.

He heard the crunch of the fallen leaves under his feet on the pavement. He stopped and watched two leaves drifting gently, slowly downwards in the moonlight. And his soul seemed to rise to the beauty and poetry of it, to the rhythm of the seasons and of life going on. He stared at the tree from which the leaves were falling. Though neither he nor anyone else could see it, he knew that before those leaves fell nature had already provided next year's leaves safely in buds with thick coats to protect them against the rigours of winter. He gazed upwards to the thinning branches. In his heightened awareness he thought he heard the branches sigh for the lost leaves. Everything was beautiful in its own time.

'You are not mine to love and pleasure' . . . beautiful sad words . . . the saddest thing . . . He said them aloud to himself as he walked along.

When he reached a corner on Great Western Road he stopped and gazed at the moon. When he looked again at the late evening traffic bowling along he realised that he was going in the direction of his wife's house in Kirklee Terrace and not his own flat in Crown Gardens.

He wondered why he was going to her tonight. He didn't know. He felt he knew nothing — except that he was alive. More joyfully alive than he had been for years, than he could ever remember being. For once he felt no pressing need to know and understand. It was enough to be.

As he approached the house he saw the lights were on in the morning room. Edwina was still up. But it wasn't late — just on eleven. The hour would boom out at any minute in a clutch of nearby church clocks.

As his key turned in the door and the familiar scent of the spicy potpourri she kept in a large bowl in the hall greeted him, he wondered if he was going home to his wife because he wanted her to save him before the insanity of being in love undid him.

'Is that you, Drew?' he heard her call as he locked up.

'Indeed you have the pleasure,' he said, entering the morning room where she looked up from the table at which she had been going over some accounts.

'Much happening in the news tonight?' she asked.

'Not to my knowledge. There's still a bit of flak flying around over Sir Douglas Campbell and Ted Heath,' he said. 'Reminds me I must just ring the office. I'll be with you in a minute.'

He crossed the hall to the room he used as an occasional study and dialled Roseanna's number.

'Hello,' she answered softly in the late evening voice which replaced the businesslike daytime 'Roseanna Warrender'.

'Thank you for the most wonderful evening in a long time,' he said.

'Thank you.'

'Till I see you tomorrow.'

'Till tomorrow.'

'I'm in love with you. How long have you known that?'

'Since you told me.'

'Don't even tell me white lies.'

'Till tomorrow.'

'Bye.'

'Bye.'

'I didn't hear the car,' said Edwina when he returned to the morning room.'

'I walked here.'

'How energetic of you.'

'I'm feeling energetic.'

He sat down facing her across the table.

I'm in love, he wanted to tell her. He wanted to tell the whole of Glasgow, the whole world, to shout it from the roof of Globe Publishing and in banner front-page headlines. Then he remembered he was married to Edwina and she wouldn't like it. He remembered, too, that it was in this room fourteen years ago that he had first taken her in his arms. They had both escaped from the drawing room upstairs where Max had been holding forth at a reception and had stood by the window in this room watching the traffic rolling home along the boulevard. Fourteen years ago! And she had needed him so much. And from that evening forth he had fallen more and more in love with her.

They had never shared, even in the beginning, the all-encompassing, all-possessing thing that flooded every niche and recess of his soul the way what he felt for Roseanna Warrender did now.

He had never thought such things happened in real life. But perhaps unconsciously he had, and that was why he'd never wanted to marry her and resisted marrying her for so long — so that he would be free to walk to his true love when he met her.

'If the day ever comes when you no longer want to live with me, I'll let you walk free.' Her words came back to him now.

But they both knew it wasn't true — as much then as it was now.

'Nightcap?' she asked softly, gathering up her papers.

'Yes. Good idea,' he said brightly.

She rose and poured two Lagavulin malts from Islay and handed one to him.

'Come and sit down by the fire and talk to me,' she invited. 'We never seem to talk much these days.'

He rose and strolled over to the settee facing the fire and sat down, though he didn't feel like sitting down. He wanted to walk for miles.

He took a large gulp of his whisky and looked at his wife over the rim of his glass. She was sitting in the same chair she had sat on that evening fourteen years ago. She was forty-four years old now, and still slim and dark and beautiful. She had been twenty-eight then and he thirty-five. And now he was forty-nine and felt younger than he had ever done.

I love you, he wanted to say. But I'm not in love with you. And then he wanted to ask for her help to save him from what was happening to him. He wanted to reach out for her understanding.

She was his friend and he wanted to talk to her about it and tell her what was happening to him and what it was like for him now. Except it would break her heart . . .

He wondered if it would have been easier if they'd never married, as he had wished. Yet he'd been glad that he was married to her as the years passed and she gave him back the family life he had lost. She had become his refuge and strength — until now when she couldn't help him in his hour of greatest need.

'You're very quiet,' she said, eyeing him intensely.

'Why don't we go to Ardnamurchan for the weekend?' he suddenly suggested. 'It would do us both good to get away.'

PART TWO

CHAPTER THIRTY-TWO

'What's happening to us?' asked Edwina. Her question had a hollow ring and seemed to fill the whole of the big kitchen in the house in Ardnamurchan where she was studying every line and muscle movement on her husband's face over the breakfast table.

'Meaning?' Drew raised both eyebrows in an alien puzzled look.

'Meaning us. You and me.'

'What's happening is that we've come away for the weekend to our home by the sea, which we've always loved and where we've always been happy.'

His voice lingered on the last word, as if he was desperately trying to cling on to something. And whatever was troubling him she found that reassuring — that he was rooted in what they had and their belonging.

Except something was different which she could not put her finger on. It was swirling in the air fragrant with the scent of freshly percolated Kenyan coffee.

'You used to say the joy of Ardnamurchan was that you could get away from the telephone,' she said. 'But you've hardly been off the phone since we arrived.'

'The Scottish *Daily News* is in trouble and could close any night,' he said sombrely. 'I need to keep in touch.'

Edwina had admired the brave attempt by a quarter of the 2,000 journalists and print workers made redundant by closure of the *Evening Citizen* and removal of Scottish *Daily Express* printing to Manchester to start their own daily newspaper. It had been launched four months ago in a blaze of publicity with the backing of the Labour government and the publishing tycoon Robert Maxwell, but it was already losing circulation, unable to get advertising and plunging into debt.

'I know it's horrid and a lot of people are going to lose their jobs and while sympathising you'll have to get a lot of extra papers out the night it goes, to mop up what circulation it has,' she said. 'But we came here to forget about those sort of problems. Can't we do that for just a few hours?'

'Of course. Of course,' he said. 'Let's go for a walk and jump in the sea.'

'Now?' she raised her eyebrows.

'Now. This instant.'

'I'll get my jacket,' she said, standing up.

'No. Don't bother. Let's just go as we are.'

'But it might be quite chilly out even though the sun's shining.'

'We'll walk fast. We'll soon get warmed up,' he said, taking her hand and leading her towards the door.

She eyed the clear outline of her husband's profile. He had been on tenterhooks to the point of hyperactive since they arrived and there was no sign of him relaxing. And his gestures were jerky and somehow lacking their usual grace.

And then he had clung to her in the night. He had seemed almost like a child after they had made love, as if he was afraid of losing her and what they had.

'I love you. I'll always love you,' he murmured before he went to sleep.

'I love you. I always will,' she whispered but he seemed to be asleep already as her lips pressed gently on his ear.

What is it apart from the *Daily News*? The words were on the edge of her tongue and she needed to know, but something held her back. Sometimes it was best not to probe but simply to wait until a person wanted to talk. Sometimes it was better not to know. There was no need to know everything about a beloved man. Sometimes mystery was sweeter and better than knowing . . . but instinctively she sensed: not now.

They needed to spend more time together, as they'd both made the effort to do when they were newly married. But then they both got busy and their special times together had somehow gone by default. The success of the Albion Model Agency meant she often worked in the evening compering shows. She was richer and more powerful and successful than ever before – but the price, which always had to be paid, was that she and her husband hardly saw each other.

She had never seen why he needed to keep his old bachelor flat in Crown Gardens. He had put it on the market after their marriage, but the right buyer hadn't come along. And then she'd often been busy late in the evening, and he'd started going to his own place to read the first editions.

'But there's no need for that,' she'd said. 'I've redecorated and furnished the study on the ground floor specially for you.'

'If I have to go home to an empty house, I'd rather it was my own,' he said. After that he gave up the idea of selling his flat.

She'd been uneasy about it ever since, but she didn't want to lose the business. And then somehow he'd started drifting over there to read the first editions even when she was at home. Sometimes he came home to her afterwards, sometimes he rang to say he was having a nightcap and going to bed alone. And she was often too tired to argue or invite him over as all she wanted to do was sleep.

She knew they really should have more time together now, especially as the children were grown up and hardly around. Marietta was now twenty and a student at Glasgow University, sharing a flat with five other girls, and Keith was in his last year at Glasgow Academy.

Things were going to have to change, she decided as they stepped on to the shore.

The sun was already high and casting a million shimmering, dancing lights on the sea and the air soft as on a summer morning.

This was where they came to renew themselves, to gather their strength once more at this place where the land reached down to the ocean and the small isles of Eigg and Rhum seemed only a finger's length away.

There was no one about on the white shell sands as their feet, light as birds' wings, began to skip over the shore.

'Shoes off,' said Drew.

She kicked her sandals into the air.

Hand in hand they put their toes and then their whole feet into the water. And then it was up to their ankles and up their calves.

'This is just playing at it,' he said, gathering her up in his arms. 'Let's go in and do it for real.'

He ran back to the dry sand with her in his arms, and she felt she was being borne along by the wind — the way she used to feel when they first came here and seemed to live only for each other no matter how busy they were.

Those were the days when the time they spent apart was just something they did so they could look forward to seeing each other again, which was their real purpose in being alive.

Now suddenly those days seemed recaptured, to be hers once more, and her heart lifted up as she ran her fingers through his golden hair.

Just like they did in the beginning, they stripped off as for battle and ran back towards the sea.

'Race you,' he cried, soaring off ahead of her.

'That's cheating,' she cried, running after him.

She seemed to be able to run as fast as ever and caught him up at the water's edge, where he was waiting to take her hand for the run into the sea together.

The ocean was its warmest in September, and its embrace was buoying.

After swimming off on his own for several minutes, he floated towards her and reached for her hand.

'Younger than in the days of our youth,' he laughed. But those eyes which were bluer than the sea were intense and pleading and she sensed a deadly purpose in his game — as if he was trying to recapture something that was gone and lost.

But she took her cue and swam into his arms.

Everything seemed the way it always had been as she looked up at the droplets of sea water dripping from his brows.

But what was it? What was this restless need he was sublimating into endless and furious physical activity? Why couldn't he tell her and talk to her about it like he used to do — in the beginning?

As he swam away from her again she realised that was what was missing from this otherwise magical morning — the old trust and ease with each other. A part of him had gone away from her.

But the morning sun was warming on her back as she bobbed up and down in the water, her fingers brushing his, their bodies gliding past each other.

And then he took her in his arms once more and everything seemed all right again.

'You're my water baby,' he murmured into her sea-soaked hair.

At that moment he felt, if they just stayed here in the water, they would be safe and nothing would happen to divide them.

But then as she swam away from him again he realised they were already divided because Roseanna was here with them – in his heart. And when he held Edwina in his arms and looked into her eyes a part of him was imagining he was with his young protégée.

I love you both, he felt like shouting out as he soared through the water. If only you could understand!

In a little while they left the sea and made love in their secret place along the shore.

'You are my refuge and strength, Edwina Hamilton,' he murmured into her ear afterwards. 'I'm glad I married you.'

But for the first time since his marriage he was no longer sure.

In the afternoon he walked to the other side of the bay to Peter and Agnes Stevenson's house, who looked after his home when he was away.

The sky was beginning to cloud over in the far west and he sensed a storm could brew up by the evening.

Though he felt physically calmed and soothed by the hectic lovemaking, his spirits were still in turmoil. He loved Edwina and needed her to be there for him, but he wondered if she would be much longer.

'Oh, Mr Hamilton, Peter will have the wood ready for you next week and bring it over,' Agnes Stevenson greeted him at the door of her cottage. 'You'll stay and have a cup of tea?'

'Of course.'

He stayed for an hour getting the local news and gossip from the Stevensons.

'The cottage at the far end of the bay is up for sale,

though the owner would also settle for a long let,' Agnes told him. 'But that's unlikely as people only want holiday lets in this area.'

'You never know,' said Drew.

'Well, let us know, if you hear, because we said we'd look out for them,' said Agnes.

'By all means.'

The sky was darkening as he retraced his steps across the shore, and a storm seemed certain now. Halfway he stood gazing towards Rhum and Eigg, which were glowering navy blue. As he went on staring at the islands as if in a trance he was filled with a sense that this weekend with Edwina was simply the lull before the storm . . .

CHAPTER THIRTY-THREE

T he storm broke days after Globe Newspaper Publishing's election night party in the seventh-floor executive suite, where Drew introduced his wife to the young woman who so obsessed him.

'Roseanna has done almost as much running around constituencies as most of the candidates,' he said to Edwina.

'From what I've read in the paper you've had a very interesting time,' said Edwina, smiling.

'Very,' said Roseanna, eyeing her rival as beadily as she would any interviewee.

She scanned the older woman's hair for grey and tell-tale root regrowth, wondered how soon plastic surgery would be needed to maintain the remarkably well-preserved face, and was amazed by the residual voluptuousness of the figure. The bitch wasn't in bad shape for a woman of her advanced years, but she would probably wake up one morning soon and discover that like the last autumn leaf on a tree her looks had gone in the night. What she couldn't handle and what sent a sharp, acute pain right through her were the echoes of ecstasy reflected in the woman's eyes. Drew had taken the

ageing creature to his house in Ardnamurchan again this past
weekend, and the glory of it was still shining out of her.

At that moment, when she felt physically sick with
jealousy, she knew The Time Had Come – to make Drew
hers to love and pleasure.

The chaste goodnight kisses, the brushes of hands, the
lacing of fingers, the simmering looks of longing and desire
became things of the past at that instant. The time for holding
back was over and gone.

She wanted him now, this night, but he was dashing up
and down between the editorial floor and the party as the
election results came in. The party would go on till breakfast
so she consoled herself that at least the older woman could
not have him.

It was the next day, Friday, before all the results were
in and Harold Wilson's Labour government was returned to
power with an overall majority of three parliamentary seats.
The Scottish Nationalists had increased the seven seats they
had in the February election to eleven and the Conservative
leader Edward Heath was now in serious trouble with his
own party.

'It's going to be as inconclusive as ever, but there are some
exciting times ahead,' said Drew as the weekend loomed.

So it was going to be Monday before she would get her
chance to make him hers.

She spent the weekend stocking up on champagne, smoked
salmon and enough food and drink to last a month if they
locked the door and stayed in bed that long.

Though she had a woman come once a week to clean the

flat, she washed and dusted from ceiling to floor, prettied it everywhere with flowers, arranged and rearranged the lighting and set the time switches so that it was warm and welcoming when she returned on Monday evening.

On Monday morning, now that she was about to make him hers, she dressed elegantly rather than sexily in a sugar-pink Wallis Chanel-style suit and a black camisole, and had her hair styled before she went to the office.

Drew was waiting for the lift in the front hall when she got there, and she wanted him at once.

Once the elevator door glided shut and they were alone she placed her arms around his neck and kissed him passionately on the mouth.

'What was that for?' he asked, his blue eyes lambent with desire.

'To say how nice it is to see you this morning,' she replied, her eyes already triumphant that he would be hers tonight.

They walked to the Malmaison in the evening because he had given his chauffeur the night off.

But she hardly ate and they left early and he hailed a taxi to take them to her flat.

At the front door she held his head in her hands and kissed him even more passionately than in the lift.

'You've made me wait a long time for this,' he murmured when she raised her head and let him go.

'I hope you find it's been worth waiting for,' she whispered.

Then she put her key in the door, slipped her hand into

his and led him across the threshold into the welcoming, softly lit hall.

The waiting had been too long. Their pent-up desires simply exploded now.

'Which way?' he murmured into her hair.

She led him through an open door where the elegant white bedside lamps were lending a gentle light to a room furnished in restful shades of yellow and green.

He undressed her quickly but expertly without rush before he discarded his own clothes and made joyous, celebration love to her for hours in her vast, luxurious bed.

'It was worth waiting for, but the waiting's been agony,' he said around eleven o'clock when they were sharing champagne and smoked salmon by the fire.

'For me, too,' she sighed.

'I'll need to ring the office to get the papers,' he said.

'Go ahead,' she said, raising her hand towards the telephone on the table beside him.

She was wearing a gorgeous ivory satin negligee when she opened the door to take the papers from the chauffeur.

Now the world would know she was Drew's mistress because the chauffeurs gossiped and that was wonderful. She had never intended to have a secret affair with him.

And then they read the papers and he rang the office to change a front-page story and it was so exciting sharing it all with him. She looked at his head bowed over the papers as he scanned them alertly and gave a silent sigh. When he was done reading and had called the office the whole glorious night lay ahead of them. It felt like the prospect of eternity.

She suspected he would want to call the older woman when he had rung the office, and she did not wish to know. The creature's days in his life were numbered now. So she vanished into the bedroom and sat at her dressing table brushing her golden hair until he came looking for her, needing her again.

They awoke to a different world in the morning as they beheld each other with wonder, if not something of awe.

'I didn't know it was possible to be so happy,' he said, holding her close before they rose. 'For once I don't want to go to the office.'

'But we must,' she said, knowing it could only harm their relationship if they took the day off. He would feel seduced and might not like her so much afterwards.

He left her flat at nine o'clock and walked the short distance to his own in Crown Gardens where he changed into a fresh shirt and suit and rang for the chauffeur to collect him at the usual time of ten o'clock.

Her hips swayed triumphantly when she crossed the big editorial room to her desk. When she had hung up her coat she dropped sleepily on to her swivel chair and looked across the room, which was comparatively empty at this time of day.

Well, she wanted to shout at the people there, I know you think I've been sleeping with the editor for months, but as a matter of fact last night was our first time. And yes, it was glorious.

Her gaze fell on her hands and her black-stockinged legs.

There wasn't one inch or centimetre of her skin that he had not caressed and loved last night. And every bit of her still tingled.

Her eyes met Ian Russell's and she sensed from the way he was looking at her that he had already heard the chauffeur's gossip. And it enhanced her glory and happiness. It was wonderful that he knew.

She gave him a smile which said, Look, don't ask me to do anything this morning. I've just spent the most exhausting night with the editor and I'm feeling rather tired.

That evening the chauffeur-driven car took them straight to Kensington Road and she was wearing her ivory satin negligee again when the driver returned later with the papers.

That was how it had to be — all out in the open from the start with no pretence at covering up.

He stayed again the following night and the one after. But on Friday morning he said at breakfast, 'I have a wife to go to this evening.'

It was the first harsh word that had passed between them.

CHAPTER THIRTY-FOUR

Now he no longer had any wish to tell Edwina about being in love. Now the time for confession was over and the time for privacy had begun.

Now he had entered another world in which she had no place and he felt quite separate from her as he had not done since their marriage. He felt no need for her now.

And when he looked at her across the breakfast table he felt he was beholding her from a riverbank, and he had left her on the other side.

More than anything he wanted to be nice to her. His desire to be nice to her was quite overpowering. Edwina was a very nice woman, but he had never been passionately in love with her the way he was now. He had never felt for her or any other woman what he felt for Roseanna. And if anyone had told him what he would feel would be so overwhelming, so all-possessing he would never have believed them.

'Were you very late last night?' she asked, a look of inquiring sympathy in her eyes.

'Uh, huh,' he nodded. 'One or two problems in the caseroom. The usual threatening not to bring the paper out if someone didn't get his tea break. The boss is getting really fed up with the way he feels he's no longer in control of the paper even though he owns it.' He was spreading out the explanation in order to delay the supplementary questions he knew she would ask. He wanted a few more minutes to get his answers pat.

'What time did you get in?'

'Oh, it must have been about half past one.'

'You didn't come to bed.'

'I didn't want to disturb you. So I camped in the study.' The words tripped easily and smoothly off his tongue.

'That was thoughtful,' she said gently. 'But as you'd stayed at Crown Gardens all week, it would have been nice to wake up beside you this morning.'

'I know,' he said, reaching for her hand across the table and squeezing it. He was glad that ever since their marriage she had understood that if she rang him at his own flat and got no reply it meant he was either still working or sleeping.

'I rang you on Wednesday.'

'It's been an impossible week. Even more than usual.'

'Every week seems to be these days. For both of us,' she sighed.

'What are your plans for today?'

'I have none.'

'Well, as we've hardly seen each other all week, why don't I take you out into the country for a nice long leisurely lunch?' he suggested, hoping to pre-empt any further questions or complaints.

The seeming spontaneity of his suggestion brought a smile to her face.

'I'd like that. Very much,' she said.

The way her face brightened almost hurt him. For the first time he felt deceitful. This woman loved him far more than he had ever loved her. That had been the danger in their marriage from the start. In her heart she probably loved him as much as he loved Roseanna. Now he knew how powerful an emotion love was. He felt nervous as well as slightly guilty. No one should love a person that much more than they were loved in return. Passion needed to be mutual – or it was dangerous.

'I'd better get dressed,' she said. 'after I've cleared up the breakfast things.'

'I'll do that,' he said. 'Just you get dressed and we'll make an early start for the country. It's a nice day to get some fresh air.'

'Thanks,' she said and he saw the tenderness and gratitude in her eyes and once again he felt he was looking at her from across a river. This very nice woman he had married because it was what she wanted – and against his better judgement – was no longer the woman he wanted to be with more than any other.

And when she returned downstairs, bright as sunshine in her Country Casual green and purple tweeds and her face almost luminous with expectation, the river seemed even wider.

It was a fine clear crisp autumn morning of bright sunshine

when Drew swung his Mercedes coupé out of Kirklee Terrace on to the broad carriageway of Great Western Road and gathered speed towards Loch Lomond. The leaves were still largely on the trees and the countryside was ablaze with the lovely marmalade shades of the season.

He seemed reinvigorated as he bowled along but the restlessness of recent weeks was quite gone. A confident controlled energy had taken its place, and she wondered what had happened to him.

She had rung him every night at Crown Gardens this past week when she knew he was likely to be there and awake, reading his beloved first editions – and got no reply. It was most unusual for him not to be there on at least one night between eleven and midnight. She almost rang the office on Thursday but she knew he preferred her not to do so.

He was working very hard, but he certainly wasn't tired.

'You're driving like a very young man,' said Edwina as he raced past an MG sports car.

'The fresh air has gone to my head. Such a treat. I never get any and so I find it heady,' he said and quickly thought: Be careful. Don't start giving her clues.

They lunched at a hotel by the loch on freshly caught fish and late-season raspberries doused in cream, and washed it down with Vouvray and mineral water because he was driving.

It was while looking at her bright and lovely face over lunch that he became aware he had to sleep with her tonight. It had been easy to kip in his study last night because he came home late and knew he was far too tired from his hectic week with Roseanna to show much interest in his wife. For the first time he was coming face to face with the new dichotomy in his life.

'You must have been very tired last night,' she said pointedly as if she could read his mind.

He grinned. 'I'll make it up to you tonight,' he promised.

He squeezed her hand and realised he would enjoy making love to her tonight. It would be pleasant exercise and relaxation compared to the wild nights of passion with his young mistress . . . a sort of canter over the foothills rather than ascending Everest.

He was as good as his word and it was every bit as pleasant and relaxing as it had promised to be over lunch. And it was just as pleasant on Sunday night as well . . .

At seven o'clock on Monday evening Drew and Roseanna made no pretence of wanting anything but each other and took his chauffeur-driven car straight to Kensington Road.

She guessed he had done a bit of duty lovemaking to his wife over the weekend and wished to wipe it from his memory fast, which she was sure she had done by the time they picnicked around midnight on smoked salmon and champagne and read the first editions of the morning papers.

'This is becoming a very pleasant habit and a lot more fun than reading the papers on my own,' said Drew across the fire.

She smiled. It was nice to read the papers together after

love, almost like a bit of gentle after-play which helped them to come down together.

It was only a week since they first made love but it seemed a lifetime ago and she felt so coupled with him now. She wondered if he felt just as coupled, though she knew it could not be exactly the same despite his passion for her. Yet.

'Is there anything you need to worry about in the first editions?' She asked.

'Inflation's starting to get out of hand,' said Drew. 'Wages are up over twenty per cent in the last year. It's not good for the country. But no, there's nothing to keep us out of bed too long tonight,' he added, giving her a large wink.

She rose and climbed on his knee and placed her arms around his neck as he rang the office. Then he carried her back to bed.

It went on like that all week – going home early to bed at seven and getting up, content and happy shortly before midnight to read the papers and share a champagne supper.

And in the morning he strolled round to Crown Gardens and changed his suit and shirt and the chauffeur picked him up at ten o'clock.

And then it was Friday morning and he said, 'I'd better see my wife this evening.'

'Must you?'

'I think it's not a bad idea. Besides she might start looking for me.'

And I'd like her to find you right here, preferably when we're in bed, she thought. She said, 'If you say so.'

It was too soon to start making demands and claims

even though she was starting to hate the weekends without him.

'I'll see you Monday.' He reached for her hand across the table.

'I'll see you Monday,' she whispered and they clung to each other before he left.

It was still October and only twelve days and nights since they had first made love, she reminded herself as she dressed for the office. But the more she had of him the more she wanted and she needed to start making the weekends theirs as soon as possible – even if it was only one in four or three . . . or two . . .

From the moment she had realised she was in love with him she had been acutely conscious of the need not to become a victim of love, not to give in and consider his marriage and the strain he was under having an affair with her and all the usual nonsense which turned women in love into victims.

That was why the sooner his wife knew of the affair and realised her marriage was over the better, though she expected to have to share him for a time.

She needed now to deliver a killer psychological blow which would make Edwina Hamilton realise her marriage was over and give up her man.

She needed to make love to Drew in the bed he shared with Edwina in Ardnamurchan . . .

The next Monday they embarked on another hectic week of early to bed and champagne suppers at midnight with the first editions in Kensington Road.

'I can never never never get enough of you,' he murmured in the middle of one of the endless nights which the days seemed hardly to separate. 'Why don't you come away with me?'

'Take me to your island,' she whispered, seeing her chance.

'My island?'

'Your place in Ardnamurchan.'

'Oh, Roseanna, I'll take you anywhere. Anywhere you wish.'

CHAPTER THIRTY-FIVE

'We need to think carefully about where we're going, what we're doing,' said Drew.

'I'm not sure I understand what you mean,' said Roseanna cautiously, alarm bells pealing in her head.

'I mean that I'm crazy about you, that in my middle years I'm involved with you body, mind and soul as I never was when I was younger or indeed have been with a woman in my life before. I love building your career. I love everything about you. But I am married. And I have no intention of becoming unmarried.'

If she had had a gun to hand, she would have pointed it straight at his head across the breakfast table and shot him dead.

She had been seething since the moment they arrived at Ardnamurchan three days ago and discovered they were staying in a rented cottage across the bay from the house where he took Edwina Hamilton. She felt used, cheap, of a lower order in his eyes than the older woman.

'Why are you talking about marriage?' she asked, pulling as pleasantly surprised a face as she could muster. 'It's not something I've thought about.'

'Perhaps not yet,' he said, 'because our relationship is still young and tender and we haven't been lovers long enough for demands and bitterness and resentment at what's not possible for us to have set in. But if we're to continue our delightful association for any length of time it's something you may very well think about — '

'I'm not the marrying kind,' she interrupted, feeling insulted and humiliated.

'Then you're even more exceptional than I already know you to be,' he said. 'Almost all women are the marrying kind eventually. And the longer a relationship continues the more of the marrying kind they're inclined to become.'

She felt more exposed than when she was naked and he was plunging deep inside her. He had seen right to the bottom of her soul and she hated him for knowing so much about her secret plans.

'But if you're not the marrying kind, then perhaps we can look forward to a long and trouble-free time together,' he said. 'I'm not the marrying kind myself.'

'But you've been married twice.' She heard the sharp edge, the snap in her voice and was furious at what it was giving away when she needed to put on a show of calm indifference.

'I was only twenty when I married for the first time. For sex,' he said. 'Marriage was the only way to have regular sex in those far-off days.

'But I had no intention of ever repeating that mistake. I never had any wish to marry my wife. She had the devil's own job getting me to the church.'

'So why did you marry her?'

'It was a case of either or. Either I married her or it was over. I didn't want to live without her. I'd lost her once before when she was still married to her first husband. I was very deeply attached to her and had no wish to lose her again.'

The words were so steeped in affection for the older woman that they wounded. But he had never talked about his wife before and she hadn't asked. However, as she'd learned as a journalist, information was power and she needed information about the strengths and weaknesses of the former Edwina Rutherford so she would know how and where to attack. She also knew she needed to keep moving quickly to establish equal status with the ageing former and future divorcee or the lesser, secondary role he wished herself to play in his life would become permanent. And that was dangerous. So her voice was calm when she said, 'So you've known her for a long time?'

'For over twenty years — since she was a young girl foolish enough to marry Max Rutherford, who was old enough to be her father.

'The first time I met Edwina was at a reception on the seventh floor shortly after she returned from her honeymoon. She was wearing a red velvet dress which clung delightfully to her figure, but though the effect on her white skin was dramatic the colour was too old for her. She looked as if she was making a tremendous effort to look older, more sophisticated than she was. What I saw was a vulnerable slightly lost young woman hiding beneath the dress and the haughty expression she assumed in those days. Even then she seemed to need me in a way I couldn't quite fathom.'

Roseanna silently drew her breath at the depth of the root and affection between him and the ageing woman, whose flesh she now wanted to rip apart with her bare hands.

'Take me to the lighthouse,' she said, choked and fleeing from the subject.

She needed to get out of the house before she screamed or hit him.

The wild incoming November tide was lashing the rocks on which the 118 foot high grey granite column of Ardnamurchan lighthouse stood atop a sixty foot cliff on the edge of a bleak moor.

'Fancy a swim to America?' Drew teased Roseanna.

'Not today, thank you,' she said quietly.

He watched her standing away from him, her golden hair swathed in a huge silk scarf, her head held proud and high and her teeth sunk into her lower lip as she gazed towards the small isles which were grey as the sea today. He knew she was hurt by what he had said about marriage being out of the question. She was being very brave and pretending that thoughts of it had never entered her head, but her pain was showing in her subdued manner and the distance she was keeping from him.

They had been lovers for five weeks now, and it was best that she understood early that there could be no long-term future for her with him. He was glad he had spoken and been honest with her. He was glad he had cleared the air before it got thick with false hopes, and hoped it would be easier for her when she got used to it. He felt less disloyal to Edwina and better about himself.

'I'm taking next week off,' he had told his wife late last week.

'But, Drew, I'm up to the roots of my hair in fashion shows next week. Can't you — '

'I want to go on my own.'

'Wherever to? What's brought this on?'

He saw the questions teeming in her eyes.

'I need to think, to get some space.'

'I thought I gave you plenty of space.'

He heard the pain in her voice.

'You do,' he said. 'But I'm a glutton for space. I need some more.'

'Have you decided where you're going?'

'A wander, but I'll probably get to Ardnamurchan at some point.'

'It's nice at this time of year,' she said. More beautiful because the colours are more dramatic in the late autumn afternoon sky.'

'I know. I love them, too.'

'Yes.'

'I mean it about my space. Don't look for me there.'

He felt guilty — and afraid of what she might ask him next.

'I've always respected your sovereignty, your right and need to be completely separate, and I've never intruded where you haven't wanted me in your life,' she said with a quiet dignity which did not completely mask the pain and suspicion clouding her eyes.

'No.'

He felt an overwhelming love for her at that moment and wanted to take her in his arms and tell her, but he was afraid because she would realise what was happening to him — and the time for telling her was over and gone.

Now he looked at the slender figure of his young mistress who had turned her head away from him completely.

'Roseanna.'

He stepped towards her and took her elbow in his hand and the fragility of it went straight into his heart.

And when she raised her head to him he saw that she was crying — pure, unrestrained tears she could not resist or help.

'I love you,' she said softly as he took her in his arms.

'I know, and it's hard for you. And you're being very brave.'

'And I need you in my life. Always.' She seemed to be losing all control. 'I've found something with you and I can't let you go.'

'I know,' he said. 'We've both found something in each other that we never want to be parted from, something too precious to lose. Perhaps we're in deeper than we imagined.' And as he looked into her eyes through the film of her tears he knew he loved her more this day than he had ever done — and there were no easy compartmentalised solutions to keep his life in nice neat tidy sections the way he liked best. 'We'll find a way.'

They clung to each other for ages on the sea-lashed rocks, their figures swaying in the west wind as if they were as much a part of the nature of this place as the earth and the things that grew there.

And when at last they parted he said, 'Come, I'll make you lunch.'

He cooked a sumptuous lunch of partridges pot roasted in port and brandy and stuffed with rice and apples, sultanas and almonds and accompanied by baked Jerusalem artichokes. And he served them with a well-warmed Chateauneuf du Pape before a blazing log fire in the house he shared with Edwina.

And as darkness fell over the ocean in the afternoon and the lights on the islands twinkled like stars, Roseanna longed to live with him in this house for the rest of her life.

'Make love to me,' she said afterwards, and he did so by the leaping flames of the fire — and much later in the bed where he had loved Edwina.

They stayed there for the rest of the week because it was warmer and more comfortable than the cottage, and they hardly got out of bed except to eat and walk along the shore when they felt in need of fresh air.

'I went to bed with a woman for a week once before,' he said towards the end of the week.

'Really?' She raised an inquiring eyebrow.

'Yes. With Elsie.'

'Elsie?'

'Yes, Elsie MacLelland,' he said. 'It was before she married Alex Regan.'

'I thought you two had known each other rather well,' she said with an indulgent smile. She loved the way she was learning little things about him as the days passed. And she felt each tiny detail he revealed to her binding them closer together.

'Yes, Elsie and I went to bed for a whole week in Venice to nurse each other better from our wounds. She'd just broken up with Max Rutherford and I'd just been parted from his wife.'

'Ed –'

'It was after I'd lost her, and I needed to blot it all out of my mind. So did Elsie. The whole office knew, but we didn't care. It did us both a power of good. We felt able and fit enough to carry on with our lives when we got back.'

Roseanna felt the shadow of the other woman fall as powerfully between them as if she was in the room.

It was essential that she established equality with the past and future divorcee in Drew's eyes as soon as possible. The woman must also recognise her equal status in the period of sharing before the marriage ended.

Before they left Ardnamurchan she made sure she had left sufficient territorial markings that the woman could be in no doubt about her importance.

PART THREE

CHAPTER THIRTY-SIX

'I've been here before,' said Edwina grimly.

'You and I both. Together,' said Max Rutherford.

'This is no time for joking,' she said sharply, giving him a pained look.

'I'm being very serious,' he assured her.

They were in the master bedroom in Ardnamurchan looking at the array of knickers Roseanna had deposited with such guile all over the place.

'Besides, this is entirely different to the unfortunate incident on our honeymoon,' he said. 'As you know, I loved Diana very deeply. She'd been in my life since I was a young man. And I'd lived with her in the house in Provence. Hamilton's little whore — '

'Drew's not a whoremonger. So don't call her that,' Edwina interrupted.

'Well, Hamilton's bint is an an imposter, an intruder who's trying to break into his life. Edwina, you're a beautiful, mature and wise woman now. You can soon see this little imposter off.'

'I will,' she said. 'I will.' And her chin took on a

chiselled, determined set. This day had been a long time
coming.

She had known from early in her first affair with Drew
that one day she would have to fight for him. She had
fought to make him her husband and now she would fight
to keep him.

And she had known from the moment he had suddenly announced he was taking a week 'on his own'
that there was someone else — probably a journalist on
the *Globe* because he had little time to meet someone
anywhere else.

For weeks there had been huge questions in her mind
when she could never get an answer to her evening calls to
his flat in Crown Gardens. But she had neither said nor done
anything because she hadn't known what was best to do if
he *was* seeing someone else.

From the day she had finally married Drew she had
been acutely aware of his need for emotional space, to
be separate from her. She had vowed she would bind
him to her in freedom, keep him by letting him go —
so that he would always want to come back to her.
But she had never expected knowingly to let him him go
away with another woman, and the pain was poignant and
excruciating. How had it happened? How had they reached
this point? How had she been so careless that it was a *fait
accompli* when he told her he was going away 'on his
own'? She had been paralysed not knowing what to do,
how to handle it in case she made it worse. She needed
information.

The moment he had driven out of sight in his Mercedes coupé she had shot straight round to Max's flat.

It was half past ten in the morning when Max opened the front door of his flat in a black velvet dressing gown which revealed both the abundant springy white hairs on his chest and that he was wearing nothing underneath it. He was now seventy and bald. People said he looked like Picasso and rampant virility glared out of him every bit as much as it did from the famous artist. Edwina took one look at him and knew he was exactly what she needed.

'Do you want it now or later?' he asked, recognising her need.

'Now.'

'Here or upstairs?'

'Anywhere.'

She didn't care so long as she got from this man what her beloved husband was off to give to someone else.

'You'll be more comfortable upstairs.'

Her hand slid easily, familiarly into his.

He slipped her skirt off on the landing and thrust his tongue down her throat as he dropped her knickers on top of her skirt.

She was still wearing the rest of her clothes when he took her on an even bigger bed than the ones they had shared during their marriage.

'I needed that,' she said, sitting up afterwards.

'I know,' he said, easing her jacket off. When he had undone her blouse he fondled her breasts for a long time before he drove inside her for even longer. 'You needed that as well,' he said when he finally slid from her and took off the rest of her clothes. 'Now I'll bring you some champers and lunch. You'll find a robe behind the door in the dressing room if you like. But I'd rather you didn't. It's warm here and I'm a great *déjeuner sur l'herbe* man.'

'I must say, Max, you've lost none of your . . . style,' she said when he returned bearing a silver tray with a bucket of ice, champagne and some smoked salmon and placed it on a table by a window.

'None of my vitality . . . either . . . wouldn't you say,' he invited her to compliment him as he sat on the edge of the bed and took her hands in his.

'But how? All I ever hear these days is that you drink too much.'

'I'm not quite the drunkard of my reputation. Besides there are one of two other things I prefer to drinking, which in excess only damages a man's performance.'

'You're amazing, Max.'

'Pleasing, too, I trust.'

'Very,' she smiled.

'And now we've sorted out your basic needs for the moment, let's talk over lunch about why you really came to see me. Her name is Roseanna Warrender — an ambitious little bitch on the *Daily Globe* who's set her cap at him.'

'Oh, I met her on election night,' said Edwina. 'She's young and very sexy.'

'I'm surprised I haven't seen you round here before, wanting to find out what I know about her.'

'I suppose because I haven't known what to do and maybe a bit of me didn't want to know,' she said. 'How long's it been going on?'

'Ah, that's a matter of some conjecture. But first things first. Come and have a little lunch.'

The room wasn't quite as warm as Max thought, so she slipped into the white towelling robe before she joined him at the window table.

'So, how long, Max?'

'It's just over five weeks since his chauffeur started taking the first editions to her flat in Kensington Road,' he said.

'And it's that long since I haven't been able to get an answer to the telephone at his flat in the late evening.'

'I'm inclined to think that's when it started, though there was a lot of dining at the Malmaison before then,' said Max.

'Working dinners is what he calls them,' said Edwina, bitterly wishing she had not been so committed to her own work in the evenings.

'Of course, you know why it's this ambitious little whore rather than any other?'

'Why?'

'She's the Lord President's half sister and her father was also the Lord President, and Drew has always aspired to be one of the Establishment. It goes right back to his Diary days. He wants to be one of the people he writes about,' he said.

'No,' said Edwina, her voice suddenly breaking. 'She's young and intelligent and I have to admit I can see what he sees in her.

'Once again I've failed, Max. I'm not good at being married.
I'm no good as a wife.

'He never wanted to marry me. I tried to coax and cajole
him and he only married me when I threatened to break it
off. Ours was really a shotgun marriage.

'I've tried to give him the space and freedom he needed.
I never wanted him to regret marrying me.' The temporary
anaesthetic of making love to Max was beginning to wear off
and tears were filling her throat.

'But it's been no good,' she whispered as the tears began
to fall. 'He's found someone else . . . But he's my life and I
don't want to be alone again or live without him.'

She cried bitter sobs on to the white hairs of her ex-husband's
chest for a long time.

'Of course if your taste is really that bad, you can get
him back instead of welcoming the opportunity to get rid of
him,' said Max, his bald head gleaming in the late afternoon
sunshine as he returned with another bottle of champagne
when she had dried her eyes.

She could not help laughing.

'Oh, Max, you're impossible and you do look like Picasso,'
she said, raising her glass to him when he had replenished it.

And she had to admit she was feeling a lot better. Loving
and crying with her ex-husband had done a lot to ease her
immediate pain. But when she glanced at the clock she
couldn't help wondering exactly where Drew was and what
he was doing at this exact minute with Roseanna Warrender.

'And your own personal Picasso is the very man to help you,' he said. 'You and I can start dining at the Malmaison, and you can accompany me to the receptions at Globe Publishing and that will bring your errant husband haring back in your direction.'

'But you don't go into the office much any more.'

'I've still got a desk and a secretary and I'm going to start being seen around again.'

'But I don't think we should become lovers again,' she said when he called at Kirklee Terrace for a late evening drink on Friday.

'Oh, I suspected you wouldn't want that part of my love and friendship package for long, but the facility remains there for you,' he said cheerfully, winking at her over his sturdy glass of Lagavulin.

'Oh, Max, you make me laugh and I don't know what I'd have done without you this week,' she said. 'You've got me through it without falling to pieces.'

Max had also been a valuable source of intelligence on the dead set Roseanna had been making for Drew for almost a year.

'Make no mistake,' he warned. 'She is utterly ruthless. You are at war.'

And now she was in no doubt about the ruthlessness and determination of the younger woman to steal her husband.

'It's fiendish,' she said to Max as he uncovered another pair of lacy black knickers at the bottom of the wood basket by the drawing-room hearth at Ardnamurchan.

'It wasn't enough to leave them in my bed. They fall out and explode in my face at almost every cupboard door I open.'

Drew had rung her on Saturday, announcing he was in Ardnamurchan and would be returning to Kirklee Terrace on Monday evening. To prepare her, Max had ordered a helicopter to take them there early on Monday morning.

'I feel as if the house has been burgled, as if it was no longer mine,' she cried. 'This is the place where we built our marriage, where we were really together, and both our families came here and became friends. It's where Drew was reconciled with his son and daughter. It was our home. And now I no longer feel it is . . .'

'And that's exactly what this little minx wants you to feel. That's why she's done it,' said Max. 'Bomb is the right word. They're psychological bombs planted to blow your mind and make you believe your marriage is over. So you give up and let her walk off with your husband. She's trying to get you to make it easy for her. Drew won't know what she's done.'

'But he brought her here. How could he do that? How could he pollute our home? If he had to have her, why couldn't he have taken her to a hotel for a week?' she cried.

'From what I know of this evil little piece, he was probably under enormous pressure from her and she somehow manoeuvred him into bringing her here. I've never liked the man but somehow I don't believe that he'd have voluntarily brought her to the home he's shared with you,' Max assured her.

'But why has it happened? I thought we were happy. How long do you have to live with someone to know what goes on inside their head and heart?'

'Ah,' said Max. 'I can't answer your last question. But it's obvious she's been out to take a sledgehammer to your marriage from the start. And there is one other thing . . .'

'Yes . . .'

'Drew is nearly fifty. His major achievements are behind him now. So are the golden days of his very golden youth. It may be that he's trying to recapture those days through his affair with a younger woman.'

'Oh . . .'

'Don't let that destroy your confidence either, Edwina. You're stronger and more attractive to a man than you've ever been. You have something better than youth – you're in the very prime of life. And you can get your husband back if you can do just one thing, which I know you have the strength to do.'

She stared at him in amazement, as if he had just announced he had discovered some elixir for eternal life.

'Yes . . .' She waited on his words.

'You must do what we all need to do at some time in our lives if we're to go on living and not become one of the living dead. You must reach beyond heartbreak.'

CHAPTER THIRTY-SEVEN

Edwina had dressed with care in an elegant scarlet wool kaftan and was watching the credits roll on *Coronation Street* when Drew entered the morning room.

Though she had talked through her pain and anger and determination to get her husband back with Max, she had no idea what she would feel when she saw him again.

Now as their eyes met she was shocked by his haggard appearance. And delighted. However passionate his week with his young mistress had been, he was in turmoil. Torn between conflicting loyalties. A ray of hope shot through the welter of emotions which his presence triggered.

Then her glance crawled over his face, the deceptive flare of his nostils, the treacherous blue of his eyes, the dishonest fullness of his lips, the crass spread of his hands. Most of all it was his lips and his hands which had betrayed her and ought to be cut off and ripped out.

She wanted to kill him.

She got up and hurled the TV remote control straight at his head.

He ducked but not fast enough.

It struck him a glancing blow on the forehead.

She smiled as she watched the blood trickle on to his eyebrows and nose.

'That is the most beautiful sight I've seen since you set off to Ardnamurchan with your trollop,' she informed him, her voice ringing with delight. 'I wonder if she'd still fancy you if she could see you now starting to bleed to death. But it's so beautiful,' she cried, reaching for a heavy glass ashtray.

She sent it hurtling towards him.

But this time he stepped out of its path.

It shattered on the frame of a picture by one of the Glasgow Boys.

'All right, I'm every sort of bastard ever born, but I'm not going to let you kill me,' he shouted, striding towards her.

He stopped just short, facing her.

As their eyes met and held she saw that he was guilty and ashamed.

She no longer wanted to kill.

She just wanted to make him suffer till he screamed in agony. Then she would give him her biggest, broadest smile.

'So you know . . .' he faltered.

'And what your little trollop might like to know is that the three score and ten pairs of knickers she left all over the house in Ardnamurchan made a splendid bonfire this afternoon. It lit the late afternoon sky brilliantly.

'By the way, you won't be able to spend any more time there with her as all the locks have been changed and the Stevensons relieved of the job of looking after it.'

'So you've been there . . .'

'Max and I deloused and disinfected the place from the rooftops downwards earlier today.'

'Max! What's it got to do with him?'

'It's got to do with the fact my first husband is a very kind and thoughtful and helpful and considerate man.'

He turned and stumbled towards the tantalus on the sideboard and poured himself a Lagavulin malt.

'You can make that two,' Edwina informed him.

He obeyed and handed her a glass.

'Why?' she demanded when they sat down by the fire. 'Why?'

'I wish I knew,' he sighed. 'I wish I knew. In the beginning I just wanted to be her mentor. I saw she had talent. I wanted to pass on what I knew about the newspaper business and she was an eager pupil. She was so eager.'

'So I gather.'

'Oh, you don't want to believe all Max tells you. He's — '

'An extremely accurate reporter.'

'Well, let's not argue about Max.' He shrugged. 'I'm obsessed. I'm in her thrall. I . . . I don't know what the answer is.'

Though she was in terrible pain, she saw a cry for help in his tortured eyes, heard it in his voice. He, too, was in pain.

Beyond that pain she saw hope.

However long it took, she would reach beyond heartbreak and get him back . . .

CHAPTER THIRTY-EIGHT

'You're living on overtime in your husband's life,' Roseanna informed Edwina.

'Really.'

'Don't you realise that?'

'The thought has never occurred to me.'

'Look,' said Roseanna grimly, 'Drew never had any wish to marry you and did so only to satisfy your desire to be his wife. You've known since before your marriage that he'd leave you when he found the right woman. And in fact you gave him a solemn undertaking that he'd be free to go once he did fall in love. Now that he's done so, you really must face up to it and take responsbility for your promises.'

'My relationship with my husband either before or after my marriage to him is really none of your business, Miss Warrender.'

They were in the sauna of the health club where Roseanna had sought out her lover's wife. And the ageing bitch was proving even harder to dislodge than she had been these past six months.

'When they affect my life and my relationship with my

lover, they do.' Roseanna spoke in a low voice and assumed an expression which suggested she was talking to a very tiresome child who refused to understand. 'It's six months now since he moved out of your house. Surely that's long enough for you to realise he won't be coming back.'

'It's also long enough for you to realise he has no intention of moving in with you, that he much prefers living on his own to living with you. I'm surprised you haven't realised he's that kind of man — who needs a lot of solitude and his own company.' Edwina affected an easy drawl as her eyes held the other woman's. 'My impression is that he's enjoying a fling — a last carouse with youth.'

Her words and pitying smile stung Roseanna.

'It's not a fling. He sleeps in my arms and makes love to me every night either at my home or his own. He no longer makes love to you. Or even thinks about it.' She saw how that hurt the ageing woman because Edwina winced. Sensing the chance perhaps of breaking through at last, she quickly followed up. 'Does that not tell you how he feels?'

Edwina lowered her eyelids and stared at her scarlet-painted toenails.

'You're not very good at marriage, Edwina — '

'Mrs Hamilton.'

'Mrs Hamilton.' Roseanna had said the name before she realised she was acknowledging the older woman's status as her lover's wife. 'Both your marriages have ended in failure — '

'I doubt if your employer, Lord Kilmacolm, would like to hear you describe a marriage which produced an heir to his newspaper empire as a failure,' Edwina lunged back.

'Well, whatever,' said Roseanna, assuming a bored expression. 'Both your husbands left you. Why don't you accept your limitations, Mrs Hamilton? Marriage is not for the likes of you.'

'As you have so far failed to persuade even one man to marry you, I don't think you really know what you're talking about,' said Edwina. 'Or indeed anything about marriage.'

'I know what I'm talking about and I know what I want,' said Roseanna grimly. 'I want your husband, Mrs Hamilton, and I am going to get him.'

'Ah, but there's something you should know, if you want to get married, Miss Warrender,' Edwina informed her. 'It takes two. And in your case three because you first have to persuade me to give up my husband. But it seems to me that in light of the danger you obviously present to his wellbeing, he needs me to be around. And I can assure you I have no intention of abandoning him to your mercies.'

'What is it you want, Mrs Hamilton? Why are you being so selfish hanging on to a man who no longer wants anything to do with you? Why do you hang about everywhere flaunting yourself under his nose?'

'I do not like the way you behave, Miss Warrender,' said Edwina in an even tone. 'But I'll tell you this. There is no security for a woman in a man, even though he may be much older than she is. It seems to me you're looking for a man to be stronger than you are, possibly a replacement for your late father who was certainly a formidable character. Such a man doesn't exist emotionally for a woman. A woman always needs to be stronger than a man and her security lies in herself.' She rose. 'Now what I badly need is a change of company and air,' she added, striding from the sauna.

After a shower Edwina sat by the pool with a cup of delicious peppermint tea and pretended to read a magazine.

She went to the health club once a week to relax and restore and take care of herself, and since Drew had left her it had been even more important to have a place where she felt cosseted.

Now though she had maintained stoicism in the sauna, the verbal assault had left her shaken and in no doubt of this young woman's determination to walk off with her husband for good.

The last six months felt like the worst in her life and she would never have got through them without the support of Max, who had been the loyal platonic friend she needed to talk to and take her out in the evenings so that she maintained the vital link of appearing in her husband's social circle while giving him emotional space.

'The important thing is that you're still his woman,' Max had told her. 'When a woman finds another man, she forgets about the man she's been with in the past. When they meet, he's history. But it's different for a man. He feels a past woman is still his woman. And that's how Drew feels every time he sees you. Every time I take you to a reception at Globe Publishing and he sees you or sees you across room when we dine at the Malmaison, he sees you as his. And there's no man he'd rather snatch you back from than me. Believe me.'

She had believed him and she sensed the tide was turning now, that the long months of giving Drew the emotional space he wanted, of loving him enough to let him go, might be beginning to pay off.

The most telling thing was that Roseanna had sought her out and not she Roseanna.

Despite her incredible, breathtaking brazenness and the way she behaved as if she was entitled to equal marital rights and status, her husband's mistress must be getting desperate.

'Oh, let me look at you. Come on, do your old catwalk number for the man who'd like to be your lover all over again,' cried Max as Edwina entered the morning room in Kirklee Terrace.

She was wearing a stunning Jean Muir leafy chiffon dress which floated around her body, hinting at its shape, and was gathered in a garland of sequins around her shoulders. And she walked up and down and pirouetted and turned on her heel and smiled just as she used to do, and taught all the model girls to do now.

'Bravo!' cried Max, clapping. 'Drew Hamilton is going to want to hit me tonight. He might even try. And he'd miss. Come on. Let's be going. I can't wait to see his face.'

'You know Marietta and Keith are delighted we've become such friends,' she said, throwing a black velvet cloak over her shoulders in the hall.

'I know,' he said. 'Marietta told me when she came to lunch the other day. She thinks we ought to get married again. I felt quite miserable having to admit we weren't even lovers. But she says it doesn't matter because you're good for me just as a friend, and she considers I'm looking a lot smarter since I got a decent woman to step out with again,' he added, ushering her down the steps and into his chauffeured Rolls.

The chatter in the seventh-floor executive entertainment suite was silenced as Lord Kilmacolm crossed the room to greet his son and former daughter-in-law.

'My dear Edwina, what a pleasure it is see you again,' he said in a loud, hearty voice. 'You've become so busy and successful in your own right you never seem to have much time for us old newspapermen.

'Your presence here this evening is truly something to celebrate.'

'Hear, hear,' echoed Alex Regan, appearing at his side.

'Oh, James, I had no idea you were going to be here this evening,' she said, looking up at his still upright figure.

Though he was now ninety-six, Lord Kilmacolm was a neat, spry figure who looked more like a vigorous seventy-five.

'I couldn't afford to miss this chance of seeing you,' he said.

Then out of the corner of an eye she saw Marietta and Keith — and realised what they had done. This party was for her. Her family were on her side, trying to lend a helping hand to mend her marriage. They loved her and were proud of her, and there to help her when she needed them.

She felt the tears at her throat and swallowed and felt very loved.

Then her eyes met Drew's. He was standing alone, handsome and golden as ever, in the centre of room. As if he had been waiting there for her all his life. Suddenly the familiar attachment of the girl with the rapt eyes clinging to his as she hung on his arm and his every word seemed a thing of the past.

It was then she knew that this party was for him, too. For them . . .

It was after ten when Drew's chauffeured Jaguar dropped him in Kirklee Terrace.

The days of long light of the Scottish spring and summer began in May and the brightness of the spring evening filled the morning room when she poured them Lagavulin malts and they faced each other across the fire as they had been doing for so many years of their lives now.

'I wondered how you were,' he said tentatively.

'Just fine,' she said. 'I've had a lovely evening. It was so nice of James to throw this surprise party for . . . I had no idea.'

'It was nice to see you,' he said, gulping his malt.

'And how are you?'

'I miss you.'

In her heart his words were like the fireflower that is the first to grow again when an inferno has left the earth where once a forest flourished unfit for any living thing — the sign that life is possible again on the scorched, seared earth.

It had been an emotional evening and she knew she must stay calm — and no tears.

'Good party.'

'Yes.'

'Nice evening all round.'

'Yes.'

'Nice of James to be there. We don't see much of him these days.'

'Yes.'

'I know you're always very busy, but it would be nice to see you some evening for dinner if you're free.'

'Yes. That might be nice.'

'I'll ring you next week.'

'Yes.'

'Are you on your own here this evening?'

'Marietta's playing chess with Max upstairs.'

'I see.' He scoffed his Lagavulin. 'Well, it was nice to see you. I'll not keep you.'

He got up and looked about the room.

Then their eyes met and his face crumpled in anguish.

'Oh, Edwina, what I'm trying to say in my stupid, silent, inarticulate way is that . . . that it's over . . . Can we . . . can we try again . . .?'

It seemed as if the ocean was at high harvest tide as her eyes held his, that the earth had borne fruit again, that there truly was a time and a purpose to everything under the heavens.

'I think you know the answer to that question,' she said as he swept her into his arms once more and held her there for a long time.

'Do you believe in God?' he asked as he let her go.

'I don't know,' she said. 'But I think I've come to believe in miracles.'

She walked him to the hall and the front door.

The long daylight was just turning to twilight as he stood on the threshold and asked her with a most solemn face, 'Edwina, you surely haven't been sleeping with that elderly drunk Max Rutherford?'

'Whoever you and I have been sleeping with in our time apart is over and gone. We should not tempt the clouds to return after the rain.'

CHAPTER THIRTY-NINE

He walked for hours round and round the streets he had known for so long in that elegant *arrondissement* that almost seemed too elegant to belong to Glasgow — Dowanhill. In one house or another it had been his home since he had become successful, a man to be looked up to and respected, 'one of them' as his first wife would have said.

But Cathy had been a long time ago and she had never belonged here or wanted to. She had not even wanted especially to belong even in Seamill on the Clyde's fair coast where he had bought a fine house for his family.

But there was no going back, and soon now, too, Roseanna Warrender, his darling and protégée, would belong in the past.

He hoped he had done right by her, equipped her to make her own way in the rough trade of journalism. She was ruthless enough to make her mark far beyond his province, which is what he suspected she really wanted. He had merely been a stepping stone over which she had passed.

But she had not yet gone from his life. She was still the

present, waiting for him. Now. Tonight. In his own place, his private world in Crown Gardens.

He looked up at the lights in the first-floor apartment. If only she had not crowded him and stayed so many nights she had almost seemed to have moved in, it might have been different. But she edged too close, till he felt he had no space left to himself and, inevitably, she'd started pressing him for commitment . . .

And now . . .

Though he hated what he had to do and what the immediate future held, he knew he couldn't stay in the street all night. He had better go in and get on with it . . .

It was two o'clock on the small gold clock which stood on the drawing-room mantelpiece when Roseanna heard him turn the key of his flat in Crown Gardens.

The first editions of the papers should have been here hours ago. So should he.

But the time had passed and neither had arrived.

She knew that woman was somewhere behind it – the elderly creature he had never wanted to marry. Except she wasn't so elderly. The most sick-making thing in the sauna had been looking at the body of a woman who was still desirable enough for Drew to want again.

She rose as she heard his step in the hall and caught sight of her sulky expression in the overmantel mirror. That wouldn't do.

She assumed a welcoming smile as she crossed the room and placed her arms around his neck.

'You're very late tonight,' she murmured, pressing her lips close to his.

'Yes,' he said brusquely, removing the bracelet of her arms around his neck. 'Look, I know it's late. But we need to talk.'

'Of course,' she said, summoning an instantly sympathetic face. 'Is something troubling you?'

'I think you know a great deal has troubled me right from the beginning,' he said gravely.

When he had poured himself a Bowmore malt from the tantalus he dropped easily into his favourite fireside chair and looked at his lovely young mistress almost as if she was his own adult daughter and he hoped he had done right by her as she set out in life.

Now he hoped again he had done right by his young protégée, that he he had equipped her well enough with the skills she would need in the profession she had chosen in preference to the law.

She would not want — it was unthinkable — to stay with Globe Publishing once she realised it really was over.

And it really was, now. Perhaps that was what it had been about — the passing of skills from one generation to the next. And now she was a journeywoman journalist she could make her own way and had no need of him.

But it wasn't going to be that easy. She would fight and resist, prolong the agony, and he would have to live with that. But for how long?

'I've put the flat up for sale,' he said, watching her expression like a stalking lion.

'This flat?'

'This very flat.'

'You mean you're moving in with me?

He saw the uncertainty in her eyes, heard the brittleness in her voice, and wished he could escape.

He took a large gulp of his malt.

'I mean that for the first time since I married my enormously understanding wife I'm going to live with her full time.'

'No.'

The tiny word escaped from her lips and her face crumpled like buckled rail track. And now she knew the fight was not to win but to avoid losing him.

Somehow she had to keep him in her life.

'Yes,' he said. 'And it's best for you that I do. I'm far too old to be starting a family, which is what you'll want.

'I'm simply far too old – point. I'm fifty and you're only twenty-eight. I'll be seventy when you're still under fifty and in your prime.

'We're too far apart.'

'No, no!' She jumped up and ran into his arms. 'It's her, isn't it? That woman you never wanted to marry,' she cried.

'It's true I never wanted to marry her, but now I'm glad she's my wife,' he said. 'She gives me the space I need to be myself and find myself, and in some funny old way we seem to belong.'

'You don't mean that! You don't mean that!' she cried and started to tear at his clothes. 'It's me you want, not that old woman!'

'Oh, Roseanna, stop this,' he said quietly. 'Surely after all we've enjoyed together we can part in a civilised fashion and be friends.'

She heard the plea in his voice, saw the pain and conflict in his eyes.

She slid off his knee, stood back and let the ivory satin negligee fall slowly from her shoulders. Till she stood before him naked and golden as the sun in the firelight.

'Make love to me,' she whispered.

And he did, as the flames warmed their bodies, and in a fury wild as a winter sea all night long.

Triumph shone in her eyes in the morning.

'You'd miss what we have,' she whispered, looking up at him as he was ready to leave for work ahead of her. 'And you wouldn't get it any better anywhere else.'

'Yes,' he said. 'It's a fact that sex can be better than ever even when the rest is all over between you.'

She raised her hand and it had landed on his face with the full force of her strength before she knew what she was doing.

'Oh, Drew, I'm sorry. I'm sorry,' she cried. 'I didn't mean that! Please forgive . . .'

But he had shot out the front door and was gone. And when she reached the street he was driving off.

CHAPTER FORTY

'No, there's nothing we need worry about in the first editions. Looks like a quiet night,' said Drew to the night editor of the *Daily Globe*. 'I need one,' he added bitterly. 'Goodnight, John.'

The clocks were still ringing out the midnight hour when he replaced the telephone receiver in the drawing room in Crown Gardens and rose to pour a Lagavulin.

The room seemed strangely, heavenly quiet. The nightmare was over. Roseanna had gone and would not be coming back because he'd had the locks changed the moment she'd shown her face in the office today. Though her things were still everywhere — like the debris after a storm — for once she had the sense not to crowd him either in person or on the phone.

He half filled the heavy lead-crystal glass with his favourite malt and returned to his fireside chair.

When he had dropped into it and stretched his legs out in front of him, he took a long draught of whisky and gazed at the papers strewn across the large glass coffee table for several minutes. Then he slowly raised his eyes

towards the empty chair facing him where Roseanna had
so often sat.

He was so glad she was gone!

He wished he didn't feel quite so happy, that his emotions
could be at least tinged with sadness.

He realised now that she had been a dream of youth who
had become a nightmare when she tried to make her own
dreams about him come true.

'I was trying to recapture what was gone and lost for ever
— my youth,' he had told Elsie MacLelland when they met
for an old pals' lunch. 'I wanted to make her youth mine.
In giving her all the chances I did I was trying to share
her youth, maybe even rob her of it. She was so young
and talented and full of promise I saw some reflection of
my younger self in her. It was all so heady and powerful
and — almost, I suppose — inevitable.'

'You're not the first man and certainly not the last it will
happen to,' Elsie sympathised.

'But I loved her. At least I was in love with her.'

'That much at least is obvious,' said Elsie.

'But I suppose it started to go wrong not long after the
beginning. She wanted to go to Ardnamurchan. So I took
her, not to my home but to cottage across the bay. But that
wasn't enough for her. She managed to move in. I didn't
like that. It seemed wrong somehow. And then she left her
knickers all over the place. Edwina found most of them the
next day. I didn't think too much of that.

'The first wild reckless abandon was over after that.
Some part of me started to close up. And the more I

closed up, the more frantic she got and the more she crowded me.

'That's when the rows started. Real blazing humdingers which almost invariably ended in equally blazing humdinging lovemaking.

'I got hooked on the sex. As we went downhill it took the place of everything right to the end. Last night was fantastic. But I knew it was the last.'

'Do you think she'll stay with the paper?'

'I don't think she'll want to. I'd rather she didn't, but I won't be getting rid of her.

'She gave up the law because she needed to make a fresh start away from Edinburgh. Now she's going to need to make another one and she must have the time she needs.'

'Very noble, Drew. But is it wise from your point of view? And I shouldn't think Edwina would want her hanging around for long.'

'Edwina's not in charge of the *Globe*.'

Talking to Elsie had helped him to sort out his thoughts and feelings.

And now at last he was leaving his bachelor flat behind for good and going home to Edwina.

'It's a funny thing,' he said to Elsie, 'but it almost feels as if I'm only marrying Edwina now that I'll be going home to her every night. But I'm glad she made me marry her because marriage has enabled us to get back together and I don't think we would have done if we hadn't married.

'There's a strength in marriage, an ability to hold together despite human weakness, which doesn't exist in other human relationships.'

'What you mean is there's a strength in your marriage to Edwina.'

'Whatever I mean, I love her.'

He heard a clock strike a quarter past twelve and as he swallowed the last of his Lagavulin he realised the first day of his new married life to the woman he loved was just beginning . . .

CHAPTER FORTY-ONE

'Features.'

Roseanna answered the telephone on her desk.

'This is Lord Kilmacolm's office,' said a woman with a southern English accent. 'I would like to speak to Miss Roseanna Warrender.'

'Speaking.'

'Oh, Miss Warrender, Lord Kilmacolm would like to see you in his office.'

'When?'

'Now. That is, if it is convenient.'

Roseanna knew this was a command, not a request.

'I'll be straight up.'

She looked at Ian Russell.

'Why do you think Lord Kilmacolm wants to see me?'

'To appoint you editor of the *Sunday Globe*.'

'Ha,' she said, getting up and heading for the cloakroom first.

'Go straight in,' said the woman with the English accent who had recently replaced Lord Kilmacolm's chief secretary on her retirement.

Roseanna had always got on well with the proprietor of Globe Newspaper Publishing when she had met him at lunch and receptions on the seventh floor and it was through his acquaintance with her stepfather that she had got a job with the company.

'Come in, Miss Warrender,' said James from behind his vast mahogany desk. 'Sit down.' He pointed to the chair in front of it.

But the cordiality with which he normally greeted her was gone and a chill filled the air between them.

She began to feel uneasy as she sat down.

'Miss Warrender, you have for some time been conducting a liaison with the editor in chief of the newspapers I publish,' he said, his steely eyes pinioning hers as her fingers closed around the sides of the chair. 'As a son of the manse, I do not approve of married men conducting extra-marital affairs, but I have learned to be fairly tolerant of human nature.

'Normally such affairs blow over, which is what I allow them time to do.

'However, there seems to be no sign of an end to your affair with Mr Hamilton, and my information is that you take your relationship so seriously that you would like to marry him.

'That is quite simply out of the question as it would cause far too much trouble within the company.

'The reason I wished to see you, Miss Warrender, is to say that you will not be seeing Mr Hamilton again.

'As of now you are no longer on the staff of Globe Newspaper Publishing.

'Two of my security people are waiting outside to escort

you from the office. Your desk will shortly be cleared by one of my secretaries and any personal effects sent on to you.

'A cheque in lieu of notice and in payment of the holiday periods due to you awaits your collection in my secretary's office.'

'But . . .'

But before she could say another word two security men entered Lord Kilmacolm's office and frogmarched her from the room.

'Drew Hamilton's office,' the dragon answered the telephone.

'Hello, Rosemary. It's Roseanna. I'd like to speak to Drew.'

'I'm afraid Mr Hamilton is in a meeting, Miss Warrender,' said the dragon in her most dragonish voice.

But it was being called 'Miss Warrender' that told her the bastard had got her fired!

He had changed the locks on his flat in Crown Gardens. And no one answered the door when she went banging round to Kirklee Terrace.

CHAPTER FORTY-TWO

'So he went back to his wife,' cried Roseanna.

'Married men usually do,' Helen sympathised.

They were having tea in Helen's first-floor sitting-room at Auchinvreck and the scent of the cedar trees was wafting through windows open to the afternoon sunshine.

'And I've lost my job as well. The whole new life I was building has been destroyed.'

There had been no end to her tears since she had fled to Auchinvreck, which her mother had kept as a country home for herself and Lord Brodie after he sold his Inverness-shire estate at Craigendhu.

'It may not seem much like it to you now, but you're young and resilient and you'll recover,' said Helen gently. 'And I'm glad you felt you could come here.'

Roseanna focused her bloodshot eyes on her mother.

'There was nowhere else I wanted to be,' she said.

'You don't know what it means to me to hear you say that,' said Helen. 'Though we've been on polite speaking terms since I married John, I've often felt that the price I paid for this marriage was that I lost you.'

'Well, now you know you haven't. When it all went wrong, I needed you more than anyone,' said Roseanna. 'And I'm sorry if I'm boring the ears off you going over and over everything again and again.'

'Going on talking about it is how you'll master what's happened to you and get over it,' Helen assured her. 'And I can listen for as long as you need to talk.'

'Oh, I did some terrible things,' said Roseanna, feeling like a small child again. 'I don't know if I can ever talk about them.'

'Then you mustn't, but you mustn't condemn yourself for them. You did them because you were in love, and women sometimes do terrible things in the name of love.'

'Like trying to steal other women's men. Like you and John when he was married?'

'I wasn't thinking about John, who wasn't married when I first met him. And I'll always think that he was stolen from me. I was thinking about my first husband. I was only eighteen and he was still married to his first wife when I became his mistress.'

'Oh, you naughty lady!' exclaimed Roseanna, suddenly shaken out of her own woes by her mother's admission about the distant past.

'Harry Dunlop was fifty-four, thirty-six years older than I was, and he would certainly never have married me if his wife hadn't died. I was on the point of leaving him at the time of her death and we hadn't been married long when he died,' said Helen. 'And maybe that was a blessing because we were too far apart in age to be happy for long.

'But I learned something important about the dreams of men through Harry.

'Middle-aged men who have affairs with much younger women are acting out dreams of their lost youth. They're indulging in a fantasy which can't withstand the demands of reality once it intrudes.'

'Are you saying that's what happened with Drew and me? That I was just a fantasy?'

'I don't for a moment doubt he was in love with you for a time,' said Helen. 'And if you'd been content to stay there, in his daydream of youth, perhaps your affair with him would have lasted longer. But as soon as you started trying to make your dreams of him become reality, your relationship was already starting to wane.'

'I suppose that makes some ghastly, horrible sense,' sighed Roseanna. 'But I loved him . . . so much . . .'

And her tears began all over again.

In the cool of the evening she went for a walk by the river and threw sticks into it for Rannoch, her favourite black labrador, to retrieve.

Later she sat on a wooden bench on the lawn gazing up at the house as the sun set over the Eildon Hills.

Somewhere the spirit of her father seemed to be blowing around. She remembered his tall erect figure stepping from his car outside the house and in her mind's eye saw herself and Rannoch running to greet him with hugs and licks and kisses.

Now he seemed to be there for her again, urging her to

have the courage when her pain and anguish were healed to live again.

Before they went to bed she and her mother stood in the hall looking up at the portrait of her father.

'He picked me up and gave me a new life when I had no one and nowhere to go,' said Helen. 'He gave me you and he was the best friend I ever had.'

Roseanna looked at her mother's slightly slanted emerald eyes which were the mirror of her own and then at the portrait.

Her spirits seemed to rise with her gaze. Somehow out of the loss and pain of recent weeks she had become reconciled with her mother, her family and her roots. Somehow she belonged again and when she healed from her injuries she would live . . . and love again . . .

CHAPTER FORTY-THREE

'The boss has lost none of his ruthlessness,' said Drew. 'He fired her.'

'As you and I both know, it's his way of doing things. Even his own family aren't spared, so he's never going to show tenderness or mercy to someone who's not,' said Edwina.

They were sitting on the terrace at Ardnamurchan on an early summer day. Bright sunlight was dancing on the ocean rolling home and the islands rose deep royal blue out of its waters. But for a moment Edwina's mind drifted back to the evening of the party James and Max Rutherford had given for her in the seventh-floor suite . . .

. . . Afterwards she dined with Max and James at a new French restaurant in the Spottiswoode Hotel.

'And what now?' James asked.

'I want you to fire Roseanna Warrender. Tomorrow,' she said in a matter-of-fact business voice.

The old man's face creased into a triumphant grin.

'Being in business has made you one of us,' he gloated. 'Congratulations. It will be done. Tomorrow.'

Her eyes met Max's across the table.

'I knew this would be necessary ever since the day we lit that bonfire at Ardnamurchan,' she said.

'But you gave him enough rope, so he had the illusion of freedom,' said Max. 'Oh, you clever woman.'

'I've let him have his affair — as I gave him my word I would before we were married,' she replied coolly. 'Now I'm simply doing what I have to do . . .'

. . . Drew would never know what she had done or how skilfully she had played her cards despite her anguish. The most important one, denied to almost every woman in her situation, was that she had been able to stay in his social circle — and she had hung in, determinedly and doggedly being there and playing every ace. The trick had been to allow him emotional space while staying in his physical and social orbit so that he could never completely forget her or relegate her to the past. That was the reason it had been essential to get rid of Roseanna Warrender — so that she could not stay near and tempt him again.

And the beauty of it was that Drew would always believe it was James Rutherford, first Baron Kilmacolm, doing what he had to do, and never guess how skilfully she had bound him to her in perilous freedom. But he was never having another love affair, she vowed now as he sent a champagne cork spinning towards the ocean . . .

'Of course it was over anyway. You knew that,' said Drew, handing her a glass of champagne.

'Yes. You told me,' she said.

'Once again we come together as different people,' he said, raising his glass to her. 'Just as we did once before. But let's make it for keeps this time.'

'Yes,' she said, lifting her own glass to him. 'For keeps.'

His wife fascinated him more than ever now and he couldn't take his eyes off her. But he couldn't tell her why because Lord Kilmacolm had sworn him to secrecy about who had been behind the firing of Roseanna.

'I was merely the executioner,' the old man had confessed.

Now he wanted to raise his glass in admiration of his wife's stunning ruthlessness.

He raised his glass again. But the only words that passed his lips were, 'To the strength of second marriages.'

She looked at him across the white wrought-iron table with his profile and still-golden mane against the deep sapphire blue of the islands and the ocean. She had fought the best fight to keep this man – and won. But losing him again had never been an option.

She pressed the glass to her lips as their eyes met again and held.

Alpha and Omega. The beginning and the end. Except there was no beginning and there was no end. Her love for this man was eternal . . .

POSTSCRIPT

In September 1975 Roseanna Warrender joined the public relations staff of the European Economic Community in Brussels.

In 1980 she married an American diplomat and today lives with her husband and two children in Bad Godesberg, Germany.

AUTHOR'S NOTE

Though it operated as a hotel from 1969 Glenborrodale Castle did not achieve luxury status until it was bought by the businessman Peter de Savary in 1987 and refurbished. It has since been sold and is now a private residence.

To the best of my knowledge there is not and never has been a Spottiswoode Hotel in Glasgow.